LADY OSBALDESTONE'S CHRISTMAS GOOSE

STEPHANIE LAURENS

LADY OSBALDESTONE'S CHRISTMAS GOOSE

A lighthearted tale of Christmas long ago with a grandmother and three of her grandchildren, one lost soul, a lady driven to distraction, a recalcitrant donkey, and a flock of determined geese.

Three years after being widowed, Therese, Lady Osbaldestone finally settles into her dower property of Hartington Manor in the village of Little Moseley in Hampshire. She is in two minds as to whether life in the small village will generate sufficient interest to keep her amused over the months when she is not in London or visiting friends around the country. But she will see.

It's December, 1810, and Therese is looking forward to her usual Christmas with her family at Winslow Abbey, her youngest daughter, Celia's home. But then a carriage rolls up and disgorges Celia's three oldest children. Their father has contracted mumps, and their mother has sent the three—Jamie, George, and Lottie—to spend this Christmas with their grandmama in Little Moseley.

Therese has never had to manage small children, not even her own. She assumes the children will keep themselves amused, but quickly learns that what amuses three inquisitive, curious, and confident youngsters isn't compatible with village peace. Just when it seems she will have to set her mind to inventing something, she and the children learn that with only twelve days to go before Christmas, the village flock of geese has vanished.

Every household in the village is now missing the centerpiece of their

Christmas feast. But how could an entire flock go missing without the slightest trace? The children are as mystified and as curious as Therese—and she seizes on the mystery as the perfect distraction for the three children as well as herself.

But while searching for the geese, she and her three helpers stumble on two locals who, it is clear, are in dire need of assistance in sorting out their lives. Never one to shy from a little matchmaking, Therese undertakes to guide Miss Eugenia Fitzgibbon into the arms of the determinedly reclusive Lord Longfellow. To her considerable surprise, she discovers that her grandchildren have inherited skills and talents from both her late husband as well as herself. And with all the customary village events held in the lead up to Christmas, she and her three helpers have opportunities galore in which to subtly nudge and steer.

Yet while their matchmaking appears to be succeeding, neither they nor anyone else have found so much as a feather from the village's geese. Larceny is ruled out; a flock of that size could not have been taken from the area without someone noticing. So where could the birds be? And with the days passing and Christmas inexorably approaching, will they find the blasted birds in time?

First in series. A novel of 60,000 words. A Christmas tale of romance and geese.

Praise for the works of Stephanie Laurens

"Stephanie Laurens' heroines are marvelous tributes to Georgette Heyer: feisty and strong." *Cathy Kelly*

"Stephanie Laurens never fails to entertain and charm her readers with vibrant plots, snappy dialogue, and unforgettable characters." *Historical Romance Reviews*

"Stephanie Laurens plays into readers' fantasies like a master and claims their hearts time and again." *Romantic Times Magazine*

Praise for Lady Osbaldestone's Christmas Goose

"Written with a light touch, deep knowledge of the period, and bracing good humor, this book recalls the best ghosts of Christmas past." *Kim H., Proofreader, Red Adept Editing*

"Readers will fall in love with Lady Osbaldestone and her adorable grandchildren as they make village life lively in this tale of mystery and romance." *Irene S., Proofreader, Red Adept Editing*

"Laurens has created an utterly charming holiday tale sure to be viewed as a most welcome gift by her readers!" *Angela M., Copy Editor, Red Adept Editing*

OTHER TITLES BY STEPHANIE LAURENS

Cynster Novels

Devil's Bride

A Rake's Vow

Scandal's Bride

A Rogue's Proposal

A Secret Love

All About Love

All About Passion

On A Wild Night

On A Wicked Dawn

The Perfect Lover

The Ideal Bride

The Truth About Love

What Price Love?

The Taste of Innocence

Temptation and Surrender

Cynster Sisters Trilogy

Viscount Breckenridge to the Rescue

In Pursuit of Eliza Cynster

The Capture of the Earl of Glencrae

Cynster Sisters Duo

And Then She Fell

The Taming of Ryder Cavanaugh

Cynster Specials

The Promise in a Kiss

By Winter's Light

Lady Osbaldestone's Christmas Chronicles

Lady Osbaldestone's Christmas Goose

Cynster Next Generation Novels

The Tempting of Thomas Carrick

A Match for Marcus Cynster

The Lady By His Side

An Irresistible Alliance

The Greatest Challenge of Them All

The Casebook of Barnaby Adair Novels

Where the Heart Leads

The Peculiar Case of Lord Finsbury's Diamonds

The Masterful Mr. Montague

The Curious Case of Lady Latimer's Shoes

Loving Rose: The Redemption of Malcolm Sinclair

Bastion Club Novels

Captain Jack's Woman (Prequel)

The Lady Chosen

A Gentleman's Honor

A Lady of His Own

A Fine Passion

To Distraction

Beyond Seduction

The Edge of Desire

Mastered by Love

Black Cobra Quartet

The Untamed Bride

The Elusive Bride

The Brazen Bride

The Reckless Bride

Medieval (As M.S.Laurens)

Desire's Prize

Novellas

Melting Ice – from the anthologies *Rough Around the Edges* and *Scandalous Brides*

Rose in Bloom – from the anthology *Scottish Brides*

Scandalous Lord Dere – from the anthology *Secrets of a Perfect Night*

Lost and Found – from the anthology *Hero, Come Back*

The Fall of Rogue Gerrard – from the anthology *It Happened One Night*

The Seduction of Sebastian Trantor – from the anthology *It Happened One Season*

The Adventurers Quartet

The Lady's Command

A Buccaneer at Heart

The Daredevil Snared

Lord of the Privateers

Other Novels

The Lady Risks All

Short Stories

The Wedding Planner – from the anthology *Royal Weddings*

A Return Engagement – from the anthology *Royal Bridesmaids*

UK-Style Regency Romances

Tangled Reins

Four in Hand

Impetuous Innocent

Fair Juno

The Reasons for Marriage

A Lady of Expectations An Unwilling Conquest

A Comfortable Wife

LADY OSBALDESTONE'S CHRISTMAS GOOSE

LADY OSBALDESTONE'S CHRISTMAS GOOSE

ISBN: 978-1-925559-07-1

Cover design by Savdek Management Pty. Ltd.

Savdek Management Proprietary Limited, Melbourne, Australia.

www.stephanielaurens.com

Email: admin@stephanielaurens.com

❀ Created with Vellum

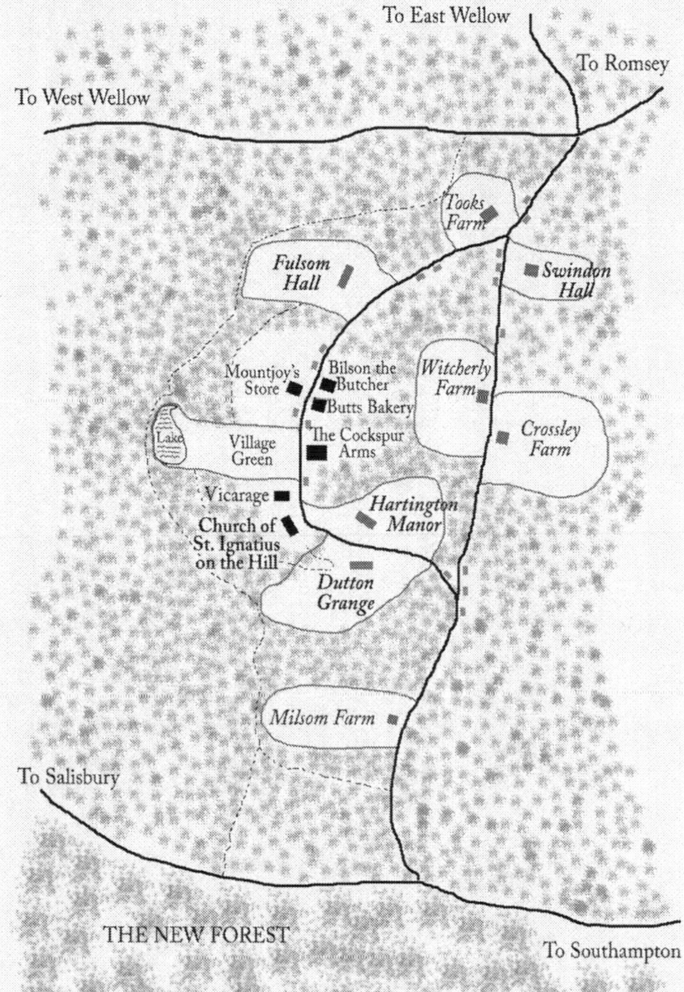
Little Moseley, Hampshire
To East Wellow
To Romsey
To West Wellow
Tooks Farm
Fulsom Hall
Swindon Hall
Mountjoy's Store
Bilson the Butcher
Butts Bakery
Witcherly Farm
Crossley Farm
Lake
Village Green
The Cockspur Arms
Vicarage
Church of St. Ignatius on the Hill
Hartington Manor
Dutton Grange
Milsom Farm
To Salisbury
THE NEW FOREST
To Southampton

THE INHABITANTS OF LITTLE MOSELEY

At Hartington Manor:

Osbaldestone, Therese, Lady Osbaldestone – *mother, grandmother, matriarch of the Osbaldestones, and arch-grande dame of the ton*

Skelton, Lord James, Viscount Skelton (Jamie) – *grandson of Therese, eldest son of Lord Rupert Skelton, Earl of Winslow, and Celia, née Osbaldestone*

Skelton, the Honorable George – *grandson of Therese, second son of Lord Rupert Skelton, Earl of Winslow, and Celia, née Osbaldestone*

Skelton, Lady Charlotte (Lottie) – *granddaughter of Therese, eldest daughter of Lord Rupert Skelton, Earl of Winslow, and Celia, née Osbaldestone*

Live-in staff:

Crimmins, Mr. George – *butler*

Crimmins, Mrs. Edwina – *housekeeper, wife of Mr. Crimmins*

Haggerty, Mrs. Rose – *cook, widow*

Orneby, Miss Harriet – *Lady Osbaldestone's very superior dresser*

Simms, Mr. John – *groom-cum-coachman*

Daily staff:

Foley, Mr. Ned – *gardener, younger brother of John Foley, owner of Crossley Farm*

Johnson, Miss Tilly – *kitchen maid, assistant to Mrs. Haggerty, daughter of the Johnsons of Witcherly Farm*

Wiggins, Miss Dulcie – *housemaid under Mrs. Crimmins, orphaned niece of Martha Tooks, wife of Tooks of Tooks Farm*

At Dutton Grange:
Longfellow, Christian, Lord Longfellow – *owner, ex-major in the Queen's Own Dragoons*
Hendricks, Mr. – *majordomo, ex-sergeant who served alongside Major Longfellow*
Jiggs, Mr. – *groom-cum-stableman, ex-batman to Major Longfellow*
Wright, Mrs. – *housekeeper, widow, sister of Mrs. Fitts at Fulsom Hall*
Cook – *cook*
Jeffers, Mr. – *footman*
Johnson, Mr. – *stableman, cousin of Thad Johnson of Witcherly Farm*

At Fulsom Hall:
Fitzgibbon, Mr. Henry – *owner, still a minor, studying at Oxford, home for the holidays*
Fitzgibbon, Miss Eugenia – *Henry's older half sister*
Woolsey, Mrs. Ermintrude – *widowed cousin of Henry and Eugenia's father, Eugenia's chaperon*
Mountjoy, Mr. – *butler*
Fitts, Mrs. – *housekeeper, widow, sister of Mrs. Wright at Dutton Grange*
Billings, Mr. – *Henry's groom*
Hillgate, Mr. – *stableman*
Terry – *stable lad*
James – *footman*
Visitors:
Dagenham, Viscount (Dags) – *eldest son of the Earl of Carsely, friend of Henry from Oxford*
Kilburn, Thomas – *friend of Henry from Oxford*
Carnaby, Roger – *friend of Henry from Oxford*
Wiley, the Honorable George – *heir to Viscount Worth, friend of Henry from Oxford*

At Swindon Hall:
Swindon, (Major) Mr. Horace – *owner, married to Sarah, ex-army major*
Swindon, Mrs. Sarah (Sally) – *wife of Horace*
Colton, Mr. – *butler*
Colton, Mrs. – *housekeeper*

Various other staff

At the Vicarage of the Church of St. Ignatius on the Hill:
Colebatch, Reverend Jeremy – *minister*
Colebatch, Mrs. Henrietta – *the reverend's wife*
Filbert, Mr. Alfred – *deacon and chief bell-ringer*
Goodes, Mr. Philip – *choirmaster*
Hatchett, Mrs. – *housekeeper and cook*

At Butts Bakery on the High Street:
Butts, Mrs. Peggy – *the baker, wife of Fred, sister of Flora Milsom*
Butts, Mr. Fred – *Peggy's husband, village handyman*
Butts, Fiona – *Peggy and Fred's daughter*
Butts, Ben – *Peggy and Fred's son*

At Bilson's Butchers in the High Street:
Bilson, Mr. Donald – *the butcher*
Bilson, Mrs. Freda – *Donald's wife*
Bilson, Mr. Daniel – *Donald and Freda's eldest son, assistant butcher*
Bilson, Mrs. Greta – *Daniel's wife*
Bilson, William (Billy) – *Daniel and Greta's son, Annie's twin*
Bilson, Annie – *Daniel and Greta's daughter, Billy's twin*

At the Post Office and Mountjoy's General Store in the High Street:
Mountjoy, Mr. Cyril – *proprietor*
Mountjoy, Mrs. Gloria – *Cyril's wife*
Mountjoy, Mr. Richard (Dick) – *Cyril and Gloria's eldest son*
Mountjoy, Mrs. Cynthia – *Dick's wife*
Mountjoy, Gordon – *Dick and Cynthia's son*

At the Cockspur Arms Public House in the High Street:
Whitesheaf, Mr. Gordon – *publican*
Whitesheaf, Mrs. Gladys – *Gordon's wife*
Whitesheaf, Mr. Rory – *Gordon and Gladys's eldest son*
Whitesheaf, Cameron (Cam) – *Gordon and Gladys's second son*
Whitesheaf, Enid (Ginger) – *Gordon and Gladys's daughter*

At Tooks Farm:
Tooks, Mr. Edward – *farmer*

Tooks, Mrs. Martha – *Edward's wife, aunt of Dulcie, Lady Osbaldestone's housemaid*
Tooks, Mirabelle – *eldest daughter of Edward and Martha*
Tooks, Johnny – *eldest son of Edward and Martha*
Tooks, Georgina – *younger daughter of Edward and Martha*
Tooks, Charlie – *younger son of Edward and Martha*

At Milsom Farm:
Milsom, Mr. George – *farmer*
Milsom, Mrs. Flora – *wife of George, sister of Peggy Butts, sometimes assists in the bakery*
Milsom, Robert – *eldest son of George and Flora*
Milsom, William (Willie) – *younger son of George and Flora*

At Crossley Farm:
Foley, Mr. John – *farmer, brother of Ned, Lady Osbaldestone's gardener*
Foley, Mrs. Sissy – *wife of John*
Foley, William (Will) – *son of John and Sissy*
Various other Foley children, nephews, and nieces

At Witcherly Farm:
Johnson, Mr. Thaddeus (Thad) – *farmer, father of Tilly, Lady Osbaldestone's kitchen maid, and cousin of Mrs. Haggerty, Lady Osbaldestone's cook, and cousin of Johnson, stableman at Dutton Grange*
Johnson, Mrs. Millicent (Millie) – *wife of Thad, mother of Tilly*
Johnson, Jessie – *daughter of Thad and Millie, Tilly's younger sister*
Various other Johnson children

Others from farther afield:
Mablethorpe, Mr. – *solicitor of Mablethorpe, Grimms, and Wrigby of Southampton*
Berry, Dr. Horatio – *medical doctor from East Wellow*

CHAPTER 1

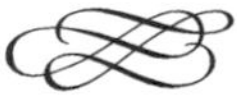

HARTINGTON MANOR, LITTLE MOSELEY, HAMPSHIRE
DECEMBER 1310

"You did *what*?" Standing in her drawing room, Therese, Lady Osbaldestone, looked upon the three slightly rumpled children, lined up quite literally on the carpet before her, with something akin to fascination. Three of her brood of sixteen grandchildren, they were proving to be remarkably inventive. Presumably, they took after their mother—Therese's youngest daughter, Celia—rather than their father, the rather stiff-rumped Earl of Winslow.

At eight years old—or nearly nine, as he was wont to insist—Jamie, Lord James, Viscount Skelton, was the eldest. With slender build and long limbs, even features, sky-blue eyes, and a mop of straight, dark-brown hair, he bade fair to grow into a good-looking young gentleman; he would be a great catch one day. He stood tall and uncowed in the middle of the small group, but as with the other two, his eyes held a hint of not exactly wariness but uncertainty; neither he nor his brother and sister knew how Therese would react. In common with her other grandchildren, they didn't know her that well.

On Jamie's right stood George, all of seven years old, a half head shorter and a trifle more solid in build. He, too, possessed the Skelton blue eyes, currently large in a face in which the features were still forming. From under a thatch of slightly curly, mid-brown hair, George, too, eyed Therese warily, yet stoically. His stance suggested he would stick by his brother come what may.

Standing on Jamie's other side and holding on to his hand was Lottie —more properly Lady Charlotte Skelton. Her blond hair fell in large, loose ringlets about an angelic face; at five years old still possessing an air of innocence her brothers could no longer so believably project, Lottie looked at Therese with open curiosity. There was an element of confidence in Lottie's blue gaze that reminded Therese that she was responsible for the three, that they relied on her to keep them safe—that she was, in effect, in loco parentis, and they had every right to expect her protection and support.

Her question still hung between them.

Rather than attempt to answer what they instinctively understood was a rhetorical question, their blue gazes unwavering, the three miscreants stared back at her as if willing her to appreciate the irrefutable logic of their actions.

The other occupant of the drawing room shifted impatiently and repeated, "They climbed to the belfry and used old curtain cords to link the bell ropes." Reverend Colebatch, who had marched the three up the manor's front path and ushered them into the drawing room, pursed his lips in disapproval and eyed the three with scant charity. "You must have heard the resulting cacophony, my lady. It was the most hideous summons to prayer I've ever heard."

Therese compressed her lips—to stop any hint of a smile slipping past her guard. She had heard the noise; all the village must have. "I see." Spurred by curiosity, she asked the trio, "Was there some purpose behind your actions?"

Jamie readily—eagerly—replied, "We wondered, if the ropes were linked so that two of the eight bells rang together whenever the rope for either was pulled, whether the music would still sound as it should—"

"But just louder," George put in.

"Or whether the peal would be all mixed up and sound awful," Jamie concluded. He glanced sidelong at Reverend Colebatch. "We just wanted to see, so we did it today for the bell-ringers' practice. We wouldn't have done it on a Sunday."

Therese knew all three normally had music lessons. In light of that, their curiosity was understandable; she was even a touch impressed by their enthusiasm in pursuing such an intellectual question. *While I might admire your ingenuity...* No, that wouldn't do. Keeping her expression stony and unrevealing, she stated, "I believe you've had your answer and now owe Reverend Colebatch an apology."

All three immediately turned to the minister and murmured their "humblest apologies."

Reverend Colebatch humphed. "Yes, well, it's not just me you scamps have inconvenienced. Poor Deacon Filbert was deeply shocked and rattled by the noise. It was he who climbed up and untangled your handiwork, but by then it was too late for the bell-ringers to practice."

"I suppose it's just as well," Therese calmly put in, "that the bell-ringers aren't preparing for any competition at the moment."

"Indeed." Reverend Colebatch frowned at the children. "But that noise was a horrendous assault on the hearing of all those about the church."

Therese eyed the three culprits. "And where were you three when the bells started?"

The trio returned her gaze as if she should have known. "In the graveyard," Jamie said. "We had to be near enough to hear the result clearly."

Once again compressing her lips against a smile, Therese nodded, then looked at the minister. "Reverend Colebatch, please accept my apologies as well. I have clearly been remiss in not keeping these three in better line. If you have any recommendations as to punishments, I will willingly entertain them."

She knew very well that with no children of his own, the reverend was a soft touch for any youngster, but having arrived in the village only four days before, her three scallywags didn't know that; they looked with faint trepidation at the minister.

Reverend Colebatch hmmed and frowned at the three. Eventually, he offered, "As there was no lasting damage done, and as it appears you were motivated by academic interest, I daresay if you will come to service on Sunday and apologize humbly to Deacon Filbert, we might say no more about it."

Jamie and George assured him they would, indeed, apologize most humbly; Lottie contented herself with a huge-eyed nod.

Therese judged it time to reassert control. "I believe," she stated in her most uncontestable tones, "that I can assure you and Deacon Filbert—and the poor bell-ringers, who must have sustained quite a shock as well—that nothing of a similar nature will ever happen again." She fixed her gaze on her grandchildren. "Will it?"

"We definitely won't do that again," Jamie vowed.

Lottie solemnly nodded.

George nodded, too, but in a mumble, added, "Now we know what happens, there's no need for us to do it again."

The irrefutable logic of children.

Therese swept forward. "Wait there," she murmured to the children as she passed them. With one graceful arm, she gathered Reverend Colebatch and turned him to the drawing room door. "Thank you for bringing them home, Reverend. Rest assured I will discipline them appropriately."

She saw the minister to the front door with assurances that she, along with the three children, would certainly attend Sunday service, that indeed, she was quite looking forward to it, which was true. Reverend Colebatch's sermons were short and succinct, and Therese now had the added incentive of seeing how her grandchildren met the challenge of placating Deacon Filbert, who was a fussy little man rather overfond of drama.

Crimmins, her butler, had been hovering in the hall. Allowing him to close the front door on the minister, Therese exchanged a look with the longtime head of her staff. "They tied the bell ropes together."

"Ah." Crimmins looked enlightened. "That horrible noise. We thought maybe some animal had got among the bells."

"If bells could caterwaul?" Therese headed back to the drawing room. "Indeed."

She walked into the room, closed the door, considered the three faces turned her way, then, stifling a sigh, walked past the trio to the chaise. She sat, leant back, and surveyed the three. "Now, what am I to do with you?"

The children had wheeled their line and stood facing her. They looked at her, exchanged swift, sidelong glances with each other, then looked almost questioningly at her again.

As if expecting her to have an answer where they did not.

She studied them as they studied her.

The linking of the bell ropes was not their first infraction since they'd arrived unheralded on her doorstep in one of their father's carriages four days before. A letter had accompanied them—a plea from Celia. Apparently, Celia's husband, Lord Rupert Skelton, the Earl of Winslow, had succumbed to the mumps and was proving a predictably grumpy and irascible patient. Normally, had all been well, Therese would have spent Christmas and the preceding week with Celia, Rupert, and their family at

Winslow Abbey in Northamptonshire, but Celia had written, putting Therese off—essentially canceling Christmas for the Winslow Abbey household—and begging her mother to house her three elder children far from any risk of contagion. Of necessity, Celia had kept the youngest of her brood, the infant Emma, with her at Winslow, but had sent the three older children to safety in Little Moseley.

The children had been dispatched in the charge of Lottie's new governess, a Miss Philby, as well as the family's dour coachman and a younger groom. Celia's intention had been that Miss Philby would take on the responsibility of overseeing the children, keeping them amused and out of Therese's hair.

From her own childhood, Celia knew that Therese had had precious little experience caring for children herself. As the wife of a very senior diplomat, Therese had been a major hostess all her adult life; her five children had been nurtured by a procession of nurses, governesses, and tutors prior to the three boys being sent to boarding school.

Beyond bringing them into the world, Therese's major personal contribution to her children's lives had been in steering four of the five into comfortably settled married life.

Sadly, Miss Philby had not arrived in Little Moseley with her erstwhile charges. John Coachman had informed Therese that the young woman had stuck it out as far as Southampton, but had refused to come any farther. "Too meek by half to manage the likes of three Skeltons" had been John's reply to Therese's question as to why the silly woman had done a bunk.

Faced with three of her direct descendants, Therese accepted, however reluctantly and with whatever degree of trepidation, that managing the trio and "keeping them amused" now fell to her.

While Monday had seen an attempt to label, apparently with a view to cataloguing, the ducks on the village pond with predictably noisy results and many ruffled feathers, not all of which had belonged to the ducks, Tuesday had seen the three tramping through the fields toward nearby Romsey, getting lost, and being brought home in a helpful farmer's cart. Yesterday, they'd tried to help deliverymen roll barrels down the ramp into the cellar of the village's public house—and nearly squashed the publican.

Today, they'd disrupted the bell-ringers and assaulted the sensibilities of the entire village.

Therese had only recently returned to Little Moseley. She hadn't as yet definitively made up her mind if she wanted to make Hartington Manor her permanent home, but she might. She didn't need the villagers to take against her and her household.

She'd been fourteen when she'd inherited Hartington Manor from an old but much-loved eccentric aunt. Therese had often spent the summer months with her aunt Gloriana in Hampshire and had retained warm, fond memories of the place. Consequently on her marriage, she'd asked for the manor to be made her dower property. After the death of her husband, Gerald, three years before, it had passed into her hands outright.

In the years immediately following Gerald's death, she'd traveled, visiting again all the places he and she had lived in over the years of his extensive and distinguished career with the Foreign Office. She hadn't known why she'd wanted to revisit those places, but she had, meeting again many of the people they'd entertained and been entertained by while ambassadors to this court or that.

In retrospect, she rather thought she'd been bidding that old life goodbye.

She'd returned to London for the Season earlier in the year and had spent the summer on her usual peregrination, visiting her longtime English friends. She'd spent August in Cambridgeshire with Helena, Dowager Duchess of St. Ives, delighting in catching up with the large and boisterous Cynster family, with whom she was almost as intimately acquainted as her own and as accustomed to meddling in their private lives alongside Helena. Steering and guiding the following generations was an occupation she still enjoyed.

Of course, those she was accustomed to steering and guiding were usually in their twenties or older. In her admittedly limited experience, those under ten years of age were rather harder to manipulate.

She'd finally returned to Hartington Manor in late November, with the fogs wreathing the forests and the chill of winter sinking into the bones of the land. She'd informed her small household that she was considering spending more time in Little Moseley, making the manor into her true home. But she hadn't yet decided absolutely definitely; there was the not insignificant question of whether village society could provide sufficient interest to keep her absorbed and entertained. They would see.

Meanwhile, however, she had three innately curious and inventive children to… She wasn't even sure what tack she should take with them.

How was she to keep them amused? Would what entertained her work for them, too?

A tap on the door interrupted their mutual weighing up.

Therese raised her gaze. "Come."

The door swung inward, and Mrs. Haggerty, Therese's cook for the last decade and more, stood framed in the doorway. "I thought you should know, my lady, that Farmer Tooks was just by to tell us that there'll be no goose for Christmas dinner."

"No goose?" Therese raised her brows incredulously. It was one of the traditions she insisted on for Christmas, and the village kept its own flock of geese especially for the event.

Mrs. Haggerty was well aware of those facts. Clasping her large hands, she nodded portentously. "*No goose*. Tooks was in a right taking—it seems the entire flock's gone missing."

"So it's not just us or a few missing out but the whole village?"

Again, Mrs. Haggerty nodded. "No one's going to be happy. As far as I've heard, every family in this village expects to have goose on the table on Christmas Day."

Therese stared at Mrs. Haggerty while, in her mind, she heard Gerald's voice as, very early in their marriage, he'd shared one of the maxims that had helped make him the diplomatic force he had already been.

When faced with adversity, look for the opportunity buried within it and seize hold of that.

Over the years, she'd frequently had recourse to that advice, and it had never failed her.

Refocusing on Haggerty's face, Therese nodded crisply. "Leave it with me. I'll look into the situation and see what can be done."

"Thank you, my lady. But late as it is, I truly don't know what else we're to serve. Perhaps I should get Bilson to put us up a nice haunch of beef, just in case."

Therese inclined her head. "Do—as a fallback. But"—she swung her gaze to her grandchildren, who had been listening with captivated interest—"I'm determined we'll have goose for Christmas as we always do."

The children had been looking at Haggerty, but as she bobbed a curtsy and reached to draw the door closed again, they turned back to Therese.

She met their gazes levelly. "I wonder… Perhaps as a way of making amends for the abused sensibilities of the village, you should assist me in finding out what has happened to the village's flock of geese."

Three pairs of eyes lit; three faces glowed with eagerness.

"You mean to track them down?" George asked.

"At the very least, we should find out where they've gone." Therese reached for the cane she'd taken to using. Not so much because she needed the physical support—not yet, even though she'd turned fifty earlier in the year—but because the cane had been Gerald's and the support she derived from feeling the ornate silver head under her palm was of a different nature.

Planting the cane's tip on the carpet, she rose, then with the cane, waved to the door. "Let's get our coats and have Simms bring the gig around, then we'll take ourselves off to Tooks Farm and see what this is all about."

Edward Tooks was a heavy man. He had a naturally dour disposition, but now glumness was piled atop his usual morose demeanor. He looked positively hangdog as, having spotted Therese driving up in her gig, he clumped across his barnyard to meet her at the gate.

Her and the three children, who had crammed into the gig on either side of her, and who scrambled down the instant she halted the gig in the lane, several yards back from the gate.

Tooks reached the gate, leant on it, and eyed the approaching children without any leavening of his expression.

The three halted before the gate. They looked up at Tooks, then wisely shuffled to the side as Therese, having hitched the piebald mare to a fence post, came walking up.

"Good afternoon, Tooks." Therese gave him a crisp nod. "I understand you have a problem with your geese."

Tooks bobbed his large head. "Aye, my lady. You have that right, though it's not so much a problem with them as that they're gone. Vanished without a trace, the lot of 'em—all twenty-three birds just gone."

"Dear me. And when did this happen?"

"Tuesday sometime, it was. Can't say as to the exact hour, but the flock was all here, right as rain and roosting in the barn, when I left for market a while before dawn. Then when I got back—long after dark, that was—Johnny said when he went to feed them late in the afternoon, they was nowhere to be found. Well." Tooks rubbed his temple with one thick fingertip. "I thought maybe they'd just got out of the yard and gone around to one of the outbuildings. It's so cold now they wouldn't want to be out in the weather, and we're fattening them up, so they get right peckish morning and night—that's why you can be sure they'll turn up for their next feed. They won't wander off. So I thought that if we looked the next morning, we'd find them tucked away in the hayshed or some such place, but Johnny and I searched everywhere, and we found not hide nor hair of them."

From beside Therese, Jamie murmured, "What about feathers?"

Tooks heard and transferred his weighty gaze to Jamie. "No feathers, either, young sir. No sign at all. They're gone, and that's all I can tell you."

Therese frowned. "Surely no one would steal them—not the whole flock."

"Aye," Tooks said. "It's hard to imagine. A vagrant or even a band of travelers—they might take one or two. I did wonder if that was a possibility, so I asked around the Arms yesterday evening, but no one's seen any outsider wandering through. And no one heard anything, either, and the whole flock makes a helluva racket—pardon me, your ladyship."

"That's quite all right, Tooks." Therese was still frowning. "But I take your point—transporting a whole flock in secret over any distance at all…it's hard to see how it might have been done, not in silence. Not without someone noticing."

"Aye, well…" Tooks shifted and straightened, turning to look south-westward. "I did wonder…"

When he said nothing more, Therese prompted rather sharply, "What did you wonder, Tooks?"

Edward Tooks grimaced. "Seems like stealing away the village flock might be the sort of lark that mob of young gentlemen visiting at Fulsom Hall might think to get up to."

"What mob of young gentlemen?"

"Mr. Henry's university friends down for the holidays. They seem the sort, if you know what I mean."

Therese could, indeed, imagine; with three sons of her own, she'd dealt with many such groups in her time. And Fulsom Hall was the neighboring property, with no great distance between.

Tooks went on, "From what I heard from Billings and Hillgate—they're the groom and stableman up at the Hall—Miss Fitzgibbon has her hands full trying to manage that lot." Tooks shook his shaggy head. "I didn't like to go and ask at the Hall, not as it's Miss Fitzgibbon I'd surely have to speak to. She's got enough on her plate and doesn't need me adding to it—and it's only suspicions I have and all."

"Hmm. Yes." Therese could appreciate that given the relative social positions, Tooks would feel reluctant to approach Miss Fitzgibbon about guests at the Hall. However, this was a situation that put the Christmas feasts of everyone in the village—those at the Hall included—in doubt. And there was nothing to prevent Therese from paying Miss Fitzgibbon and her brother, Henry, a social call. "Leave it with me, Tooks." She met Tooks's gaze. "I'll call at the Hall and see what I"—her gaze fell to the three children, who had listened avidly throughout, and she amended —"what we can learn about any sightings of geese."

"Thank ye, my lady." Tooks bobbed his head. "If you'll let me know…?"

"If we learn anything that points to the whereabouts of the flock, I will send word immediately." With a crisp nod, Therese turned to the gig.

She didn't even have to collect the children; they were already running back to the carriage to eagerly pile in.

CHAPTER 2

Therese hadn't yet called at Fulsom Hall since returning to the village. The last time she'd made her way up the drive had been at least a decade ago, during one of her and Gerald's short visits to the manor.

"Other than a university-aged Mr. Henry Fitzgibbon," she mused as she steered the mare up the gravel drive, "Tooks mentioned only a Miss Fitzgibbon. Sir Harold and Lady Fitzgibbon were alive when last I was here. Now, what was her name?" Unsurprisingly, Jamie, George, and Lottie, although listening attentively, couldn't supply it. "Ah yes! Lucinda. The first thing we need to do is to determine the situation here and learn who's in charge."

She glanced at her assistants. All three solemnly nodded.

She looked ahead to where the drive ended in a neat forecourt. It was oddly flattering to have three such bright and inquiring minds hanging on her every word.

After drawing the gig to a halt, then handing the reins to a young groom who came pelting around the side of the house, Therese descended and started walking toward the front porch.

The day had been overcast, and the light was fading, the afternoon waning toward evening. The cold was intensifying, but they were all well rugged up in thick winter coats and had scarves wound about their necks.

Somewhat to her surprise, she felt small fingers slide into her free hand. She looked down to find Lottie pacing beside her; the little girl's gaze was fixed on the front door.

Therese held Lottie's hand a trifle more firmly as, with her other hand, she gripped her cane and caught up her skirts and climbed the two shallow steps to the porch. There, she paused to consider Jamie and George, who had halted at the bottom of the steps. After a moment, she suggested, "Perhaps, boys, you might do better waiting outside." She glanced around, then brought her gaze to rest on the archway in the hedge that stretched past the corner of the house to the right. The archway gave onto the gardens and was on the same side of the house as the stable and presumably any other outbuildings near the house. Raising her eyebrows, she met Jamie's and George's alert gazes. "Who knows what you might stumble upon?"

The boys didn't know whether to grin or not. They exchanged a swift glance, then, with lips not entirely straight, eagerly bobbed bows. "Yes, Grandmama," they chorused.

Jamie clarified, "We'll go and look around."

"And keep out of mischief," she added. "I'll call for you when Lottie and I are ready to leave."

With ducked heads, the boys vanished in a soft clatter of feet on gravel.

Turning to the door, Therese grasped the bell chain and tugged.

A minute later, the door was opened by a tall, stately butler; to Therese's eyes, the man looked strangely tense. Her well-trained memory supplied a name. "Mountjoy, isn't it?"

Instantly gratified, the butler bowed low. "Indeed, ma'am. How may I assist you?"

"I am Lady Osbaldestone. I've taken up residence at Hartington Manor—you might have heard. I wonder if I might speak with Sir Harold or Lady Fitzgibbon."

Mountjoy's face clouded. "Sadly, my lady, both Sir Harold and Lady Fitzgibbon have passed on."

Therese sighed. "I feared that might be so. In that case, I believe I need to speak to whoever is in charge."

"That will be Miss Fitzgibbon, my lady. Sir Harold's daughter—Miss Eugenia." Mountjoy stepped back, holding the door wide. "Please come inside, and I'll fetch Miss Fitzgibbon."

Mountjoy showed them into an unremarkable drawing room.

Therese sank onto one of the twin chaises set at right angles to the fireplace and drew Lottie down to sit beside her. Once Mountjoy had departed to seek his mistress, Therese glanced at her golden-haired granddaughter and murmured, "Something strikes me as odd. There's no reason that, even at your age, you can't observe and learn." When Lottie looked at her inquiringly, Therese went on, "Miss Eugenia was in pigtails the last time I was here—I doubt she can be more than twenty-five years old at the most. So there should be a guardian, a chaperon at the very least, yet Mountjoy didn't mention any such person."

Lottie's eyes conveyed that she was duly drinking in those facts.

Footsteps in the hall, swift and light, drew their eyes to the door. It opened, and a young woman in a morning gown of blue kerseymere walked into the room. Golden-blond hair streaked with light brown was piled in a loose knot on the top of her head. Her blue eyes, wide and long lashed, with a definite frown swimming in their depths, met Therese's with a directness she rarely encountered in young gentlewomen. "Lady Osbaldestone?"

"Indeed." Gripping her cane, Therese rose. She was tallish for a woman; Eugenia Fitzgibbon was several inches shorter. "Miss Fitzgibbon, I take it." Regally, Therese extended her hand. "I knew your parents and was saddened to hear of their passing."

Recalled to her manners, Miss Fitzgibbon blushed faintly, endeavored to banish her frown, politely touched fingers, and bobbed a curtsy. "Good afternoon, ma'am."

"As to that," Therese said, "I'm not entirely sure. I have only recently returned to the village, and as you've no doubt heard, village communications being what they are, I have settled at Hartington Manor, which was my late aunt's house." Therese glanced at Lottie, who had popped to her feet beside her. "This young miss is my granddaughter, Lady Charlotte Skelton, who is visiting the manor."

Without further prompting, Lottie executed a wobbly curtsy.

Her features softening, Miss Fitzgibbon solemnly bobbed in response, then with a gesture invited Therese and Lottie to resume their seats and moved to sit on the chaise opposite. "I had heard you had taken up residence at the manor. Would you care for some refreshments, ma'am?"

"Thank you, my dear, but no. This is not, strictly speaking, a social call."

"Oh?"

"I learned not an hour ago that Farmer Tooks's flock of geese, the one the village relies on for their Christmas dinners, has vanished. Apparently into thin air."

Eugenia Fitzgibbon's frown returned. "Vanished?"

"So it seems." Therese waited until Eugenia raised her gaze to her face. "Fulsom Hall is the nearest holding to Tooks Farm. I've come to inquire whether anyone here—staff, family, or guests—have seen anything of the birds. I understand there are twenty-three in the flock, and all are missing."

Eugenia's gaze fell. Her lips compressed, and her frown deepened. After a moment, she glanced up and met Therese's eyes. "As I daresay you might have heard, my brother, Henry, has four friends staying at present."

"Four, is it? I hadn't heard the number." Therese waited a heartbeat, then offered, "Young gentlemen down from Oxford—I well know what such groups are like. My sons, all three of them, went through that stage." When Eugenia searched her eyes, Therese smiled in steely fashion. "They can be quite a handful to rein in."

Eugenia studied her for a second more, then blew out a breath. "You could say that." The starch seemed to go out of her. "Although I don't believe I can claim to have yet mastered the art. Of reining them in, I mean."

"They can be a challenge. But as to the geese…?"

Eugenia sighed. "While I admit that on the face of it that seems just the sort of prank Henry and his friends might get up to, I seriously doubt they had anything to do with the geese going missing."

Therese opened her eyes wide. "You seem very sure."

Eugenia's lips tightened. "Indeed, I am, for the simple reason that they've been half drunk or worse ever since they arrived and couldn't catch or even round up a flock of geese to save themselves."

"Ah." After a moment, in a matter-of-fact tone, Therese offered, "You might ask Mountjoy to water the wine. I've even been known to order that a few drops of vinegar be added. That tends to fairly quickly wean them off the claret and on to ale, and they need to drink far more of that to reach the same level of intoxication." Therese glanced down to find Lottie's big blue eyes fixed on her face. She inwardly shrugged and looked at Eugenia, to find that young lady regarding her with a mixture of hope and awe.

Tripping footsteps pattered in the hall, then the drawing room door eased open. A faded lady with pale, wispy hair, her thin, not to say gaunt, figure clad in an unseasonably filmy gown in a very pale pink with a thick, knitted maroon wrapper wound about her bony shoulders, peered myopically around the door. "Eugenia? Have we visitors?"

Eugenia seemed to stifle another sigh. She rose. "Cousin Ermintrude."

Therese rose as the vision in pastel draperies drifted across the room. Lottie, apparently viewing the apparition as strange and therefore more dangerous than Eugenia, slipped off the sofa and pressed close to Therese's skirts.

Eugenia indicated Therese and Lottie. "Lady Osbaldestone has returned to the village to live at Hartington Manor, and her granddaughter is visiting." To Therese, she said, "Mrs. Woolsey is my father's cousin and acts as my chaperon."

"I see." Therese nodded politely to Mrs. Woolsey, who dropped into a twittering curtsy.

"My lady! It's a pleasure to welcome you to Fulsom Hall." Mrs. Woolsey's expression abruptly blanked, and she glanced around. "Eugenia, dear—where are your manners?" To Therese, she gabbled, "I'll send for refreshments right away."

Therese held up a commanding hand. "No need, I assure you. We only called to inform Miss Fitzgibbon of a village matter."

Eugenia looked relieved that Therese hadn't mentioned the geese.

Heavier footsteps sounded in the front hall, then the door, which Mrs. Woolsey had failed to close, was thrust open, and a young gentleman, nattily dressed in what, Therese suspected, was the latest style for Oxfordians-in-the-country, strolled in. "I say, Genie." He was a robust-looking specimen of average height, with curly brown hair, his countenance faintly and rather suspiciously flushed. He didn't quite slur, but it was a near thing. "You can tell old Mountjoy we won't be keeping him from his bed tonight—we're off to Romsey to find some…"

The gentleman's gaze had slowly swung past Mrs. Woolsey to take in the fact that his sister was entertaining visitors. His gaze encountered Therese's, and his voice petered out.

Behind the gentleman—presumably Henry Fitzgibbon—four others somewhat unsteadily tripped in, jostling shoulders as they pushed through the doorway.

"We're off to find some fun and frolics!" one of the four—a dark-haired, long-limbed, distinctly pale gentleman—announced.

Then he noticed Therese and came to a weaving halt. Close behind him, the other three stumbled on his heels.

A muttered oath, imperfectly suppressed, reached Therese's ears.

In the pocket of her gown, her fingers closed about the handle of her quizzing glass. She hadn't thought to use it in the country; she carried it out of habit rather than design. As a sudden silence engulfed the room, she withdrew the glass and slowly raised it to her eye.

Leveling the quizzing glass on the first of the four, the dark-haired one who had finished Henry's sentence for him, Therese scanned the young man's aristocratic features. "Dagenham, I believe."

The young man rocked back a trifle, weaving in shock that she had pulled his name from thin air.

Therese held him skewered with her gaze. "I will be sure to let your mother, the countess, know that I ran into you when next I write to Carsely." Leaving Viscount Dagenham goggling in near terror, she looked at the next young man's paling face and humphed. "Kilburn. Venetia will be pleased to hear of you, also." She passed on to the next now-horrified young sprig. "A Carnaby, obviously. Hmm—I believe you must be Roger."

Slowly, as if frightened to move quickly, the young man nodded.

"Yes, I thought so. Gertrude is your mater, as I recall." She swung her glass to take in the last of the four, a tall, thin young gentleman now holding himself rigidly still at the rear of the small crowd. Her eyes narrowed. "Good heavens. I hadn't realized any of Letty's offspring were of such an age. But you're the eldest, I take it. George, isn't it? Viscount Worth's heir?"

George Wiley managed to unhinge his jaw sufficiently to croak, "Yes, ma'am."

"Indeed." Therese swept her magnified gaze over the group one last time, then lowered the glass. "I am Lady Osbaldestone. I live nearby. And as you've just realized, I'm well acquainted with your families, most especially with your mothers." She paused, then added, "I trust you will henceforth bear that in mind."

A chorus of "Yes, my lady," "Indeed, my lady," and "Of course, my lady" was accompanied by four rather wobbly bows.

Therese arched her brows in supercilious fashion. "I believe you were about to take your leave of Miss Fitzgibbon and Mrs. Woolsey."

The four, joined by a distinctly subdued Henry, did so, performing the simple task with the exemplary manners of which they were entirely capable. Satisfied, when they glanced her way, Therese dismissed the five with a sharp nod. With barely concealed relief, they quit the room, and an instant later, the front door opened and shut.

Mrs. Woolsey fluttered her hands. "So delightful that you knew the young gentlemen's families, dear Lady Osbaldestone."

Eugenia had simply stared, wide-eyed, throughout Therese's performance. Now she turned to Therese and said, "Thank you. That was"—she looked back at the door, now neatly closed—"amazing."

"Nonsense, my dear." Therese reached for Lottie's hand; the little girl had watched the proceedings from the safety of Therese's side. "Dealing with impulsive young gentlemen becomes second nature after a while. One simply has to ensure they recollect that the names they carry bring with them a certain responsibility. Reminding them of that responsibility is really all it takes."

Noticing that twilight had descended and from the corner of her eye catching Mrs. Woolsey's vaporous gestures, before that lady could invite them for dinner, Therese fixed her gaze on Eugenia's face. "My dear Miss Fitzgibbon, to return to the matter that brought me here, I would ask that you permit me and my helpers to check through your outbuildings, purely to ensure you are not unwittingly harboring any feathered fugitives."

Mrs. Woolsey blinked and frowned, entirely at sea.

Eugenia glanced at her chaperon and quickly nodded. "Yes. Of course." She gestured to the door. "I'll come with you myself."

Swiftly, Therese took determined leave of Mrs. Woolsey, giving that lady no chance to further engage. With Lottie skipping beside her, she followed Eugenia from the room.

Eugenia led the way into a morning room and, via a set of French doors, out onto a terrace. She waited for Therese to join her, then walked down a set of stone steps to the lawn. "We only have the stable, a barn, and a toolshed and workshop, and our stableman and groom and the gardener have said nothing about any geese."

"Indeed. I gather Tooks spoke with a Billings and a Hillgate. They reported no sign of the birds, but they hadn't until then known the flock was missing, so couldn't have searched."

"Billings is Henry's groom, and Hillgate is our stableman. I would think they would know if we've had a visitation in the stable." After a moment, Eugenia glanced at Therese. "Does this mean the entire village will not have goose for Christmas?"

Therese nodded. "The entire flock has gone missing, which does not auger well for Christmas dinners in Little Moseley."

Jamie and George must have seen them coming. The boys duly presented themselves when Therese and Lottie, with Eugenia, reached the stable yard. Therese introduced the pair, who politely made their bows. The boys had spoken with the young stable lad who had been hauling bales of hay, and together, the three had checked the barn and found no trace of the missing geese.

Eugenia led them to the toolshed with its adjoining workshop, but that, too, was devoid of all signs of feathered occupancy.

"Geese make rather a mess, as I recall," Eugenia said. "If they had been here, there would be some sign."

They all agreed.

Just to be certain, and given they were there, they entered the shadowy stable. From a hook, Eugenia collected a lamp, lit it with the tinderbox left ready, then held the lamp high as they walked down the central aisle.

Jamie and George helped search the boxes, most of which were occupied by horses, but there was no sign of geese—not even a feather—to be found.

The aisle led into an open area in which various carriages and curricles were stored. Therese noticed three curricles of recent vintage.

Seeing her take note, Eugenia explained, "Our visitors drove down with Henry from Oxford."

Therese nodded her understanding.

"Oh—that doesn't look good."

Therese and Eugenia, along with Lottie, turned to see Jamie, with George, staring at a rather dashing, bright-blue curricle with fine gold-paint trim. The boys were staring at the side not lit by the spill of light from the lamp.

Eugenia's lips set. She strode quickly around to play the lamplight over the curricle's side, illuminating a long, deep gouge across one side panel and a crushed section at the rear corner. "Damn!" Recalling who she was with, she colored and shot an apologetic glance at Therese and Lottie. "My apologies, ma'am. But…" Her voice faded, and she gestured at the damage. "That's Henry's curricle."

Therese sighed commiseratingly. "Sadly, my dear, that saying that boys will be boys is entirely true, even when the males in question are long past boyhood." She turned to Jamie and George. "I hope you two are taking note. What do you do if you damage something—a curricle, for example?"

Jamie glanced at George, then volunteered, "Confess immediately?"

"Correct." Therese nodded approvingly. "It's always best to get such things off your chest, and waiting to be found out later is just asking for more trouble." She turned to the stable doors. "Come along. I saw our gig tied up outside. It's getting dark, and we really should get home."

Home. By which she meant Hartington Manor.

She gathered the children, sent them ahead, and followed, Eugenia by her side. "Thank you for your assistance, Miss Fitzgibbon. We're sure to meet again in the village now that I've decided to take up residence, at least for a time."

Eugenia's gaze was on the three youngsters, now scrambling up into the gig. "Are you entertaining your grandchildren for the season?"

"Yes. Their parents are sadly indisposed, so the three will be celebrating Christmas with me."

"I—ah—heard of their exploits." Eugenia's lips twitched, and she shot Therese a glance. "The bells were…interesting."

"I've been given to understand that was a serious experiment, apparently, in discord." She added, "I've been assured that, having once been conducted, said experiment will not need to be attempted again."

Eugenia chuckled, then her amusement faded and her frown returned.

They reached the gig. Therese climbed to the seat and took the reins from Jamie, who'd been carefully holding them. She reached for the brake and met Eugenia's eyes. "Should you require any further assistance with your four guests, by all means, send to the manor, and I'll come. That said, I doubt you'll have more trouble with them, at least not directly. And don't forget about watering the wine."

"I won't. Thank you for all your help."

"Not at all. And if we manage to find Tooks's flock, I'll send word."

Therese turned the gig and, with a flick of the reins, sent the mare trotting smartly down the drive.

Once in the lane, she said, "Jamie, George—report, if you please."

The pair wriggled with eagerness, and Jamie quickly said, "We checked all over—in the shrubbery and the dovecote and all over the place. That was why we hadn't yet checked in the stable. But we didn't find anything, and like Miss Fitzgibbon said, geese do make a mess."

"We found no mess." George shook his head. "Not anywhere there."

"All right. So it seems that, despite Farmer Tooks's suspicions, we must cross Fulsom Hall off the list of possible places the flock might be."

Murmurs of agreement came from the three, even Lottie, who to that point had said very little. But she did seem to be highly observant, spongelike in absorbing all she saw and heard.

As if feeling Therese's gaze, the angel's face turned up. Lottie met Therese's eyes, then in her high-pitched voice piped, "Miss Eugenia's very worried, isn't she?"

Therese reviewed all she'd seen and heard. Slowly, she nodded. "Indeed, she is."

"She's running that big house all by herself," George said. "The stable boy, Terry, said the groom, Billings, said she's at her wit's end, what with her brother still being at the stage of playing larks rather than taking on the running of the place."

"Hmm" was all Therese returned. Deftly, she swung the gig out of the Hall's drive and into the lane that led through the village. Yet as they bowled down the village street—referred to as the High Street—on past the village green and the Cockspur Arms public house with its windows now shining as the evening's gloom took hold, past the vicarage and the Church of St. Ignatius on the Hill and around the wide bend and into the drive of Hartington Manor, she was very much of the opinion that with respect to Miss Eugenia Fitzgibbon's situation, something needed to be done.

After dinner, to which Therese had sat down with her grandchildren as a family at the country hour of six o'clock, she led her three young assistants to the library. There, they hunted, and eventually, George found the map of the village Therese had been sure had to be there somewhere.

"Excellent." She carried the rolled map to the round table in the room's center and spread it over the polished surface. A cheery fire crackled in the grate, and the heavy curtains were drawn across the windows; with the weighty presence of the packed bookshelves all around, the room felt comfortably cozy.

She held the map down and leant over it. The children quickly drew chairs up to the table, scrambled up, and lent their assistance in holding the map flat.

"Right, then." With one hand freed, Therese pointed out Tooks Farm, to the north of the village proper. "First, let's consider the possibility that while Farmer Tooks was away to market, someone drove a cart into his barnyard, loaded up the geese, and drove them away. If the cart headed south—either down the High Street and through the village or via the more direct route past Swindon Hall and Crossley and Witcherly Farms—it's hard to imagine the cart not being seen."

"Or heard," George put in.

"Quite." Therese pointed in the other direction. "But if the geese were loaded into a cart and taken north, along the road to Romsey, well—"

"We were there." Jamie met Therese's eyes. His were alert and interested. "The geese went missing on Tuesday, and that was the day we went walking toward Romsey."

"Indeed. And you were out along that road for most of the day until that farmer returning from market brought you home." Therese surveyed her three adventurers. "I take it you encountered no squawking cart on your excursion."

All three shook their heads. "There were some carts," Lottie offered, "but none had any geese."

Therese nodded solemnly and looked back at the map. "In any venture, it's usually wisest to follow the most likely track. While one doesn't wish to imagine the geese were stolen, perhaps there was some other reason to account for their removal. Regardless, at this point, as all we want is to have our goose for Christmas dinner, our principal aim is to find the flock—explanations can come later." She studied the map, wondering where on earth the birds might have gone.

Jamie, also surveying the map, crossed his forearms and leant on them. "We should ask around. If the flock is anywhere near, someone will see or hear them—or see feathers or their mess if they've continued to move."

Therese switched her gaze to him.

George stirred. "We need to ask everyone on all these estates." He waved a still-pudgy hand over the village and surrounding land. "Not just the owners—they might not know. But there are sure to be workers and grooms and gardeners—they're the ones who are out and about in the fields and meadows and woods."

"There are lots of woods." Lottie pointed to the stylized trees denoting woods that were liberally dotted around the village.

"You all make good points." Therese straightened. "Right, then. Milsom Farm is perhaps a little too far south. Let's start at Dutton Grange tomorrow morning. If we learn nothing there, we can work our way northward along the village street."

Jamie nodded and pointed. "Until we reach Fulsom Hall and Tooks Farm again."

The sound of the door opening had them all turning to see Mrs. Crimmins, the housekeeper, and Orneby, Therese's dresser, walk in. Both women halted just inside the door. "It's time for you three scallywags to head for your beds," Mrs. Crimmins said. "You've had a big day, and you'll need your rest."

"Indeed." Therese looked meaningfully at all three as they glanced at her. "If you want to continue our investigations in the morning, you'll need to get a good night's sleep. Off with you now."

All three grinned at her. It was the happiest—the most openly happy —she'd seen them since they'd arrived.

"Goodnight, Grandmama." Lottie came close, caught Therese's hand, and tugged on it.

It took Therese a second to realize the child wanted her to bend down. When she complied, Lottie placed a soft kiss on her cheek. Therese felt her face soften. "Sweet dreams, my poppet."

George had sidled closer, and before she could straighten, he stretched up and kissed her cheek, too. "Goodnight, Grandmama."

"Goodnight, George," she murmured as he scampered off.

Jamie, with the weight of all his nearly nine years on his shoulders, hung back, clearly uncertain. Therese smiled; she had three sons and vaguely recalled this awkward stage. She reached out, wrapped an arm around Jamie's shoulders, and hugged him to her side. "And you, too, Jamie. Sleep tight."

He grinned up at her, then tipped his head against her for an instant before moving out of her hold. "Goodnight, Grandmama."

Mrs. Crimmins and Orneby—the former a round, comfortable, motherly sort, the latter a prim, starchy, rigid female who to everyone's surprise had readily taken on the task of helping Mrs. Crimmins with the children, especially with their washing and dressing—gathered the trio and herded them out of the door. Orneby reached back and closed the door behind her.

Therese stood for several minutes, staring at the door, then she collected the map, now rolling onto itself again, and returned it to its place on the shelves.

Her three imps seemed to be settling in; previously, they'd been more fractious about retiring, but tonight, they'd gone willingly. Even eagerly. No doubt it was the prospect of potential excitement on the morrow.

Smiling to herself, Therese walked to the wing chair angled to the hearth and sank into its padded comfort. Despite the poor start to the day, once she'd accepted her responsibilities, she felt she'd acquitted herself rather well. Hopefully, incidents like the tying of the bell ropes would remain in the past.

A tap on the door heralded Crimmins. "Did you want anything else, my lady? A nightcap, perhaps?"

She considered, then shook her head. "No, thank you, Crimmins. Nothing else." A thought occurred, and she amended, "Or at least, nothing of that nature. You might, however, be able to help me with some information."

After Gerald's death, while Therese, with Harriet Orneby in tow, had traveled hither and yon, Crimmins and Mrs. Crimmins, along with Mrs. Haggerty and John Simms, the coachman-cum-groom, all of whom had been a part of the Osbaldestone household for decades, had repaired to Hartington Manor to put everything in order for Therese's eventual arrival.

All four could have continued at Osbaldestone House in London—Therese's eldest son, Monty, now Lord Osbaldestone, was shrewd enough to recognize the worth of such experienced and loyal staff—but all were middle-aged and had elected to leave the bustle of London and follow Therese into the country.

Crimmins closed the door and came to stand nearer. "It will be my pleasure, my lady. On what subject?"

"Dutton Grange. I haven't called there for years, and as was borne in on me today, with the years, people die, and others inherit. The last time I was at the Grange, Lady Longfellow was already long dead, but Leslie, Lord Longfellow, was alive, and I believe he had two sons, although I only met the elder. As I recall, the younger son was away with our troops in the Peninsula."

"Indeed, ma'am. The current Lord Longfellow is the younger son. The elder son—I believe his name was Cedric—died about four years ago, a little before we came to the manor, then Lord Longfellow died last year. A stalwart old gentleman, he was. The whole village turned out for his funeral. The younger son—Christian, the new lord—couldn't attend as he was still in hospital recovering from wounds he received in Spain. When he was released, Lord Longfellow sold out and returned home, but by then it was last summer. Since then, I understand he has been busy getting the estate running smoothly again."

Therese angled a questioning look Crimmins's way. "No rumblings?"

"None, my lady. I gather the staff and tenant farmers are relieved to have someone at the helm again, and I've heard nothing against the new Lord Longfellow's ability to steer, as it were." Crimmins paused, then went on, "The only thing I have heard about his lordship is that he's a recluse—that because of his injuries, he eschews local society and remains inside the house."

"A wounded recluse." Therese considered the prospect. "I wonder how severe his injuries are?"

"As to that, my lady, I cannot even speculate. Since his return, few in the village have set eyes on him, although apparently, he is definitely in residence."

"Hmm. Well, the imps and I will call on him tomorrow, and no doubt, we shall see."

"Yes, my lady. Shall I tell Simms you'll need the gig again?"

"Please. Although the Grange is within walking distance, I think arriving in a carriage, albeit a gig, puts a visit on a more formal plane." Therese glanced up at Crimmins. "Tell Simms to bring the gig around just before eleven."

"Very good, my lady." Crimmins bowed, and when Therese smiled faintly and nodded a dismissal, he retreated.

The door quietly shut, leaving Therese with the soothing warmth of the fire playing over her hands and face and the peaceful sounds of her house, occupied but calm, wrapping about her.

Relaxed and at ease, she reviewed the events of her day—a long-ingrained habit after a lifetime of events, functions, and political maneuverings by Gerald's side.

After several moments, she murmured—and she really could not say to whom she was speaking, yet it felt very much as if Gerald hovered near, and it was to his shade she said, "Who knows? This matter of the missing geese has already helped with managing the children. They really are such an alert and observant lot—very like Celia when she was that age, interested in everything that was going forward. If I'm any judge at all, our hunting of the geese has fired their blood—with luck, that purpose will keep them occupied for several days yet. And me as well, of course. Although in my case, I can see another benefit to chasing the geese—namely as a way to reintroduce myself to the village and the local families. If I am going to make this my home henceforth, then establishing my place among them is something I need to do."

She'd been a pillar of society for too long not to feel that need.

The need to be an active participant, to be known, to have influence—to carve out a place and make it her own.

CHAPTER 3

The next morning at eleven o'clock, Therese discovered that neither her name nor her standing, and not even her presence, was sufficient to get her over the threshold of Dutton Grange.

Standing on the front porch with Lottie's hand once more in hers, Therese stared narrow-eyed at the mountain blocking the doorway. The day was cool, a chill December wind whipping the last leaves from the branches and harrying the thick clouds racing overhead. Together with the children, she'd driven the short distance down the manor drive, then up the graveled track that ended in the forecourt before Dutton Grange, only to encounter this rather large and somewhat unexpected obstacle.

Undeterred, she tried another tack. In her most imperious tone, she inquired, "And you are?"

The man—who was like no butler she'd ever known, garbed as he was in an ordinary hacking jacket, breeches, and boots, with a kerchief knotted about his throat—blinked, then frowned. After a moment, he replied uncertainly, "Hendricks."

"Very good. And what position do you hold in this household?"

Hendricks's frown grew blacker; he patently had no idea if ladies turning up on the doorstep and quizzing him in such a fashion was a normal occurrence or not. After another long moment, he said, "I'm Lord Longfellow's majordomo."

"I see. In that case, Hendricks, the proper procedure is to invite me into the house, show me into the drawing room to wait, then inform your master that I have called and wish to speak with him."

Hendricks's lips set, and he shook his head. "Won't be any use. Quite aside from the drawing room still being under covers, he won't see anybody, not for any reason. Those are his orders."

"Really?" Therese allowed her brows to rise. She wondered if Jamie and George were having any better luck tracking down Lord Longfellow.

On the way there, she'd told them of Crimmins's belief that Lord Longfellow was a recluse and kept to the house. Neither boy had thought such a thing at all likely and had suggested that as they'd done at Fulsom Hall, they would go around the side of the house in the hope that Lord Longfellow would be in the stables or perhaps walking his rear lawn.

Therese wasn't about to retreat yet. She skewered Hendricks with her most censorious gaze. "I cannot believe that Lord Longfellow is so lost to the edicts of common courtesy—"

Bang!

A door had crashed open at the rear of the front hall, in the gloomy depths somewhere behind Hendricks. He turned to look; Therese leant forward and peered past his bulky frame.

Cursing freely, a man strode out of the shadows, one leg dragging slightly. His left hand was wrapped around Jamie's upper arm. Despite his damaged leg, the man half dragged and half lifted Jamie along, all but shaking him as the man demanded in a tone one notch down from a roar, "Who the devil is this little beggar?"

Therese didn't hesitate; she didn't even think. She stepped to the threshold, struck the hall tiles with her cane, and in arctic accents commanded, "Unhand my grandson at once, sir!"

The figure's head jerked up, and he halted. Apparently recognizing the voice of female authority, he immediately released Jamie.

The man—presumably his lordship—stared at her.

Therese glared daggers back.

Apparently unperturbed by his rough handling, Jamie calmly resettled his jacket, drew himself up in a surprisingly relaxed fashion, and in an even, unthreatening tone, said, "If you had allowed me to introduce myself, sir, I would have told you that I am Lord James Skelton, Viscount Skelton, of Winslow Abbey."

Everyone—Therese, his lordship, Hendricks, and Lottie—looked at Jamie. Not at all rattled, he executed a neat bow to his lordship. Straightening, he looked up—all the way up into his lordship's face—and inquired, "And you are…?"

Therese felt pride—grandmotherly pride—well and swell. *If only Gerald could have seen...* Really, Jamie was a true chip off the family block; it was on the tip of her tongue to inform him that his grandfather could not have done better.

But now was not the time. Instead, she followed Jamie's limpid gaze to Lord Longfellow's face.

His lordship's scowl turned his features harsh. Despite the prevailing gloom of the front hall, she could see he had sustained some damage to the left side of his face, but oh, the right side, illuminated by the weak light that fell through the doorway, was nothing short of manly perfection. His features were classical and eye-catchingly striking, as if chiseled by some grateful goddess. Thick, slightly wavy black hair that looked as if he'd been raking his fingers through it contrasted sharply with his very pale complexion; hardly surprising if he'd been an invalid and subsequently had decided to keep to the house. And regardless of the imperfection of his dragging limp, his figure lived up to the promise of his face. He stood more than six feet tall, with broad shoulders and the long, lean build of a cavalryman. He was dressed in topcoat, breeches, and boots, with a cravat knotted about his throat; even in the poor light, the quality of his clothes marked him as a gentleman, as did his stance and the air of command that, even now, brought to book by a mere boy though he'd been, wrapped about him like an invisible cloak.

Eventually, he cleared his throat. "Christian Longfellow. Lord Longfellow of Dutton." The words were gruff, as if it had been some time since he'd spoken in polite company. Rather stiffly, he inclined his head; Jamie, after all, outranked him.

Her quarry confirmed, Therese didn't give him a second to regroup. "Lord Longfellow!" She swept past the mountainous majordomo, apparently rooted by surprise to the floor, and advanced. "Just the gentleman I wished to see. I am Lady Osbaldestone." She sensed Lottie and then George slip inside in her wake. With the full weight of her years as one of the ton's most powerful grandes dames, she extended her hand. "I knew your father, my lord. You, I believe, are Leslie's younger son—you were away with our troops the last time I called."

Ingrained good manners were wondrous things. No matter how reluctant the present Lord Longfellow might be to welcome her into his home, her presenting her hand in such a way had him reaching for it before he'd realized.

Then he did, yet by then he had no real option but to continue with the courtesy, grip her fingers, and bow over her hand. "Lady Osbaldestone. I…ah, hadn't realized you were in the district."

"I have come to take up residence at Hartington Manor. It's my dower property, but I've been visiting the place since I was in plaits—it used to be my aunt's house. Consequently, I was acquainted with your parents." She paused in some surprise. Now she was in the hall, she could see that the deep shadows and gloom owed much to the hangings drawn over every window, even the large leadlight window over the half landing on the stairs. "Good gracious! This place is one step away from a mausoleum." Turning, she surveyed the hall. "I understand, my lord, that you returned to Dutton Grange last summer. I'm amazed that your housekeeper has yet to properly open up the house."

His lordship's jaw set; Therese suspected he was gritting his teeth. "Mrs. Wright does as I wish. I have no need of further light."

Now Therese was closer, she could see why he might think so. The left side of his face was not merely damaged. It was *ravaged* by scars that had pocked and puckered the skin of his cheek and jaw. His left eye had escaped the carnage by a whisker; it appeared unmarred, as was his wide brow. In that moment, she could sympathize with his wish to hide away.

In some strange way, the riveting perfection of the right side of his face made the wreck of the left side all the more shocking.

She was far too experienced to allow any reactive emotion—not shock and certainly not revulsion—to show in her expression or her voice, much less to allow it to interfere with her direction. She met his hostile gaze directly, noting his understandable tendency to turn his face to the left. "As I said, I knew your parents, and I recently heard of your father's death. I had not, until then, heard of your brother's demise. How did he die?"

From between quite ridiculously long and lush black lashes, bright hazel eyes stared—almost glared—at her.

She wasn't at all sure he would answer, but to his surprise as well as hers, the mountain moved, then the majordomo murmured in his very deep voice, "I'll fetch a tea tray to the library, my lord, seeing as the other rooms aren't fit to receive guests."

Therese allowed her brows to rise in muted incredulity.

His lordship shot the mountain a malevolent glance, but in the circumstances, had little option other than to behave with passable grace. Christian, Lord Longfellow, stepped back and waved Therese toward the rear of the hall. "As you are here…perhaps you will allow me to offer you some refreshments."

Therese smiled and patted his arm. "Thank you, dear. I'm quite parched. Tea would be very welcome."

Through the shadows, the mountain met her gaze and almost imperceptibly nodded.

Christian gestured to the library door, which remained ajar. His gaze fell to the children—taking in George, who had been hovering with Lottie in Therese's shadow. After a moment, still in his gruff, rusty voice, he asked, "Your grandchildren?"

"Indeed. They're staying with me for the festive season as their father is currently ill." Therese swept into the library and paused to look around.

Ushering the children before him, when she glanced back at him, Christian waved to a sofa and a lone armchair arranged before the fireplace.

Therese walked forward and sank onto the sofa—in the middle, so the children could sit on either side of her, Jamie to her left and Lottie and George on her right.

Christian limped to the armchair, then slowly lowered himself into its well-padded depths.

She gave him no time to grow difficult. "You were about to tell me what happened to your brother."

He looked at her as if considering telling her he hadn't been about to do any such thing. Instead, he eventually said, "Cedric was killed in a carriage accident in '06."

"Hmm. Your father was still alive then." She eyed him. "You didn't think to return at that time?" Many young gentlemen would have.

His shoulders lifted in a slight shrug. "Neither my father nor I saw any pressing reason for me to leave my regiment and the fight at that time."

"I understand you were wounded in Spain in '09." She eyed his long frame. "I assume at Talavera. You were with Fane's heavy cavalry?"

He blinked. After a moment, he nodded. "The Fourth *Queen's Own* Dragoons." After another moment of staring at her, this time in puzzlement, he asked, "How did you know?"

"My late husband was in the Foreign Office. Although he passed on in '07, our eldest son is now with the ministry, and consequently, I saw the dispatches."

He snorted. "Reading dispatches is one thing. Remembering the details…" He tipped his head to her. "That's something else again."

"Gerald—my late husband—maintained that details were the lifeblood of diplomacy."

He continued to meet her gaze. "Is that why you're here? Diplomacy?"

She smiled easily. "In a way."

His chair sat to the left of the hearth; the glow from the flames fell on the right side of his face, leaving the left side wreathed in shadows. Nevertheless, she'd seen enough to appreciate that the disfigurement was severe. The scars ran over his jaw and down the side of his throat to disappear beneath his cravat.

The door opened, and the mountainous Hendricks carried in the tea tray. The tray looked almost ridiculous in his meaty hands. He nudged a small table into place before the sofa and carefully set the tray down.

Therese finished pulling off her gloves. "Would you like me to pour?"

"If you would," Christian replied.

Therese picked up the teapot; while she poured, she said, "The reason we are here is that we are pursuing a flock of geese." She prattled on, describing the flock's disappearance and what that meant for the local families.

At the news that there would be no goose for Christmas dinner, not for anyone, not unless they located the flock, Christian glanced at Hendricks, who rumbled, "Mrs. Wright heard from Tooks this morning. He still hasn't found the birds."

"Indeed." Therese handed Christian his cup, then lifted hers and sat back. "Which is why we are here, doing…er, reconnaissance, as it were." In response to the children's expectant looks, with a nod, she gave them permission to help themselves to the three glasses of milk and the shortbread biscuits Mrs. Wright had arranged on a plate on the tray. While they did so, she looked at Christian, then raised her gaze to Hendricks's face. "We wondered if your people had heard squawking or seen anything—feathers, goose droppings—anything at all that might suggest in which direction we should look for these wayward birds."

Christian glanced at Hendricks. "Ask around and see if anyone has anything relevant to share."

"Yes, sir."

Therese watched Hendricks retreat; the burly man had all but come to attention and snapped off a salute before leaving. "I take it Hendricks was with you in the Peninsula."

"He was a sergeant in the corps." Christian sipped, then added, "He helped carry me from the field. When he heard I was selling out, he asked to come home with me."

Therese studied him over the rim of her cup. "Did you bring any others from the army home with you?"

He shifted. "Only Jiggs—my batman. He's excellent with horses, and he'd served his time. He's my groom. Most of the others here hail from my father's tenure. If any of my people have reported anything of your geese, Mrs. Wright or Johnson, the stableman, will know."

Setting her cup back on its saucer, she quietly asked, "Do you plan on joining in village life eventually?"

Moving with careful deliberation, he set his cup and saucer down on the tray. His voice had hardened when he replied, "As you might imagine, I'm not comfortable among others, and there's no compelling reason for me to inflict my presence on the general public."

She could think of several sound reasons—his own sanity being one—and she could have argued that going about the village in no way equated to exposing himself to the wider public, but on both counts, she held her tongue. She and the children had won their way inside; patience, Gerald had always counseled, was a virtue worth cultivating.

The door opened, and Hendricks walked in. Therese set her cup and saucer on the tray and looked at the would-be majordomo as expectantly as the children.

Hendricks halted by his master's chair and pulled a glum face. "Johnson likes his Christmas goose—he'd already asked around, but no one on the estate has seen anything of the geese."

Therese heaved a sigh and gathered her gloves and reticule. "Thank you, Hendricks, and Lord Longfellow, for your assistance and the refreshments." Smoothly, she rose, bringing a faintly puzzled Christian to his feet; he'd expected her to try to persuade him to change his reclusive ways. "Come, children." She waited until they had returned their glasses to the tray and bounced to their feet, then she looked at Christian Longfellow, met his eyes, and smiled. "We should leave Lord Longfellow in peace."

Lord Longfellow looked as if he didn't know whether to take her at her word or not. He grasped a cane that had been leaning against the side of his chair; using it to steady himself, he limped after them as Therese led her party to the door.

Hendricks had moved surprisingly quickly to hold the door for her. As she drew level, he met her eyes, then inclined his huge head.

Therese swept into the hall, wondering just what it was she had glimpsed in the big man's eyes. Had it been hope?

Christian saw them to the front door, which Hendricks strode around them to open. When she paused on the threshold and glanced back at Christian—he'd halted several yards from the door, where he remained wreathed in shadows—he tensed, but all she did was smile serenely and incline her head in farewell, then she turned and, with her spine ramrod straight, walked out onto the porch, and, with her small retinue falling in alongside her, crossed the forecourt to where a groom now stood holding the mare's reins. Presumably Jiggs.

The ex-batman cut a slight figure, lean and wiry, and possessed a sharp-featured face.

Jiggs nodded politely to Therese, handed the reins to Jamie, and came to help her to the gig's seat. Perforce, that meant his back was to the still-open door. As he helped her up, Jiggs murmured, "You're the first to win your way across the threshold, ma'am."

Settling her skirts, she arched a brow. "Is that so?"

Jiggs nodded. "Aye—and if you could see your way to getting his lordship to step over it and outside, we'd all be in your debt."

"Hmm." She accepted the reins from Jamie and waited until he'd scrambled up. Then she met Jiggs's brown eyes and smiled faintly. "Clearly, I'll need to see what I can do."

Jiggs stepped back and tugged his forelock. "Thank you, ma'am."

Therese started the horse plodding, then as they passed out of the forecourt and into the drive, on impulse, she handed the reins to Jamie. "Here—let's see how you manage."

Jamie's eyes lit. He took the reins and, she noted, carefully arranged them between his fingers in the approved manner.

She nodded. "Good. Just let her plod along as she is. She knows the way, and I need time to think."

All three children glanced at her. As they swayed gently with the movement of the gig, they continued to shoot looks her way, as if expecting to be able to see her thoughts in her face. Eventually, she confided, "I've been wondering, you see, whether there would be enough of interest to hold me in such a small village—to give my life purpose for the months of the year in which I will be living here rather than in London or visiting elsewhere in the country."

George looked questioningly at her. "You mean if there will be enough to do so you don't get bored?"

"Yes." She nodded. "Exactly." After a moment, she said, "I suppose it's the same for you children—you need something to do to fill your days. Of course, for someone of my age, the things I might do are different from the things you would like to do, or even the things people such as Miss Fitzgibbon and her brother and his friends, or Lord Longfellow, would want to do. But regardless, one must have *some* activity to give one purpose."

Lottie slid her hand into Therese's. "What sort of things would you like to do, Grandmama?"

"If you were to stay in Little Moseley," Jamie said.

"Well, I'm considered a grande dame, and grandes dames organize and manage."

"Manage what?" George shot her a wary glance.

"Society, mostly, but of course, that means people. People who need a bit of a push to get their lives moving in the right direction, in the right way." Therese considered that, then went on, "If I'm to establish myself as, essentially, the grande dame of Little Moseley—and I rather think that would be the best thing all around—then one of the first issues on my plate would be to do something about the situation with Lord Longfellow. I can understand his sensitivity over his appearance, but it's simply not appropriate for him to continue to hide himself away as he is. And as I did know his parents over many years, one might almost say it's my duty to set him right."

"To give him a push in the right direction?" Lottie had been listening carefully.

"In a manner of speaking." Therese thought, then pulled a face. "Doing that, of course, will be easier said than done."

They'd reached the end of the drive. Therese stretched out one hand and closed it over Jamie's as he drew the mare to a halt. "Let's go right and up the other lane toward Romsey. We have time before luncheon, and I want to consult with Mrs. Swindon."

She removed her hand, and Jamie carefully steered the mare to the right, away from the Hartington Manor drive and on along the lane that led away from the village to eventually join the larger lane that ran north to Romsey and south to the highway connecting Salisbury and Southampton.

The mare judged it was time to trot. The gig had just started to bowl along when George clutched Jamie's arm and pointed ahead to the right. "Look! That gate's been smashed."

"Pull up, Jamie." Therese put her hand over the boy's and helped him draw evenly on the reins until the mare somewhat grudgingly halted. She shook her shaggy head as if exasperated. The gig came to rest, gently rocking, almost directly opposite the old field gate that had been dented and crumpled inward.

George leant from the gig and squinted. "Isn't that paint?" He pointed. "There, along the smashed bit?"

"Yes." Jamie's eyes were sharp. "And it's the same blue as the paint on that damaged curricle at Fulsom Hall."

Looking over the boys' heads, Therese confirmed their assessment. "Well." She faced forward, then murmured, "Fancy that."

Puzzled by her tone, Jamie glanced at her. "That gate's on the Dutton Grange estate, isn't it, Grandmama?"

Still gazing ahead, Therese smiled. "Indeed, it is, my dear."

After a moment, Jamie ventured, "Shouldn't we tell Lord Longfellow about his broken gate?"

"Yes, we should." Therese couldn't stop smiling. "But that broken gate, my dears, is known as a gift from the gods. A helping hand, if you will, and it's wise to learn to recognize such useful occurrences as the opportunities they are."

The children looked at her somewhat cautiously, but Therese couldn't mute her grin. "You'll see. But for now, drive on, James, and take us to Swindon Hall."

CHAPTER 4

After spending a pleasant hour at Swindon Hall, Therese and the children returned to the manor for luncheon, then leaving the mare to a well-deserved rest, they walked down the long drive and across the lane to the church and the vicarage.

With a view to sparing Reverend Colebatch's sensibilities, Therese left the children playing with the vicarage cats on the lawn in the shadow of the hedge between the church and the vicarage, then she climbed the steps to the vicarage porch and rapped smartly on the door.

As she had hoped, the door was opened by Mrs. Colebatch.

"Lady Osbaldestone! Do come in, my lady." Mrs. Colebatch stepped back and waved Therese in. "Jeremy's just gone to his study to work on his sermon, but I know—"

"No, no—I haven't come to disturb the reverend." Therese smiled. "It's you I've come to consult, Henrietta."

"Oh! Well." Henrietta Colebatch blushed. "In that case, please come into the sitting room, and we can talk in peace."

Once they were settled amid a profusion of chintz, after denying any wish for tea, Therese got straight to the point. "I visited Lord Longfellow this morning—a courtesy call given I knew his parents in years gone by and I now intend to make the village my home, as well as to learn if any of his people had any knowledge of our missing geese."

"Oh, dear me, yes. Poor Tooks! And now all the village without their

Christmas dinner. Bilson has said he'll do his best to get in enough cuts of beef, but really! What could have happened to those dratted birds?"

"Indeed, the dearth of birds continues to be a concern. However, while that was my principal reason for calling, I discovered that all is not as it should be at Dutton Grange."

"You mean his lordship shutting himself up and not seeing anyone." Mrs. Colebatch primmed her lips disapprovingly. "I assure you, dear Lady Osbaldestone, that all of us have called—indeed, Mr. Colebatch has been around several times—but to no avail. I assume that large brute of his turned you away?"

"Actually, no. Thanks to the good offices of my grandson, Lord James, we—the three children and I—managed to breach Lord Longfellow's walls and gain an audience."

"Did you, indeed?" Henrietta Colebatch was agog. "And you spoke with his lordship?"

Therese inclined her head. "We took tea with Lord Longfellow, but it's clear he intends to cling to life as a recluse. Tell me, how long has he been hiding in Dutton Grange?"

"He arrived in July. The first we knew of it was from Mrs. Wright and Cook, and then Jeffers—he's the Grange footman—and Johnson, the stableman, told those at the Cockspur Arms the next evening. They'd known he was on his way home from the war after being injured, and he had to stay recuperating in some army hospital on the coast. But then he arrived without even a day's warning, along with two men. One is that hulking brute who says he's his lordship's majordomo."

"Hendricks," Lady Osbaldestone said. "He appears devoted to his lordship."

Mrs. Colebatch sniffed. "That's as may be. Of course, the others have been a part of the household since the old lord's time, but that Hendricks and the other weaselly-looking one, Jiggs—I believe he's his lordship's groom—they keep to themselves, even in the Arms. Not given to talk—not at all."

"I daresay," Lady Osbaldestone murmured, "that the army trains men to be discreet when in situations where they are unsure of their welcome."

Mrs. Colebatch all but bridled. "As to that, if they weren't so set on keeping us from his lordship, we might see our way to being more welcoming."

"I believe that in the matter of enforcing his lordship's privacy, they are acting entirely—and if I read the signs aright, reluctantly—on his lordship's direct orders."

Mrs. Colebatch blinked, then she frowned. "We thought…well, that maybe Christian wasn't yet strong enough to override his keepers, if you know what I mean. It sometimes does happen, and as we haven't seen him, we have no way of knowing if he's in his right mind…you do hear stories of those who return from the wars, and they are not the same people…"

Firmly, Therese stated, "It's nothing like that, I assure you. Lord Longfellow is very definitely running his own show."

Mrs. Colebatch's frown deepened. "Then why on earth would Christian want to keep us at arm's length? We've all known him since he was an infant."

"I rather suspect it's because you—all the village—did know him before. No doubt you remember him as a very handsome young man."

Mrs. Colebatch's face softened as she smiled. "Oh, dear me, yes. He was like an angel fallen to earth—quite beautiful, but in a masculine way."

"Well, in his eyes, he is now only half that man you knew. He's not beautiful anymore."

"What?"

"I take it none of his staff have mentioned his disfigurement?"

"Disfigurement?"

Briefly, Therese described the scars she'd seen. "And I suspect they extend significantly beyond his face. His left leg is also damaged in some way—he walks with a dragging limp."

"And him who was always so energetic!" Mrs. Colebatch's expression had sobered. "The poor boy—although I'm sure he wouldn't want my pity."

"Indeed." Therese paused, then added, "More than anything else, I suspect it's a fear of pity that keeps him hiding away."

"But…it's not healthy." Mrs. Colebatch's voice strengthened. "Major Swindon heard that he—Christian—was very highly regarded as a fine and courageous officer. His command was sorry to lose him. We can't have him hiding away for the rest of his life—what sort of a reward would that be?"

"Precisely." Therese nodded approvingly—encouragingly—at the minister's wife. "While I can understand Christian's reluctance to go about in wider society—society outside Little Moseley—my feeling is that the village is his home, and he needs to be reminded that those who live here don't believe that scars define the man or in any way lessen his worth."

"Oh, indeed. We need to make him understand that we consider him a member of the village regardless of anything so superficial as scars."

Therese smiled. "I'm so glad we see eye to eye on this."

"I'll tell Jeremy the instant he's free." Mrs. Colebatch paused. "But how are we to reassure Christian when he won't even meet us face to face?"

"Even disfigured, and then perhaps even more so, gentlemen do have their pride. We will need to tread warily, my dear Henrietta, if we are to rehabilitate Christian Longfellow to his rightful place in the village. Leave it with me." Therese rose, bringing Mrs. Colebatch to her feet. "Having succeeded in breaching his walls once, I believe I know of a… weapon, as it were, that will allow me to widen the breach. I will keep you and Jeremy informed of progress, and when and how I believe you can help. But for now, I must away and speak with Miss Fitzgibbon."

"Miss Fitzgibbon?" Mrs. Colebatch accompanied Therese to the vicarage's front door. "In that case, you won't have to go far." Mrs. Colebatch opened the door and met Therese's questioning look. "It's Saturday—Miss Fitzgibbon always does the vases in the church every Saturday afternoon. You'll find her there."

Therese smiled. "Thank you. I'll go and speak with her directly."

As she descended the porch steps, she couldn't help but feel that God was smiling on her enterprise.

The children deserted the cats and came running to join her as she walked across the lawn and through the archway in the high hedge. The church, a fine Norman nave with a square tower, rose before her; the front entrance lay to the left, in the shadow of the tower.

The path she was following cut through the gravestones to the vestry door, which was presently set wide.

Lottie slipped her hand into Therese's and skipped along by her side. The graveyard, however, proved irresistible to Jamie and George. They started playing a game of tag around the stones and monuments.

Viewing the boys' antics with an indulgent eye, Therese murmured, "I believe we'll leave them to it." She glanced down and met Lottie's curious gaze. "Meanwhile, you and I can proceed in our quest to put right those things that are presently amiss in village life."

Lottie smiled and looked ahead with transparent eagerness.

Therese's smile deepened; she felt much the same.

They walked through the vestry and into the church. Therese paused by the lectern to survey the nave, which was helpfully deserted. With Lottie's hand still in hers, she walked on and turned to view the sanctuary; a semicircular dais raised three steps above the nave, it housed the altar and the choir stalls beneath the church's lovely stained-glass rose window.

Handsome brass urns stood on twin pedestals, one on either side of the altar. Eugenia was putting the finishing touches to a massive arrangement of evergreens, holly, and Christmas roses in the urn nearer the vestry. The other urn had already been completed and stood resplendent in its Christmas glory.

On hearing their footsteps, Eugenia glanced around and saw them. She was fetchingly gowned in a walking dress of pale blue with a warm wool coat of peacock blue over it. She hadn't worn a hat—leaving nothing to dim the glory of the gold-and-brown curls piled atop her head —but a scarf of patterned blue Norwich silk hung loose about her neck.

Therese smiled. "Good afternoon, Miss Fitzgibbon."

Eugenia bobbed a curtsy. "Lady Osbaldestone." *What brings you here?* hung in the air.

Still smiling easily, Therese nodded at the bloom Eugenia held in her hand. "How lovely. Those Christmas roses are perfect for the season—a touch of white against all the dark greens. Hope blooming in the darkest days, as it were. Are they from the Hall's hothouse?"

Eugenia nodded. "We provide them every Christmas."

Therese nudged Lottie toward the front pew. "Winter is about to descend on us in earnest, I fear. The cold is intensifying." Therese sat; Lottie leant against her knees, observing Eugenia with an unwavering gaze. "This morning's frost was decidedly crisp."

Somewhat warily, Eugenia nodded. She turned back to the urn and carefully slid the white Christmas rose into place. "The village lake has already frozen over. They're predicting we'll have a good solid surface for the skating party." She glanced at Lottie. "That's usually in six days' time, on the twentieth of the month, provided the ice is solid enough." She raised her gaze to Therese's face. "Will the children still be here?"

"Yes, they will. Their father's illness will keep them banished from their home until at least the end of the year."

"Ah, well." Eugenia smiled at Lottie. "At least they'll have plenty of village activities to enjoy. We have the carol service soon and the re-enactment of the nativity as well."

"So Crimmins was telling us." With one hand, Therese stroked Lottie's neat plaits. "The children plan to participate in everything. And as I plan to make Hartington Manor my permanent home, I'll be attending, too. I'm quite looking forward to it."

"I see." Eugenia slipped the last of her blooms into place, then glanced at Therese, plainly wondering if there was a reason for Therese being there.

Therese smiled; Eugenia Fitzgibbon was not at all slow. "As part of my settling into village life, I called at Dutton Grange this morning."

"Ah." Eugenia nodded crisply. "And you were turned away as all others have been."

"No, as it happens. We took tea with his lordship. But that wasn't why I wished to speak with you, my dear." Without giving Eugenia a chance to ask about that meeting with Lord Longfellow, Therese smoothly continued, "On leaving the Grange, we turned into the lane to the east, on our way to call on the Swindons. And on the right a little way beyond the Grange drive, we discovered a gate that has been staved in. Smashed, more or less."

Eugenia frowned. "That must be on the Grange estate."

Therese nodded. "Indeed. Rather more pertinent to you, however, is that there are streaks of bright-blue paint on the smashed gate."

Eugenia stared at Therese for several seconds, then her shoulders fell. A moment later, her features set, and her expression darkened. "Henry! I might have known."

"He didn't mention it?"

"No. He didn't." The anger that had sparked in Eugenia's blue eyes subsided to a smolder, and her chin firmed. "Yet another mess I'll have to clear up and put right." She surveyed the arrangement in the urn, tweaked one branch of conifer, then with sharp, abrupt movements collected her trimmings and stepped down to the nave. "I'm finished here. I'll go home immediately and see about putting things right."

"As to that"—Therese rose and, with Lottie beside her, trailed behind Eugenia as she carried the detritus of her flower arranging into the vestry—"as I mentioned, I called there this morning. Although we did win through to converse with his lordship, that wasn't a concession easily gained."

Eugenia dumped the clipped stems and leaves into a basket, then plied a small pump handle set over a trough and washed her hands—and angled a questioning look at Therese.

Therese leant against the counter a few feet away. "It transpires that as well as being afflicted with a dragging limp, his lordship is badly scarred on one side of his face. Consequently, he believes himself to be so hideous that common decency requires that he hide himself away." Therese looked down at Lottie. "But he wasn't frightening to look at, was he, poppet?"

With all the gravity of her five years, Lottie shook her head from side to side. "He was grumpy and growly and yelled when Jamie first found him, but when we went inside, he behaved and was gentlemanly."

"Exactly." Therese looked up and caught Eugenia's eyes. "Yet he believes his scars and injuries preclude him from rejoining society. That's not at all true, yet, men! They can be so vain, they quite put us ladies in the shade."

Eugenia humphed, but distractedly. After a moment of gazing vacantly into space, she offered, "I remember him, of course, but he's six years my senior, and we were never friends. That said, anyone in the area would remember him—he was so exceedingly handsome, yet he was also…cheery, and easygoing, gregarious, and always ready with a laugh, and never one to put on airs." She met Therese's eyes. "People liked him despite his outrageous handsomeness."

"Oh, he's still outrageously handsome when seen from one side. Indeed"—Therese lightly frowned as she pondered the effect—"I would suggest that the destruction of beauty on one side makes the unmarred perfection shine even more dramatically."

Eugenia raised her brows. "He was the gentleman all the young ladies around about dreamed of, but thinking back, I suspect he would have been that even had he been much more plain featured. His beauty caught the eye, but it was his character and temperament that drew one in, drew one closer."

Therese studied Eugenia Fitzgibbon with a discerning eye and saw rather more than that young lady might have wished. More, what Therese perceived spurred her on. "Well," she said, straightening from the counter, "contrasting your view of Christian Longfellow-as-was with the brooding presence I encountered this morning, I believe it behooves us—all of us in the village—to make a push to correct his rather disparaging view of our intelligence."

Eugenia uttered a scoffing laugh. "Given the extent of the Peninsula campaigns, I doubt there are many villages in England that haven't learned the truth that scars and injuries do not make the man." Somewhat exasperatedly, she continued, "And great heavens! Everyone knows that in Christian's case, his scars and injuries were gained fighting for our country, rather than in some idiotic curricle race, like his brother."

Therese blinked. "Is that how he died?"

Eugenia nodded. "Cedric Longfellow's death was all of a piece with his life. He was irresponsible in every way. There are more than a few who were close to his father—my father among them—who were of the opinion that it was almost a relief to Leslie Longfellow that Cedric took himself off, leaving Christian to inherit. Christian was always the steady, sensible, reliable son."

"Hmm." Therese pondered that insight as, with Eugenia, she and Lottie stepped out of the vestry into the increasingly gloomy day. "I daresay that reliability is why Christian is here at all—he will see the estate and his workers right, even if he deems himself unfit to join even village society."

"Yes, well. Now I have to attend to this business with the gate."

Therese bent a shrewd gaze on the younger woman. "If you don't mind me asking, dear, how do you propose to approach the matter? Send Henry to apologize?"

Eugenia halted; her expression grew more harassed as she thought the matter through. "I *should* send Henry—it's his apology to make, after all. Only if I do..." After a moment, she sighed. "With matters standing as they are with Christian, I'm not sure I should risk it. I certainly can't be sure of Henry's tactfulness. There's no saying what he—or even more likely, one of his stupidly arrogant friends—might blurt out."

"Indeed. I have often noted that young men can be quite thoughtless over issues such as extreme disfigurement. Especially to a previously strikingly handsome man."

"Exactly. And I definitely do not want, much less need, any bad feeling giving rise to awkwardness between the Hall and the Grange."

Clasping her hands on the head of her cane, Therese nodded sagely. "Being one of the two major households in the village does bring with it a certain responsibility."

Eugenia sighed again. "Yes, it does, and at this time, that responsibility rests entirely on my shoulders." She glanced at Therese. "I'll go and speak with Christian myself and explain about the gate and that we—the Hall—will have it repaired."

Therese nodded. "A wise decision." She was conscious of Lottie watching her expectantly, as if the little girl knew there was one step more to be achieved in Therese's subtle maneuverings. "However, with regard to speaking with Christian—and I agree entirely that you should speak directly to him and not simply leave a message with his majordomo—the fact that my imps and I managed to inveigle our way past Christian's barricades should not be taken as a sign that he has in any way stepped back from his habit of having his people deny him to all callers."

Eugenia frowned. "Well, I have to see him. I am certainly not going to apologize by proxy. Even if I am, in effect, a proxy myself."

"Quite so. Which, my dear, is why I believe I should accompany you on your mission. I—" She broke off as Jamie and George came pelting up to join them; they looked like nothing so much as happy, exhausted puppies with their tongues lolling out. She smiled and amended, "We have already breached Lord Longfellow's walls once today. I'm perfectly certain we can replicate the accomplishment and ensure you get to speak with Christian face to face." She arched an eyebrow at Eugenia. "If you're of a mind to accept our help, of course."

Eugenia thought for only a moment, then her chin firmed, and she nodded. "Thank you. I would be glad of your company"—she looked at the three children—"and your help in getting past the door of Dutton Grange."

Therese smiled. "Right, then. When would you like to storm the Grange?"

Eugenia's lips twitched. She looked at the sky, which was heavy with dark-gray clouds, but the sun, screened by the louring mass, had not yet sunk too far into the west. She glanced at Therese. "No time like the present. There's hours still left in the day. If you're free, that is?"

Therese's smile deepened. "You're a lady after my own heart, my dear. I—and my retinue—are entirely free and ready to assist you. If you will wait in the lane in your gig, we'll fetch ours and join you."

Eugenia nodded.

Dramatically, Therese waved across the lane toward Hartington Manor. "Onward."

The children grinned, then, laughing, pelted across the lawn toward the lane.

CHAPTER 5

Eugenia drew her gig to a halt in the forecourt before Dutton Grange.

Jamie carefully steered the Hartington Manor gig alongside, drawing back on the reins to halt the mare next to Eugenia's cob.

"Good work." Therese patted Jamie's shoulder. She spotted the groom, Jiggs, looking out from around the corner of the house. She put her finger to her lips, then beckoned him over.

The children scrambled down. Jiggs gave Therese his hand to help her to the gravel. She handed him the reins. "We've come to see your master on a matter of village importance. Is he skulking in his library again?"

"I wouldn't say skulking, my lady. More like brooding darkly. But aye, he's there."

"In that case"—Therese turned to Jamie and George, who were awaiting orders—"I rather think you two should go around to the terrace as you did this morning and inform his lordship that I have arrived and wish to speak with him. We will be waiting in the hall." She met both boys' eyes. "Make sure you get him to come out of the library."

"Yes, Grandmama!" they chorused.

At her nod, they took off around the house.

Jiggs watched them go, a slight frown on his face.

Therese touched his sleeve. "You couldn't have stopped them, and you need to wait here and look after our gigs."

Jiggs met her gaze and nodded. "Aye, ma'am—my lady." He duly moved to stand between the gigs and accepted the reins of Eugenia's from her.

Eugenia looked inquiringly at Therese. "Now what?"

"Now, my dear, you keep to my shadow until we get inside and have Lord Longfellow before us." Therese took Lottie's hand and, once again, marched to the porch, climbed the steps, and halted before the front door.

"May I?" Lottie pointed at the bell chain.

Therese nodded. "Go ahead. Nice and firmly."

Lottie stretched up, gripped the chain's triangular handle, and all but swung on it. From where Therese stood, with Eugenia directly behind her, she could hear the pealing deep inside the house. Even Christian must know he had visitors at his front door.

Heavy footsteps approached, and the door was wrenched open. Hendricks saw Therese and Lottie and blinked.

"Good afternoon, Hendricks." Therese swept past him and on into the hall proper. "I have brought Miss Fitzgibbon"—with an imperious wave, Therese indicated the young lady who had stuck close behind her and was now standing on the hall tiles, too—"who has a matter of some importance to discuss with his lordship."

Hendricks had taken in the vision that was Miss Eugenia Fitzgibbon. With an expression caught between fascination and disbelief, he asked, "What should I tell him?"

Sounds emanated from farther down the hall as the library door was opened.

Therese looked that way. "I don't believe you'll need to summon his lordship. I've arranged for him to be fetched."

At that moment, Christian Longfellow emerged from the shadows, being all but propelled by the two youngsters at his back. His head was turned as he remonstrated with them. "All right, all right, you terrors. I'm here, aren't I? Now"—Christian turned to face Therese—"what does your grandmama want with me this time?"

Eugenia took that as her cue. Stepping out from behind Therese, she faced Christian, still three yards away. "Actually, Lord Longfellow, it's I who must speak with you."

Immediately he'd seen her, Christian had planted his feet and refused to budge another inch regardless of the boys' prodding. He swung slightly so the left side of his face was half hidden.

For a long moment, no one in the hall moved or spoke. Therese watched as Eugenia and Christian stared at each other.

She hadn't actually known, but she'd made enough matches in her time to wonder...and if her eyes didn't deceive her, and they rarely did, there was more than enough attraction here for her to work with.

Eugenia cleared her throat. "I daresay you don't remember me—"

"You're Eugenia Fitzgibbon. Young Henry's older sister."

Eugenia nodded. "Yes, that's right. And as it happens"—her chin set more firmly—"it's due to Henry that I'm here. I'm afraid I have to inform you that Henry crashed his curricle into one of your gates." She waved in the general direction. "The one on the village lane. I'm afraid the gate is smashed and needs repair. I came to let you know that, of course, we—the Fulsom Hall estate—will take care of repairing or replacing the gate."

Christian's frown had been steadily deepening. "Where's Henry? If he's old enough to drive a curricle into a gate, then he's old enough to face the consequences..." He paused for only a heartbeat, but his voice sounded hollow when he went on, "To face me and make his own apologies."

Eugenia's head rose. "As to that, my brother is still a minor, and I manage the day-to-day running of the estate. It's in that role that I'm here, purely to let you know that Fulsom Hall will, naturally, bear full responsibility for fixing the gate."

All but scowling, albeit apparently not at them but rather at the absent Henry, Christian waved dismissively. "There's no need to bestir yourself over such a thing. My people will mend the gate—it's of no consequence and nothing Fulsom Hall needs to be concerned about."

Therese opened her eyes wide. "You haven't even seen the damage yet."

"Regardless." Christian bit off the word. His eyes met Therese's, his expression one that stated he knew exactly to whom he owed the second interruption to his day. Then he transferred his gaze, hard and unyielding, to Eugenia's face. "I neither wish for nor will I accept any reparation from anyone in this matter."

Therese bit her lip to stop her smile. Evidently, no one had taught Christian that making statements of that sort in such domineering and dictatorial tones, while no doubt very useful in the army, when directed at a certain type of female tended to convert the issue under discussion into an outright challenge.

The equivalent of flinging down a gauntlet no red-blooded woman would let lie.

Sure enough, Eugenia's eyes flashed, and her chin rose another notch. "Nonsense! In this village—"

Christian snapped his gaze to Hendricks. "See that the gate is repaired immediately."

Hendricks only just stopped himself from saluting. "Yes, sir—my lord."

Eugenia all but fumed. "Lord Longfellow—"

"I'm afraid, ladies, that you've called at an inopportune time." Ruthlessly, Christian gestured to the door and advanced—essentially forcing them to give ground. "I was engaged in a matter of business that requires my immediate attention."

His swift glance at Jamie and George didn't escape Therese. Jamie looked at her, but she quickly shook her head. No need to give Christian away—he was doing an excellent job of infuriating Eugenia all on his own.

That lady all but spluttered, but was forced to yield—to fall back toward the open front door.

"Come, children." Therese caught Eugenia's eyes and signaled that this was not the right battleground on which to engage. "Come, my dear Miss Fitzgibbon. I can bear witness that you did your duty, even though your appropriate and generous offer fell on such deaf ears and stony ground."

Christian shot Therese a glance, but she had long been immune to such intimidatory tactics. Gathering the children with a gesture, she herded them, along with Eugenia, outside.

Christian halted just inside the front door. He cast a swift glance at the sky, then looked at them as they formed up on the porch. "Good day, ladies." There was a finality in his tone impossible to mistake. "And given the weather is closing in, I suggest you hurry to your homes." With that, he shut the door.

Eugenia glared daggers at the panel, then whirled and marched down the steps.

Therese followed a great deal more calmly.

"Wretched man! Whoever would have thought he'd turn into such a bear? And saying a smashed gate was of no account! What does he think we are? Or does he believe the Fulsom Hall estate isn't able to stand the cost of the repairs? Huh! He all but insulted us!"

"I don't think," Therese murmured, "that insulting you or your family was his intention. He wanted to get you out of his orbit as rapidly as he possibly could, and that was the fastest way."

"Humph!" After a moment, her color still high, Eugenia muttered, "He's insufferable."

"Yes, indeed—it wasn't well done, but I suppose one has to excuse him given it is the first time anyone has sought to directly confront him, and he was a soldier, after all—by now, barking orders like that comes naturally to him, I expect."

"Even so."

They'd almost reached the gigs and Jiggs. In more pensive tone, Therese remarked, "Of course, there's more than one way to make reparation, if you were of a mind to attempt an alternative approach."

Eugenia shot her a sidelong look. She halted by her cob's head, accepted the reins from Jiggs, then, with a determined light in her eye, faced Therese. "What alternative approach?"

Therese smiled. She nodded at Jamie to take the reins to their gig, then directed her smile at Jiggs. "Thank you, Jiggs. In the interests of deniability, I suggest you take yourself off."

"Not sure what that is, but if'n you mean so his nibs can't ask me about what you're going to talk about, then aye—I'll be off." After a brief bob to Therese and another to Eugenia, he turned and strode off.

Therese seized the chance to look back at the Grange, at the two stories of rooms, all with their curtains drawn tight. "It looks like no one lives there, doesn't it?"

Eugenia had followed her gaze. "It was so gloomy in the hall—it must be just as bad throughout the house, at least in all those rooms."

"Indeed. No light, no life. And certainly no Christmas spirit. So sad at this time of year. I daresay even the staff must feel it." Therese turned to regard Eugenia. As the younger woman looked away from the house, Therese continued, "From what I've gathered, if some determined and resolute lady were to arrive and insist on opening up the curtains and placing holly and fir on the mantels and so on, the staff wouldn't object. Indeed, I rather think they would cheer such a lady on."

Glancing back at the house, Eugenia arched her brows. "We have plenty of holly and fir at the Hall."

Therese nodded. "Of course, it would require someone to distract his lordship and get him out of the house. As it happens, although he did get Hendricks to inquire of his staff, I'm fairly sure no one has undertaken a search of the outbuildings—not with sufficient thoroughness to be categorically certain the geese were never there."

The three children had been listening avidly. Now, Jamie piped up, "If we're to track down the geese, then we need to be absolutely sure that they never came this way."

"Exactly." Therese nodded approvingly and glanced at Eugenia. "As you can see, my three assistants and I are willing to get his lordship out of the house, thus leaving the way clear for some intrepid lady to bully her way inside and deck his halls."

For what might well have been the first time that afternoon, Eugenia grinned.

They swiftly made plans for the next day, then, in companionable accord, climbed back into their gigs and drove away.

From between the heavy curtains covering the drawing room window, Christian watched the two ladies disappear down his drive.

He hadn't liked the way they'd been conferring. He'd got the distinct impression they were planning, and their plan, whatever it was, had something to do with him.

Worse, they'd both been smiling when they'd left.

That, he felt sure, did not bode well.

After dinner that evening, Therese allowed the children to follow her into her private parlor. Although the room had originally been the manor's morning room, she considered it her personal sanctum to which she admitted only her closest confidantes.

Realizing that she'd elevated the three imps to that restricted status, she inwardly smiled. Settling into her favorite wing chair beside the hearth, she watched the trio amble about the room, examining this and that before gravitating toward the nice blaze that leapt and danced in the hearth.

Outside, the wind had risen to a mournful howl and was blowing sleet against the windowpanes. But the curtains were drawn, and it was warm and cozy inside.

One by one, the trio came to sit on the floor before her feet.

Settling, their expressions childishly open and eager, they looked up at her, clearly expecting some further discussion of their plans.

"I believe," she said, "that for our purposes, the best time for us to call at Dutton Grange will be eleven o'clock. No later, or Miss Fitzgibbon won't have time to do all she needs before his lordship's stomach reminds him of the advancing hour."

"But we're going to go to the Hall first, aren't we?" George bounced on his legs, folded beneath him. "To help Miss Fitzgibbon gather holly and ivy and fir?"

"Indeed, we are," Therese replied. "And that means you three will need to bestir yourselves in good time. Breakfast at eight, I think. Then we can be at the Hall before nine, which should give us and Miss Fitzgibbon plenty of time to gather the required amount of greenery."

She regarded her three helpers. "I wonder," she continued, "aside from holly, ivy, and boughs of fir, what other Christmassy greenery the Hall woods might offer us."

Jamie sat up. "We should hunt for mistletoe."

"Yes!" George and Lottie chorused.

"Mama hangs mistletoe all over our house," Jamie went on, "at least in the rooms downstairs. She hangs bits over every doorway—she says it's important to have the white berries on the bits you hang."

"Mama says Christmas isn't Christmas without mistletoe," Lottie said.

Pleased—quietly chuffed to hear one of her own sayings repeated to her after all these years—Therese nodded. "I'm sure there'll be mistletoe if you look, but…it occurs to me that, being an unmarried young lady, Miss Fitzgibbon might balk at hanging mistletoe in Lord Longfellow's house. A house not her own, you see. She might view it as not being appropriate."

It was Lottie who looked at Jamie, then George, then turned her face up to Therese and asked, "Miss Eugenia might not want to hang mistletoe, but is there any reason we can't, Grandmama?"

Therese smiled her approval and leant forward to ruffle Lottie's curls, released from their plaits for the evening. "No, dear, none at all. Your mama has it right—Christmas isn't Christmas without mistletoe, and our purpose tomorrow is to bring Christmas to Lord Longfellow and the household of Dutton Grange.

"However," she went on, sitting back in her chair to survey her troops, "that means you'll have to exercise discretion regarding the mistletoe. Firstly, while gathering it—as it grows higher in the trees, I suggest Jamie should take a large satchel and collect it while you, Lottie and George, help me keep Miss Fitzgibbon occupied gathering the holly, ivy, and fir. As you'll be journeying to the Grange with me in our gig, transferring the mistletoe to the Grange will not be a problem. But once at the Grange…again, I think Jamie will have to do the honors. I'll be herding Lord Longfellow around his outbuildings, and again, Lottie and George, you will need to ensure Miss Fitzgibbon is absorbed with laying out the other greenery."

Understanding by their nods and eager expressions that the younger two were willing to allow Jamie to be responsible for the special mission, Therese turned her gaze on him. "You, meanwhile, can hang as much mistletoe as you can carry into the house. Don't forget to get pins from Orneby in the morning. I daresay Jiggs, and even Hendricks, might be prevailed upon to help you pin the pieces over the doorways." She smiled. "Unless I miss my guess, they're sensible sorts—I rather think they'll help if they can."

At that point, Mrs. Crimmins and Orneby arrived. The children readily scrambled to their feet and went off, happily chattering, to wash and be put to bed.

Therese sat and stared at the flames and felt her own expectations for the morrow swell. It was, she reflected, nothing short of amazing what benefits accrued from having three small persons to guide and mentor through having them join her in furthering her aims.

CHAPTER 6

The following morning dawned cold and clear, with a crisp frost limning every blade and branch. But the clouds had vanished, and the sun shone steadily if weakly from a sky of pale cerulean blue. It had been chilly in the shadows of the Fulsom Hall woods, but by the time Therese turned her gig into the Grange's drive, the sunshine had melted the ice, and the gravel crunched softly under the gig's wheels.

At eleven o'clock on the dot, devoid of her usual entourage, she drove into the forecourt of Dutton Grange.

She'd dropped off her grandchildren thirty yards down the drive, where a bend gave them cover from the house. Lottie and George would wait for Eugenia there, while Jamie was already making his way into the gardens. He would keep watch and go into the house once he saw Therese exit with his lordship in tow.

Christian Longfellow was not going to know what had hit him.

Smiling, Therese drew up with a flourish, and as soon as Jiggs appeared, she handed him the reins. "I expect to be here for an hour or so, Jiggs."

"Very good, my lady. I'll take your beast around to the stable yard. Just have them send when you're ready to leave."

"Thank you." Therese was already on her way to the front door.

At her peremptory tugging on the bell chain, Hendricks opened the door, saw it was her, and immediately stepped back. "My lady. His lordship is in the library." The large man paused, then inquired, "Would you like to wait here, or should I announce you?"

Therese beamed. "Good man—indeed, there's no sense in wasting time. Do simply announce me."

Hendricks bowed, closed the door, and led the way down the hall to the library. He opened the door, walked in two paces, and declaimed, "Lady Osbaldestone, my lord."

Christian jerked to attention, his gaze rising from contemplation of the chessboard laid out on the small table before his armchair. He was playing against himself. Hardly exciting, but none of the other males in the household had mastered the game well enough to provide any decent competition.

As Hendricks's words sank in, he didn't even have time to roll his eyes before her ladyship swept into the room. Her black gaze skewered him. Perforce, he pushed awkwardly to his feet.

He hadn't been walking enough lately, the weather being what it was, and his leg was stiffer than it should have been, leaving him feeling unbalanced even when he was not. He planted his cane and made it to his feet without toppling over. "Lady Osbaldestone." He sketched a bow, then bluntly asked, "How can we help you today?"

Instead of answering, she came forward, apparently drawn by his game of chess. She studied the chessboard for several seconds, then pointed. "Knight takes the castle, and then you're in check."

He frowned at the board. He hadn't noticed that move, but she was correct. From beneath his brows, he glanced at her. "You play?"

"My late husband was an aficionado. I helped him practice."

He would study the move later. Straightening, he repeated, "How may we assist you?"

He had to be polite to her. After yesterday's encounter, he'd endured an evening of reproachful looks from Hendricks and Jiggs, and even Mrs. Wright. Apparently, they all felt he should have been kinder to Miss Fitzgibbon, who had merely come by as a neighbor to confess to damaging his property and discuss putting matters right.

Perfectly understandable, only he hadn't seen it that way.

He remembered Eugenia Fitzgibbon quite well, and if he hadn't paid much attention to her in the past, now, she represented everything he felt his injuries had taken from him—any hope of a decent marriage, of children. Of family and a true home.

Pushing such maunderings deep, he fixed his attention on Lady Osbaldestone.

She was still frowning at the chessboard. Then she looked up and met his eyes. "You're playing against yourself?"

He nodded.

"Well, someday, I'll have to invite you for dinner, and we can see if you measure up to my mark."

He swallowed a snort; he'd had a great deal of time to practice while waiting for his injuries to heal, and he was just short of being considered a master.

"Meanwhile, however, I'm here to beg your indulgence over searching your outbuildings for any sign of these infernal geese. I realize none of your people have seen any sign of them, but it's unlikely that they specifically searched for any hint of the geese having passed this way. If we're to track the wretched birds, then we need to eliminate the areas through which they haven't been."

He could appreciate the logic of that approach, but… "It seems unlikely that the geese reached here without first crossing any of the properties in between."

She opened her eyes wide. "Who can tell with geese?"

That was unarguable. He glanced outside and was surprised to see that it wasn't raining or snowing or sleeting. He hadn't been out for days, and he really should stretch his legs.

The door opened, and Hendricks walked in. "Your pardon, my lord, but Johnson wants to know if you want the gate exactly as it was before or if it's all right to alter the position of the struts when he puts on the new ones?"

That was another sore point; his staff had not been at all pleased with his order to replace the gate immediately if not sooner. Especially as it seemed the Hall had the right sort of tools and were usually the ones to build the gates in the locality, but Christian had insisted his people repair the gate themselves. Which they could certainly do, but the price, apparently, was a great deal of grumbling.

If he allowed Lady Osbaldestone to search through his outbuildings, then he really should accompany her, shouldn't he?

He nodded to Hendricks. "Tell Johnson to do whatever he thinks is best. Meanwhile"—he waved Lady Osbaldestone to the door—"her ladyship and I will be checking the outbuildings to ensure no sign of the missing geese has been inadvertently overlooked."

As he followed a transparently approving Lady Osbaldestone into the hall, then led her to the side door, Christian reflected that this was all to the good. Opening the side door, he stood back to allow her to precede him. "I haven't done more than take a cursory look at the outbuildings since I returned. I can check over the structures while we search."

Lady Osbaldestone smiled and stepped out onto the side terrace. "Of course, dear. We've plenty of time to take a good look around."

With a huge bag of holly hanging from one hand, Eugenia dragged in a breath of cold winter air, held it, and knocked smartly on the door of Dutton Grange. She didn't use the bell; she didn't know how loudly it rang and where in the house it rang. Lady Osbaldestone had said fifteen minutes would do for her to winkle Christian Longfellow out of his house. With Lottie and George holding a basket full of fir boughs and ivy and waiting impatiently beside her, Eugenia had had no option but to place her faith in their grandmother's abilities.

The door opened. A curious Hendricks looked out.

Before he could say anything, Eugenia asked, "Is his lordship still in the house?"

Hendricks frowned. "He's just stepped out with Lady Osbaldestone."

"Excellent!" Eugenia stepped forward, all but pushing Hendricks back with the prickly bag of holly.

"Ow!" Hendricks gave way. "What's that?"

"Holly." Eugenia set the bag down and waved at George and Lottie as they tottered in behind her. "And fir boughs and ivy."

Hendricks looked as if he wasn't sure what expression he should adopt. Eventually, he said, "I suppose you're absolutely set on putting this stuff about."

"Indeed." Eugenia was already surveying the hall. "And I intend to open up all the rooms, so please explain that to Mrs. Wright later. It's all a part of our plan to bring Christmas to his lordship and this house."

"Hmm." Hendricks pondered for a moment more, then slowly—as if working through the train of thought—said, "If you're not to be dissuaded, then as his lordship's representative, as it were, I should probably help you rather than cause a flap, because it would surely be worth my head if you"—he switched his gaze to the two children standing innocently nearby—"or either of these tykes were injured." He looked at Eugenia. "That sound right to you, miss?"

Eugenia met Hendricks's eyes, read the message therein, and crisply nodded. "Quite right, Hendricks. Viewed in that fashion, it would be worth your position *not* to help us."

Hendricks nodded heavily. "That's what I thought." He went to lift the basket Lottie and George were dragging. "Here, let me get that." Lifting the basket in his arms, he turned to Eugenia. "So where do we start? The drawing room?"

They started in there, dragging the curtains wide, removing the shrouding Holland covers, and draping fir boughs artfully accented with sprigs of holly over the wide mantelpiece and on various side tables. At one point, Mrs. Wright bustled in, saw what they were doing, primmed her lips for a moment, then nodded and walked to the pile of Holland covers and swept them into her arms. "I'll be right glad to see the last of these."

With that, she bustled out.

Eugenia exchanged a glance with Hendricks, then, smiling, continued decorating.

From the drawing room, they progressed to the morning room and the dining room and eventually girded their loins and tackled the library, a room Eugenia gathered was Christian's lair for brooding. She hung as much holly, bright with red berries, as she could about the mantelpiece in there.

Lord James put his head around the door. He patted the satchel hanging from his shoulder. "I have more stuff here. I'll just put it out, shall I?"

Eugenia nodded. "Do." George and Lottie came to hand her more holly. When she looked up again, James had vanished.

Hendricks was staring at the door. "I think I'll just go and help him."

Leaving Eugenia, George, and Lottie putting holly all over the library, Hendricks moved silently through the downstairs rooms until he heard the telltale scrape of furniture being dragged.

He tracked the sound to the dining room and found Lord James trying to haul a carver closer to the door.

Hendricks halted in the doorway. Lord James looked up at him.

Then Jamie smiled a sweet, beguiling smile, reached into his satchel, and showed Hendricks what he had to hang. "I want to put it up over the doorways. I have pins." Jamie showed Hendricks those, too.

"Mistletoe." Hendricks humphed. "Complete with berries."

"My mama says it's not much use without the berries. No kisses."

Hendricks nodded his great head. "That's true." He swiveled to look at the top of the doorway, within easy reach for him. "Here." He held out a meaty paw. "Give me that and a pin, and I'll get it up for you. No need to disturb the furniture."

Jamie grinned and complied.

Meanwhile, having done their best in the library, Eugenia carried the bag with the remaining fir boughs, tendrils of trailing ivy, and the last bunches of holly into the front hall. "I'll use what's left in here, I think." She set the bag down by the huge hearth that dominated the end wall of the long hall. "Why don't you two find your brother and then go out to the gig and wait? I won't be long, and then we really should be on our way."

George, carrying their now-empty basket, nodded. He took Lottie's hand. "We'll wait out there. Jamie will find us." With that, the pair headed for the front door.

Eugenia turned to the fireplace. Her hands on her hips, she surveyed the massive stone coping above it; she had little doubt it dated from medieval times. From the corner of her eye, she saw the groom—Jiggs, wasn't it?—watching from the corridor leading to the staff's quarters. Distinctly, she stated, "I'm going to need a ladder if I'm to manage this." After a second, she added, "But first, I think I'll go upstairs and open some of the curtains up there."

She turned on her heel, went to the stairs, and swiftly climbed. She paused on the half landing to haul the curtains covering the large stained glass window wide; she spent a few minutes tying the curtains back with the cords that dangled on either side. Then she quickly climbed to the first floor and opened every curtain along the gallery.

Then she went back down the stairs—and grinned when she saw a tall ladder propped against the wall beside the fireplace. "Thank you," she sang and hurried to it.

The outbuildings of Dutton Grange were extensive. As well as the usual barn and stable, there was a sizeable toolshed, a small forge, a workshop, a gardener's shed, and three long, glassed greenhouses, two of which were not presently in use.

Therese insisted on walking through every building, surveying the floors, the rafters, looking into corners. Christian paced alongside her, also taking note, but he was patently more interested in the fabric of the buildings than in any evidence of feathered occupancy.

She wasn't entirely surprised they found no trace of the missing geese. "It's a mystery as to where those birds have gone," she said as she stepped out of the last greenhouse. Their wanderings had taken them far from the house.

Christian joined her. He pulled the door of the greenhouse shut behind them, then gestured to a path that wound through the gardens. "We can go back to the house that way."

Therese was perfectly happy to stroll in that direction. She glanced sidelong at Christian as he fell into step beside her. "The estate seems to be prospering."

He shrugged. "It's doing well enough." She remained silent and waited, and after a minute, he went on, "I've spent the last months, ever since I returned here, overhauling everything to do with the estate. My father was a decent manager, but he wasn't inclined to try new methods, and over the last years, his health had been failing, and the estate had largely been left to manage itself. As you probably know, no estate does well under such circumstances for long. But I was lucky, and the base was still there—the fundamentals were sound. I just needed to reshape things, invest here and there as needed, and encourage the tenant farmers and our own workers to go forward with their best plans, to implement their best ideas."

"But that's largely completed now, isn't it? Your taking up of the reins, as it were?"

He nodded. "Now, it's simply a matter of keeping things on track."

"So what are you going to do with your days? What challenge is next on your list?"

A frown slowly gathered in his eyes and bleakness invested his expression, then he shrugged and looked down. "I'm sure I'll find something."

Therese eyed him with a mixture of compassion and impatience; she had a shrewd suspicion he knew what he wanted, but had convinced himself that courtesy of his injuries, that prize had moved forever beyond his reach.

We'll see about that.

Almost as if he could hear her thoughts, he grew more uncomfortable

—positively twitchy. She was perfectly capable of walking briskly, but had been deliberately pacing slowly and making overt use of her cane.

He glanced at the house. Then he blinked and frowned.

Following his gaze, she realized he'd noticed the now-open curtains. However, judging by his puzzled expression, she didn't think he'd pinpointed what precisely about his house had changed.

He took an impulsive step forward, then swung to her. "As there was no trace of the geese, if you'll excuse me, I should get back to the house. There are matters I need to deal with."

If only he knew…

Regally, she inclined her head. "Of course, dear. And thank you for your time. By all means, go ahead. I'll stroll back more slowly."

With a crisp nod, he turned and strode rapidly for the house.

Therese watched him go. Slowly, she smiled. She'd kept a mental note of the minutes ticking past; she rather thought the timing of his return would prove particularly fortuitous.

She arched her brows and started walking more briskly. "In one way or another."

Christian was mentally shaking his head and trying to fathom just what his still-well-honed instincts were attempting to tell him when he walked into his house via the side door and paced into the rear of the front hall.

The sight that met his eyes halted him in his tracks.

A slender figure in a cherry-red pelisse was clinging to the very top of a long ladder and reaching—stretching—to place a bough of dark-green fir over the very top of the stone coping above the fireplace.

Shock and a sharp spike of an unfamiliar fear had him barking, *"Good God, woman! What the devil do you think you're doing?"*

He'd forgotten how powerful his voice—accustomed to vying with the roar of battle—was.

Eugenia jumped and swung around—far too fast.

The ladder shifted, then started to slowly slide to the side…

She fought to regain her balance, but that only made things worse.

Uttering a small cry, she let go of the ladder and fell.

Appalled, Christian saw it all.

He would have sworn he couldn't have made it in time, that his injured leg would never have permitted it.

He was every bit as surprised as she when he was there to snatch her into his arms, taking her weight, and even though he stumbled back a step, he managed to keep them both upright.

The ladder clanged and bounced on the flagstones.

Hendricks, Jamie, and Jiggs had been hanging the last of the mistletoe in the drawing room; on hearing Christian's bellow, they'd cautiously peeked out into the hall.

They saw the pair before the fireplace—Eugenia held safely in Christian's arms. Her hands on his shoulders, she was staring down at him, shock and a type of wonder very clear in her face, while Christian, unmoving, stared up at her.

The three glanced at each other, then, as one, silently withdrew.

Christian felt stunned on more levels than one. He stared into Eugenia's lightly flushed face, into eyes of summer blue that to his starved senses seemed to hold the promise of sunny days stretching into a halcyon future. His body responded to the feel of a woman in his arms, to the supple feminine strength, the seductive curves.

Parts of him he'd regarded as virtually dead stirred to unabashed life.

He might be hideously disfigured, he might be permanently lame, but he was still a man.

His senses, his nerves, his very skin clamored with that message while his blood pounded a steady, relentless, insistent beat in his veins.

He'd once been precisely the sort of gentleman his handsomeness had entitled him to be; ladies had always been easy come, easy go. In those days, his bed had rarely been cold. Even in the army, wherever they'd been billeted, he'd had his pick of the ladies.

He told himself the intensity of his reaction to Eugenia Fitzgibbon was merely due to the enforced celibacy of the past year. But only a small part of him believed that. The better part of his mind was curious and intent on pursuing what it sensed was…something different.

Something desirable.

Potentially exceedingly desirable in many more ways than one.

All sorts of ideas—all sorts of witty ripostes—started to bubble up in his mind as the man he'd thought he'd left on the battlefield at Talavera staged a resurgence, returning to life…

No. No, no, no. That self no longer fitted. That couldn't be him—he couldn't be that man, not as he now was.

Throughout, he'd been drinking in the startled beauty of Eugenia's face. Tracing her features, recognizing her fluster—taking a distinctly masculine delight in it.

Then her hands tightened on his shoulders. He sensed she was about to push back and away—to struggle.

He didn't want that.

Moving carefully—still not sure his leg wouldn't give way—he eased his hold on her and bent slightly, letting her slide down and gently setting her on her feet.

Gripping her waist, narrow enough that his long fingers nearly spanned it, he set her away from him.

She blinked, then faintly frowned.

It took more effort than he'd expected to peel his fingers from her, to release her. He forced himself to take a step back, just to be on the safe side.

Her frown darkened a trifle, but then she cleared her throat and, in a rather husky voice, said, "Thank you." A second passed, then her eyes narrowed. "Of course, I wouldn't have fallen if you hadn't roared at me."

He looked up at what she'd been doing. Finally saw the fir boughs draped over the mantel and higher, carefully arranged around the high stone coping.

Registered the scent—one that evoked so many memories and brought them flooding back to him. Childhood Christmases with his mother still alive, and him and his brother running about the house, laughing and playing.

His hands rising to his hips, he turned away. In that instant, he didn't know what the emotion filling him was.

Didn't know who he was as he felt it.

His eyes focused, and he raked the front hall; glancing through the open dining room doorway, he took in the entirety of the decorations. He filled his lungs. "What the de—deuce have you done to my house?"

His tone would have had his troopers cringing.

Eugenia Fitzgibbon merely sniffed. "You were the one who refused to allow me—the Fulsom Hall estate—to make proper reparation for your damaged gate."

When he swung to face her, she calmly continued, "This"—with a gesture, she encompassed all the greenery—"is the means of restitution left to me. I've decorated your house for the season." Her gaze was sharp as her eyes met his. "It was the least I could do."

"I fail to see the logic."

"There's logic, and then there's common courtesy—the way things are done, at least here in Little Moseley. You might have forgotten, but we haven't."

He couldn't swear at her. He glared instead.

She glared back.

The front door opened, and Lady Osbaldestone swanned in. "There you are, Eugenia, dear. I saw your gig outside and wondered."

From the rear of the hall, Hendricks stumped forward. He nodded briefly to Lady Osbaldestone and Miss Fitzgibbon, then fixed Christian with an exasperated look. "Johnson has more questions about the gate. Best if you come and speak to him directly."

Lady Osbaldestone seized the opening. "We won't detain you, Lord Longfellow." She beckoned Eugenia to join her. "Come, my dear. We can drive out together."

Eugenia swiped up her bag, then dropped Christian a perfunctory curtsy. "Good day, Lord Longfellow." *You ungrateful wretch.*

Christian clearly heard the words she forbore to utter aloud. He forced himself to nod—a distant, arrogant nod—to her, then directed a less fraught courtesy at Lady Osbaldestone.

Women!

Lady Osbaldestone smiled, nodded, and whisked Eugenia Fitzgibbon out of his door and drew it closed behind them.

Christian shook his head, then turned to Hendricks. Christian hesitated, then said, "Tell Johnson I'll be there in a few minutes to talk about the damned gate."

Beside Lady Osbaldestone, Eugenia walked with brisk, agitated strides across the forecourt to the waiting gigs.

Once she felt far enough removed from the house, she muttered, "That didn't go well. No doubt he'll tear everything down again. Or get Hendricks and Mrs. Wright to do it."

Therese smiled and patted her arm. "Have faith, my dear. In actuality, we've made an excellent start. Your true accomplishment today doesn't lie in greenery and pleasant scents but in opening his lordship's eyes and forcing him to see again. That will, I judge, greatly aid his household in rehabilitating him as far as they are able. That is the real repair going on here, not anything to do with any gate or the house, much less seasonal decorations, however festive."

They reached the gigs, and Therese halted and smiled at Lottie and George, already on the seat, and at Jamie, who was holding the reins of both carriages. "Now," Therese declared, "we need to plan our next move."

Eugenia relieved Jamie of the reins to her gig. The sidelong look she cast Therese declared she was aware that she was being manipulated, but in the circumstances—given the target was Christian Longfellow, who was the principal source of her present irritation—she was prepared to go along with Therese's direction. "So what," Eugenia asked, "is our next move to be?"

Therese tipped her head, clearly thinking, then admitted, "That, I fear, requires further cogitation. Leave it with me, my dear. I'll send word once I decide."

Eugenia was ready enough to leave the scene of their most recent rout.

Therese waved Jamie up, then paused to ask Eugenia, "Have you had any further trouble with your brother's friends?"

Settling on her gig's seat, Eugenia, faintly puzzled, replied, "No. They appear to be behaving themselves. At the very least, they're much quieter."

Therese climbed to the box seat of her gig, sat, and took the reins from Jamie. She smiled rather intently. "Do let me know if they cause any further difficulties. Just send word, and I'll drop around."

Clearly recalling the effect Therese had had on the Hall's visitors, Eugenia nodded. "Thank you. If they revert to their worst, I will."

"Excellent!" With a salute, Therese sent her mare clopping out of the forecourt and on down the drive.

Behind her, Eugenia brought her gig around and followed.

From his vantage point behind the drawing room curtain—now opened, forcing him to peek around the curtain's edge—Christian watched the pair of gigs roll away. Turning from the sight, he humphed. He'd seen them talking—plotting. No doubt planning their next assault. He knew a tactical retreat when he saw one.

"Damned females!"

He started back toward the front hall—and only then saw the mistletoe tacked above the doorway. "Good God!"

He reached up and ripped the straggly greenery down. Then he thought to look into the other rooms. Lips tightening, he pulled down the bunches pinned above each door.

He tossed the leaves onto the hall table, then stalked to the library. He opened the door and looked up.

"Damn it! Even here."

He pulled the last small bunch down. He stared at it—at the thin leaves, fine twigs, and firm white berries spread on his palm.

For a full minute, he stared at the sight while one part of him—the sane, logical, disillusioned part—prodded him to go into the hall and fling this last bunch in with the rest to be removed by his staff.

He had no idea why, instead, his fingers curled, and his hand moved and slipped that last bunch into his pocket.

He tried to find a reason, but couldn't; all he knew was that keeping that last little bit of mistletoe somehow soothed him. Somehow, in some way, keeping that—holding on to its promise—felt right.

The following day, the weather turned utterly miserable. Gray clouds loured threateningly, and alternating gusts of sleet and snow kept everyone indoors. Therese vetoed any thoughts of attending Sunday service even though the church lay only across the lane. She was not about to risk her grandchildren coming down with colds or even something worse, especially not so close to Christmas. She felt sure Reverend Colebatch would understand. She wasn't even sure he would hold services that day; she consulted Crimmins, but like her, he hadn't heard the church bells that morning, although they agreed that could be because the wind was so atrociously strong it might have blown the sound away.

All that being so, Therese did not appreciate being confined within her walls, even such comfortable walls as those of Hartington Manor. Thick and in perfect repair, the walls held in the warmth of the fires that by her orders were kept glowing in all the hearths. She'd had the windows attended to that summer, and all fitted snugly, denying entry to even the most determined draft. But while the atmosphere was cozy and undeniably comforting, her interest in the usual indoor pursuits with which ladies of her station filled their time was severely limited. Embroidery had never been her forte.

Letter writing was the one ladylike indoor activity she had always considered useful—indeed, worthwhile. Consequently, that morning, she had taken refuge in her private parlor.

Her grandchildren had slipped through the door in her wake.

As she'd settled at the desk set beneath one window, she'd wondered whether she would be able to concentrate on her correspondence with the three imps in the same room, but somewhat to her surprise, she found their chatter—suitably muted—a pleasant background sound, and their antics more often provided fodder for her scribing rather than inhibited her eloquence.

By eleven o'clock, she'd written two thick letters to close friends, and a general report to Celia on her children's well-being.

While she'd been thus engaged, her mind had continued to examine her latest plan for drawing Christian Longfellow back into the village fold. Having found nothing in that plan over which to cavil, nothing she thought needed further adjustment or alteration, she set the finished letter to Celia on top of the other two, then opened the second drawer on the left of her desk and drew out a small stack of thick ivory cards.

After setting the cards to one side, on a sheet of plain paper, she scrawled a quick outline of what she intended to inscribe, then listed the recipients. She paused to consider the list, then nodded to herself, positioned the first invitation on the blotter, dipped her nib in the inkpot, and started to write.

After finishing the first invitation, she sat back to examine it, then she blotted it, placed it with the letters, and paused to glance at her grandchildren.

Jamie and George were playing on the hearthrug with a set of toy soldiers that, thank heaven, they'd brought with them. The boys were apparently engrossed in recreating some battle that involved much cannon fire and explosions, along with cavalry charges, if the noises emanating from before the fireplace were any indication.

Lottie, meanwhile, had lost interest. Clutching her doll, she had climbed up on the chair beside the desk and, on her knees, leant over to study the card Therese had laid atop her letters. "Your writing is very pretty, Grandmama."

"Thank you, my dear." Therese lifted another card from the stack and set it on her blotter. As she picked up her pen, she glanced at her granddaughter. "You'll have to practice your writing when you grow older. A gentleman may scrawl, but a lady's hand should be clear and legible, yet elegant and refined."

She carefully transcribed the second of her invitations, with Lottie's eyes following every stroke. Sitting back, Therese scanned her effort, then smiled, blotted, and placed that invitation with the first. Almost to herself, she murmured, "It doesn't do to rush things—indeed, timing is everything in almost every sphere."

After a moment during which Therese started on her third invitation, Lottie wriggled around and sat properly on the chair. She swung her legs, then asked, "Are we matchmaking with Miss Fitzgibbon and Lord Longfellow, Grandmama?"

From the mouths of babes...

Therese paused in her scribing and regarded her granddaughter. After a moment, she replied, "Only so far as we're able. Making excellent matches requires a light touch and is not something anyone can force. We do what we can, as we can, and then allow Cupid to do the rest if he's so inclined."

Lottie's brow puckered. "Who's Cupid?"

Softly, Therese laughed and dipped her nib. "He's the god who bestows love on us mere mortals."

Lottie's lips formed a soundless "Oh." After a moment, she asked, "Will he come for Miss Eugenia and Lord Longfellow?"

"As to that, my dear, I can't say, but I do have hope."

Ten minutes later, Therese set down her pen and blotted the last of the invitations. She set the card on the small pile, met Lottie's eyes, and smiled. "And that, my dear, will set in train my next attempt to lure Cupid to Little Moseley."

CHAPTER 7

Weak sunshine greeted the inhabitants of Little Moseley when they woke the next morning. Snow had piled inches thick and was topped by a crisp, crunchy crust that had the children, once rugged up, leaping around the front lawn, squealing with delight while they and Therese waited for the gig to be brought around.

Over breakfast, they had discussed their quest to track down the missing geese and had decided that a concerted effort to question all the villagers was a sensible next step. As Jamie had pointed out, it was difficult to believe that an entire flock of geese had vanished with nary a squawk or a fallen feather, and the villagers had now had time since learning of the geese's disappearance to cast their eyes around their own domains.

John Simms led the mare and the gig onto the sweep of drive before the house. Therese left the porch and carefully picked her way across the snowy gravel. "Come, children!"

The three came running, their cheeks and noses rosy red, their faces alight, their eyes shining.

John patiently held the mare steady while the trio clambered up. Therese followed, then John handed her the reins. He tipped his head at the mare. "She should find her way well enough. The drive's mostly clear, and the snow in the lane isn't deep. Just be wary of any drifts or deeper sections."

"Thank you, John. I will." Therese settled on the seat, cast a swift glance over the children, then set the mare trotting slowly down the drive.

Adhering to their prearranged plan of campaign, they drove all the way up the High Street to where Tooks Farm lay at the northern end, just before the lane joined the road to Romsey. As had happened previously, Tooks was in his yard when they drove up and came to the gate to speak with them.

Even before they asked, Tooks shook his head. "Not a single sign of those blasted birds, begging your pardon, your ladyship. It's a right worry and all."

"No suggestions from anyone?" Therese asked.

"Not a squawk." Tooks looked glum.

Therese glanced at the children. "Well, we're on the hunt, Tooks, so don't despair. I have no idea if we'll find your birds before Christmas Day, but we're certainly going to try."

The three children cheered and managed to raise a smile from Tooks.

From there, they turned the gig around and returned to the lane, this time rolling south. They didn't bother diverting to Fulsom Hall, reasoning that if anyone there had any news of the flock, Eugenia would send word.

"Those fields"—Therese tipped her head toward the cleared expanse glimpsed through the woods to their left—"belong to Witcherly Farm, but our Tilly who works in the kitchen with Mrs. Haggerty comes from Witcherly—her parents run the farm, and she lives there and comes to the manor every day. I think we can be sure that if anyone at Witcherly knew anything about the geese, we would have heard." Therese consulted her mental map of the village. "And we checked with the Swindons the other day, so if they find anything, they'll let us know. The only other farm in that direction is Crossley Farm."

"And your Ned, the gardener, lives there, doesn't he?" Jamie asked.

"Indeed, he does, so we don't need to venture out that way, either." Therese looked ahead. "We can safely leave the church and vicarage to Mrs. Colebatch—she'll report if their staff find anything or the reverend hears anything from his parishioners. As for all the cottages, there's too many to call at, but everyone uses the shops and the inn—we can ask there."

They tied the mare to the hitching post outside Mountjoy's General Store and walked across the lane to Bilson's, the butcher. Donald Bilson was the main butcher, assisted by his son, Daniel; Daniel's wife, Greta, was behind the counter when Therese led her troop of investigators into the shop.

"Aye," Greta said at mention of the geese. "Even though we're getting the extra orders, it's still a shame. We like our goose as well as anyone, and I can't think what Tooks will do, not having all those birds to sell. All but a handful spoken for, I hear."

"I take it none of your family have seen any sign of the geese?" Therese inquired.

"No, my lady. Not a feather. And my Daniel and his mates were out hunting rabbits in the woods north of Tooks's place night before last, out along the lane to West Wellow, and he said they all kept a good lookout, but they didn't see any sign the flock had gone that way."

"Thank you. We can but keep looking." With a nod, Therese ushered her troops out of the door and back into the lane.

They asked at Mountjoy's Store, which was also the local post office and therefore a hub of village life. Cyril Mountjoy, the owner, was behind the counter when they walked in, and as luck would have it, Flora Milsom, the farmwife from Milsom Farm that lay south of the village beyond Dutton Grange, had dropped in to buy some flour.

Flora had heard all about the missing geese and assured Therese and her helpers that none of her brood had seen any hint of the birds in their fields or coppices. "Mind you, seems like they'd have to come through the Grange to reach us, and Johnson, who works for his lordship, told me they hadn't had any sightings, either."

Mr. Mountjoy added that he'd asked everyone who had darkened the shop's door since he'd heard the birds had vanished. "But seems no one has any inkling as to where the geese have gone." He paused, then added, "Odd, really. I can understand Tooks losing one or two, even a handful, but the whole blinking flock—begging your pardon, my lady, but that's a lot of birds to go missing."

Therese thanked Mr. Mountjoy and Mrs. Milsom, and Therese and the children continued on their way—to Butts Bakery, where the children were each rewarded with a fruit scone fresh from the oven by Peggy Butts, who was, in fact, the baker and also sister to Flora Milsom.

When Therese inquired as to the geese, Peggy shook her head. "I've not the slightest clue, my lady. None of us have."

Therese stifled a sigh. Tempted by the aromas wafting about the shop, she put in an order for a fruitcake for the New Year. "One can never have too much of your fruitcake, Mrs. Butts."

Peggy preened and said she would have her daughter, Fiona, deliver the cake to the manor three days after Christmas. "For you'll be wanting it fresh baked, and I won't be stoking up the ovens again until the morning after Boxing Day."

With smiles and farewells, they departed the bakery and walked on to the Cockspur Arms. At that hour, the taproom was filling with workers from the nearby farms, coming in for their lunch and a pint with which to wash it down. Therese led her small band into the room opposite the tap—a small parlor reserved for ladies and private parties. After claiming the empty table by the window, she ordered a pot of tea, three glasses of milk, and a plate of scones with jam.

The public house was owned and operated by the Whitesheaf family. It was the daughter, Enid, better known as Ginger, a pleasant lass of seventeen summers with a fine mane of carroty hair, who had taken their order. In less than five minutes, she bore a tray to their table, a bright smile on her face. She set out the pot of tea and the cup and saucer, then carefully put down the three glasses of milk, and at the very last, moving even more slowly, she placed the plate of scones and the pot of jam on the table—and laughed as the children, who had waited with bated breath, fell on the scones and jam.

Smiling broadly, Ginger shook her head and met Therese's eyes. "They all do it, my lady. You'd think they was starving waifs."

"Indeed." Therese directed a mock-severe glance at her grandchildren, but they simply smiled and continued to munch their way through the scones, smearing jam over their cheeks in the process. She blinked, then said, "Strange to say, I recall their mother behaving in much the same way."

That elicited even wider grins all around.

Therese looked up at Ginger. "I take it your family has heard about the missing geese?"

"Oh yes, my lady. And we—whichever of us is at the bar or the counter—have been asking everyone who's come through the door, but there's been not so much as a distant sighting of poor Tooks's birds."

Therese sighed. "That is becoming a depressingly familiar refrain." When Ginger looked faintly puzzled, Therese explained, "No one's heard or seen anything."

"Not even a feather or droppings," George volunteered.

Ginger commiserated, then left them to serve two new customers.

Jamie had been looking out of the window. The village green lay across the lane, a snow-spattered, grassed, gently rising expanse stretching up to the low ridge that hid the village lake from view. Jamie swallowed the last of his scone and turned to Therese. "I've noticed that the village boys play on the green in the afternoons. There are some girls, too, although they sit around and talk. I thought perhaps we"—he glanced at George—"might go there this afternoon and see if any of the children have noticed anything. Adults often forget to ask the children."

Slowly, Therese nodded. "That's an entirely valid observation. If you promise to come home before it gets dark and to take care of Lottie, too—she can ask the girls—then yes, you can go questing on the green this afternoon."

The sun was shining from what was now a cloudless sky, and the wind had dropped.

After she'd finished her tea and the scones had vanished to the last crumb and the jam was but a memory, they fetched the gig and returned to the manor, disappointed but not defeated.

Later, after luncheon, through the drawing room window, Therese watched the three children, Jamie in charge and George holding Lottie's hand, set off for the village green.

They returned two hours later, the boys sporting numerous wet splotches, indeterminate stains, and a skinned knee each, with plenty to say about whom they had played with and asked about the geese, but with not a single clue to alleviate the dearth of evidence of the geese having even existed.

Lottie, who had returned unscathed and as neat as when they'd ventured forth, summed up the considered opinion of the village children. "It's as if the flock have vanished—*poof!*—into thin air. Perhaps a witch or a warlock has got them."

Before Jamie could scoff, Therese tactfully suggested that was unlikely, there being no witch or warlock living close enough to have known of Tooks's flock.

The three children looked at her, and she looked back at them. Then she sighed. "Unfortunately, my dears, we are no further forward than we were this morning—or, indeed, since we first heard of the geese being lost."

Jamie frowned. "With respect, Grandmama, that's not quite right. We know quite a lot about where the geese aren't and haven't been."

Therese had to smile. She reached out and ruffled Jamie's hair—an action he still allowed, although she knew all too soon he would duck away. "Sadly, my boy, that doesn't get us any further with the vital question we need to answer. Namely…" She paused to draw breath, and the children chorused with her, "Where on earth have those wretched geese gone?"

That evening, clad in a fashionable winter evening gown of heavy purple silk, Therese was sitting in her drawing room, in a wing chair angled before a roaring fire, when Crimmins showed Christian Longfellow into the room.

"Welcome, my lord." With a smile, Therese rose and extended her hand. As he took it and bowed, she continued with patent sincerity, "I am pleased to see you at Hartington Manor. Tell me—is this your first visit, or did my aunt entertain you here?"

Straightening, Christian met her eyes. "I was here once before, with my parents and brother and several others for another dinner." He glanced around. "I appear to be somewhat early."

"The Colebatches will be along shortly." She waved him to the chair opposite hers. "Please, take a seat."

He did, lowering himself carefully into the other armchair. As she resumed her seat, Therese noted he'd eschewed his cane for the evening. Despite that minor sign of social engagement, his expression remained hard, almost stern.

She was perfectly certain that if given the choice, he wouldn't have come. But she'd worded her invitation very carefully—at least her invitation to him. She'd phrased her request for his company in such a way that refusing would have been an outright insult. Further, she'd described her proposed dinner party as "intimate" and had mentioned only the Colebatches as fellow guests.

She'd seen no reason to make him take fright.

Or even flight, although she judged his responsibility to his estate and his people would keep him chained to Hampshire, at least for the foreseeable future.

He was clearly uncomfortable in the even light cast by the lamps dotted about her drawing room, as if unsure which way he wished to hold his face. Oddly, it was only then—when she noticed his discomfiture—that she registered the scarring, although of course she'd seen it the instant she'd laid eyes on him.

She regarded him steadily and wondered whether she ought to tell him that the scarring made him look not older but his age. Like a stamp, it marked him as the man he truly was—the experienced officer of dragoons who had ridden through death and glory on the battlefield and had survived. There was steel in him now that wouldn't have been there when he'd graced the village in his unmarred state.

He had not only been younger then; he had also been untried. Unforged.

The doorbell pealed, and noise in the hall heralded the Colebatches. They came in on a gust of frigid air, clapping their hands and stamping their feet. "We walked," the reverend explained as he crossed the room to bow over Therese's hand.

Straightening, Jeremy Colebatch turned to where Christian waited—as if hanging back in shadows that weren't there. "Lord Longfellow!" Jeremy smiled warmly and gripped Christian's hand. He shook it enthusiastically. "Very happy to see you home again, my lord."

Christian scanned the minister's face, but detected not a hint of pity, nor of any real reaction to his disfigurement; Therese had known she could count on Jeremy to look straight past the scars. "Thank you, sir. But please, just Christian. That was the name you used to call me all those years ago."

"Indeed, indeed!" Jeremy shifted to include his wife. "I daresay you remember Mrs. Colebatch. Henrietta, my dear—here's Lord Longfellow at last."

Again Christian tensed; again he was disarmed. Henrietta beamed up at him. "Your lordship, it's a pleasure."

Christian bowed over her fingers. "Christian, remember."

"Oh, I do remember—you were always such a scamp."

"But a fine voice," Jeremy said. "You were in the choir when you were younger, weren't you, my lord?"

To Therese's great satisfaction, Christian was actually smiling when her next guests were announced—Major and Mrs. Swindon. Christian shot Therese a look, but she pretended not to notice.

The major—who had seen action in the earlier years of the Peninsula campaigns—was a bluff, good-hearted soul. He wrung Christian's hand, then nodded openly at his scarred face. "Badge of honor, what?" With a buffet to Christian's shoulder, he said, "It's good to see you hale and whole. The village needs a firm hand at the Grange. Lopsided in leadership without it, you see. Especially with no man at the Hall. Miss

Fitzgibbon and I have done our poor best, but the whole village is glad to have you back and taking up the reins at the Grange."

Mrs. Swindon, a warm, generous, and shrewd matron, shooed her husband aside so she could exchange greetings with Christian. She, too, pondered his ravaged face for an instant, then squarely met his eyes. "Men—badge of honor, indeed. For my money, your injuries are a badge of courage, and no one will make me think otherwise." Then Mrs. Swindon smiled warmly. She pressed Christian's hands. "We truly are delighted to have you back with us, my dear."

Noting that Christian looked faintly stunned, Therese intervened to wave everyone to seats. "I'm disappointed to have to tell you that we—my young troops and I—are no further forward in solving the mystery of the missing geese."

Major Swindon reported that he'd had a word with the gypsies who, with his permission, used his far field en route to Salisbury Downs. "He—the fellow in charge—agreed that none of their people would have taken the whole flock. Too dangerous for them—inviting the backlash."

Christian asked if they saw many itinerants in the area, and the exchange veered into a discussion of local affairs.

Then the bell pealed again. Watching Christian, Therese was pleased to note that he didn't immediately tense, but then the voices in the hall reached his ears, and tension flashed through him, and he looked at the door.

It opened to admit Mrs. Woolsey. Her expression vague, a somewhat silly smile wreathing her faded face, she fluttered into the room. She was gowned in a concoction of gauzy draperies that to Therese's eye was quite unsuitable for a chilly December evening, but her face radiated serenity as she greeted Therese, then acknowledged the Colebatches and the Swindons before reaching Christian.

Halting before him, she smiled into his face.

Then she did something not even Therese would have dared and raised a hand and gently patted Christian's damaged cheek. "Such a pity in one way, yet it makes you more human, and to all the other young gentlemen's chagrin, you indubitably still rank as the most handsome man in the area."

With that airy pronouncement, Mrs. Woolsey turned and busied herself settling onto the sofa beside Mrs. Swindon.

For a fraction of an instant, her words held everyone else in stasis—while their simple honesty sank in.

Therese had invited the vaporous female only because she was Eugenia's chaperon, but she was now very glad she had. Who would have thought she had such insight in her?

With a stern reminder to herself not to judge books by their covers, not even in the country, Therese smiled as her last guest, having consigned her thick coat and scarf into Crimmins's care, walked into the room.

Christian—perhaps predictably—frowned.

But standing beside him, Therese sensed not even a hint of his walls going up—not even the vaguest suggestion of retreat. He was irritated and annoyed at Eugenia, and if the swift sidelong look he cast Therese was any indication, he was also irritated with her for having jockeyed him into meeting Eugenia socially.

Therese wasn't the sort to work in concealment, not when she didn't see any reason to. It would be perfectly obvious—certainly to the ladies present—that she was, if not precisely matchmaking, then at least, as she'd explained to Lottie, facilitating Cupid.

Eugenia was on her mettle and refused to allow Christian's frown to impinge on her composure in any way. She greeted the Colebatches and the Swindons, then reached Therese and curtsied.

"Thank you for the invitation, my lady." She straightened and glanced at Christian. "It's been some time since this company enjoyed a dinner together. Not since the previous Lord Longfellow was alive."

Smoothly, Eugenia moved to Christian and extended her hand. "My lord. It's a pleasure to see you here."

That, of course, was sheer provocation, and for an instant, Christian transparently debated whether to convert his frown into a scowl. But then —no doubt to confound Eugenia—he banished the frown, grasped her hand, and executed a commendably elegant bow. "Miss Fitzgibbon. The pleasure is all mine. And I daresay you will be pleased to hear that the gate we discussed earlier is completely restored."

Eugenia's smile almost slipped. "How...wonderful. I will inform Henry, of course."

Therese hid a grin as Eugenia retrieved her hand—which Christian had forgotten to release—and moved to sit beside Mrs. Colebatch on the love seat.

The evening was going even better than Therese had planned.

The conversation reverted to news of the locality, to which Therese and Christian—both recently returned to the area—listened with unfeigned interest.

They posed several questions, seeking enlightenment, which the company was happy to provide.

Under cover of the exchanges, Christian studied Eugenia Fitzgibbon. Despite her outwardly polite greeting, there'd been a touch of wild color on her cheekbones and a certain glint in her eyes when they'd met his; it seemed she was not best pleased with him—which was ludicrous. If either of them had a right to feel aggrieved with the other, surely it was he. She'd smothered his house—at least the downstairs rooms—in fir and holly, for heaven's sake. He'd got rid of the mistletoe—all except the smallest bunch, and he still didn't know what malignant impulse had made him put that in his pocket—but when he'd frowned at the fir and holly wreathing the mantelpieces, Hendricks and Jiggs, and even Mrs. Wright, had narrowed their eyes at him.

As one who had commanded men in the field, he knew better than to issue orders his troops might refuse to obey.

So his house now smelt of fir, insidiously evoking memories of Christmases long past.

He was dwelling on Miss Fitzgibbon's iniquities when her ladyship's butler entered the room. At an inquiring look from Lady Osbaldestone, the butler intoned, "Dinner is served, my lady."

"Thank you, Crimmins." Her ladyship rose, as did her guests, Christian most slowly—most carefully—of all. He could manage without his cane, but only for so long; Jiggs had driven him in the carriage from the Grange. He'd originally intended to walk, but his staff apparently had very clear ideas of what was due his dignity. Still, Jiggs's and the others' insistence meant he hadn't needed to bring his cane.

Lady Osbaldestone had busily paired up her guests. Christian wasn't the least surprised when she finally turned to him and, with a glib, hostessly air, directed, "If you would be so kind as to give Miss Fitzgibbon your arm, my lord, I believe we can proceed."

No actual question, of course. Resolutely strangling the irritation that leapt and pricked beneath his skin whenever Eugenia Fitzgibbon was close, he courteously offered her his arm.

With a small inclination of her head, she placed her hand on his sleeve, and together, they turned to follow the other couples—Mrs. Colebatch on the major's arm, and Mrs. Swindon with the reverend—from the room.

The dining room was just down the hall. As he paced with Eugenia by his side, a flash of white on the half landing caught his eye. The three children were sitting behind the balustrade, watching them. From the corner of his eye, Christian saw Lady Osbaldestone, bringing up the rear with Mrs. Woolsey, wave imperiously, directing the trio to their beds.

Christian hid a grin. When he'd been their age, he could remember doing the same thing with his brother when their parents had entertained.

He steered Eugenia into the dining room. A huge fire burned in the hearth there, too, and the table—its length adjusted to suit the size of the company—had been laid with the season in mind. Sprigs of holly, splashed red with berries, had been plaited with small branchlets of fir, and the resulting long chain snaked down the table's center, circling the foot of a low crystal vase sporting a profusion of the hellebore blooms commonly referred to as Christmas roses.

Those blooms had been one of Christian's mother's favorites. The sight made him wonder if there were any plants still surviving in the greenhouses; he hadn't noticed any when he and her ladyship had walked through.

The couples had milled before the fireplace, behind the head of the table.

"I'll sit at the foot, of course." Lady Osbaldestone continued, "Henrietta, my dear, if you would take the place on my right, and Mrs. Woolsey, if you would sit opposite, then the reverend can be next to you, with Sally beside him and the major opposite. Christian, if you will take the carver at the head, and please seat Miss Fitzgibbon on your left, and that, I believe, will be perfect."

Christian inclined his head and obeyed, as did all the others, although the word he would have used to describe the arrangement definitely wouldn't have been "perfect." He would quite happily have sat next to Mrs. Woolsey…then again, that strangely vague lady had already rattled him once.

After seeing Eugenia to her chair, then sliding into the heavy carver that her ladyship's butler held for him, Christian decided that perhaps he'd been hasty. Given he and Eugenia were the only representatives of their generation, in the interests of furthering absorbing conversation, Lady Osbaldestone might have a point.

The meal commenced with a rich lobster bisque, followed by a remove of poached salmon.

At first, contrary to Christian's expectations, the conversation remained general, something their hostess encouraged. Their relatively small number meant it was easy to listen to whomever was speaking, and not having to restrict oneself to addressing one's neighbors meant a much wider range of subjects were explored.

Inevitably, the talk turned to the Peninsula campaign. Christian tensed, but to his relief, no one asked about his service or even commented on battles past. The major led the way; although long retired, he had friends in the hierarchy and was well informed as to Wellington's intentions. Lady Osbaldestone, too, was surprisingly knowledgeable, especially as to political strategy. Despite himself, Christian was drawn into the exchanges, and the company as one turned to him for his insights into the enemy's likely next moves.

Like the major, although he'd sold out, it hadn't proved possible to cut himself off from the arena in which he'd spent the past decade. Moreover, he still had friends among the officers fighting for king and country.

As the company progressed through the courses and the conversations swirled, he found himself—entirely unexpectedly—relaxing. Other than Mrs. Woolsey, he'd known everyone there since childhood, and as they'd all…not overlooked but either ignored or dismissed his injuries, he discovered to his amazement that he had no difficulty interacting with them in a perfectly normal way.

It was the first such event he'd attended since being hauled half dead from the field at Talavera.

The first time he'd found himself completely ignoring his injuries, too; in the Hartington Manor dining room, they seemed of no account.

When the main course—a large roast duck and a side of venison—was laid before them, the talk turned to farm management. Christian wasn't surprised to be included very much as a matter of course. What did make him blink was that the young lady seated on his left was equally included—if anything, more so.

From her answers, it became obvious that, at present, she was critically involved—indeed, the lynchpin—in the management of the Fulsom Hall estate.

Inwardly frowning, Christian tried to recall what the situation with her family was, but simple ignorance defeated him. He assumed her parents had died, and he knew she had a younger brother, Henry, and, courtesy of the smashed gate, that he was old enough to drive a curricle, but Christian had never known the boy's age.

Finally, in the lull before the dessert course, he turned to Eugenia and, lowering his voice, asked, "I gather you oversee your brother's holdings. How old is he?"

Briefly, she met his eyes. "Nineteen. Old enough to drive a curricle, but not yet old enough to have acquired any great degree of circumspection."

"He's what—at university?"

She nodded. "Oxford." She looked down the table. "That's where the four friends staying at the Hall hail from. It's my belief they're all much the same and egg each other on."

"As youths of that age are wont to do," he drily stated. After a moment, his voice low, he added, "I can remember some of my own exploits at that age, and they weren't episodes to be proud of." He glanced at her as she looked down at the empty sweet dish the butler set before her. Christian hesitated, then, in a nonchalant tone, offered, "If you have any trouble managing the group, I'll be happy to speak with them."

She chuckled and looked up, meeting his eyes. "Thank you, but Lady Osbaldestone met them. She claimed to have their mothers on her correspondence list. I don't know if she truly has or not, but the implied threat worked wonders."

He grinned. "I can imagine. At that age, just the thought of one's mother being informed of one's misdemeanors is guaranteed to induce a high level of caution in any young gentleman."

She nodded. "That's precisely what has happened. Since they encountered Lady Osbaldestone, they've been exceedingly careful. I haven't heard a peep of complaint from our staff, where previously there'd been a litany every day."

The tension between them had faded sufficiently that he felt able to say, "From all I've heard, you've been managing the estate for quite a few years, yet you can't be that old yourself."

Her lips twitched. "No, indeed. I'm only five years older than Henry, but when his mother—my stepmother—died, our father encouraged me to take over the household, which I did. I was fourteen at the time, and as the years passed, Papa allowed me to become his right hand in running the estate as well. Whether he realized he wouldn't live to see Henry reach his majority, I don't know, but as Papa died three years ago, his foresight proved wise. Our solicitor, Mr. Mablethorpe, has his chambers in Southampton, but he was a longtime friend of Papa and knows us well. Under his aegis, I've continued to run the estate."

Although she didn't quite sigh, Christian sensed her present state did not meet with her unqualified approval. After a moment, he asked, "Have you started involving Henry in managing the estate's reins? Even in small ways?"

Now, she sighed, and her shoulders slumped. "I would dearly love to involve him in the day-to-day decisions, at least while he's at home, but he keeps putting it off. And given that he does, I have to ask myself whether he's yet ready to take on the responsibility." Briefly, she met Christian's eyes. "If he isn't yet ready to take up the mantle, I suspect forcing the responsibility on him would be a grave misstep."

He thought of his father's attempts to train his brother, Cedric. After a moment, he said, "You're right. If the weight falls on shoulders not yet willing or prepared to support it, the risk of collapse, in one way or another, is very real."

That was what had happened with Cedric. He'd fought against what he'd seen as a yoke—and ended in a ditch with a broken neck.

She'd turned her head and was studying him. When he glanced her way and arched a brow, she hesitated, then quietly asked, "I wondered if you…resented the responsibility of the Grange falling on your shoulders. You couldn't have expected it."

He held her gaze while he considered the question; he hadn't actually thought of it before and had to look inward to seek the answer… He blinked, somewhat surprised by what he saw. "You're correct in that I hadn't anticipated inheriting the estate. But when I heard of Cedric's death and realized it would fall to me, I discovered I was…ready." He met her eyes again. "I hadn't been, earlier, but by the time I inherited, I knew I had all the right training and abilities to make a success of it."

He paused, looking inward and back, and in a tone of quiet understanding, said, "When I was wounded and recuperating, through all the long days and nights, the Grange—the role of Lord Longfellow of Dutton Grange—shone like a beacon. I knew it would be here, waiting for me, when I…got through the worst."

That—knowing he had work to do, that people needed him—had played a large part in saving his sanity.

Looking around the table, he added, "My only regret is that it took me so long to get home."

Mrs. Swindon, on his right, heard his last comment. She patted his arm. "Well, you're home now, dear, and one of us again."

The rest of the table had, it seemed, been discussing the possibility of putting on some sort of theatrical show to coincide with the village fair.

Mrs. Swindon looked at Eugenia and asked for her thoughts on the notion.

Christian watched, amused, as Eugenia glibly sidestepped the issue, endeavoring not to become embroiled in the pending organization.

The conversational ball rolled on down the table.

Christian continued to listen and learn. After a little while, he realized he was smiling.

He hadn't smiled like that, relaxed and at peace—his old quietly arrogant, confident, and easygoing nature surfacing—for…a very long time.

Again, he looked inward. He could all but see the prickly walls he'd built to protect himself dissolving, thinning and fading away.

He felt…as if he'd come home.

As he'd imagined he one day would, hale and whole and able.

The feeling was so tempting—so attractive, so addictive—he instinctively drew back, reminding himself that although the company around the table were those with whom he would interact most frequently, they were only a small fraction of the village community.

From the other end of the table, Therese watched her latest project unfold. She was entirely content with the way the evening had gone, and as the company rose from the table and ambled back to the drawing room—no port and brandy for the men in this group—she smiled approvingly at Eugenia and deftly stepped in to divert Mrs. Woolsey, who had seemed to be drifting back to her charge's side. Eugenia could take care of herself, and better she should do so within Christian's orbit.

Back in the drawing room, the major, Christian, and Eugenia gathered in a group, discussing the impact of the weather on their fields and the outlook for the next year's crops. Meanwhile, the Colebatches, Sally Swindon, Therese, and Mrs. Woolsey continued their discussion of possible plays that might prove suitable for the village players, with Mrs. Woolsey once again surprising them all by revealing a decidedly thespian bent.

By the time Crimmins wheeled in the tea trolley, they had almost settled on Goldsmith's *She Stoops to Conquer* as the most appropriate selection. "An old play, true enough," Mrs. Swindon stated, "but quite unexceptionable, and it does tend to satisfy the audience."

"It also doesn't require too many players." Mrs. Colebatch accepted a cup and saucer. "In a village this size, that's a real consideration."

"If we can pull it off," Lady Osbaldestone said, "I daresay we'll have a goodly crowd, especially given we intend to run it on the evening of the fair." She looked at Reverend Colebatch. "Does the fair still draw people from as far afield as Romsey?"

The reverend allowed that it did. "I expect we'll have to beg the use of the Witcherly Farm barn to accommodate the crowd."

Soon after, the Swindons declared they must away, and the company broke ranks. Therese stood in the front hall and saw her guests off. Mrs. Woolsey and Eugenia prepared to leave on the Swindons' heels. In the doorway, Therese lightly gripped Eugenia's sleeve and, smiling, caught the younger woman's eye. "Good work. I daresay I'll see you at the carol service tomorrow."

Eugenia admitted she would be there. "I have no idea if Henry and his friends will attend—I suspect the verdict will be that such bucolic entertainment is beneath their notice."

Therese gave her a commiserating look. "Young men, sadly, are still men."

Eugenia laughed and left with a wave. Their coachman drew their carriage up before the steps, and Eugenia helped Mrs. Woolsey in, then followed.

Therese turned back into the hall, to the Colebatches, who were rugging themselves up. Christian was assisting Mrs. Colebatch, who had tangled herself in a very long knitted scarf.

"If I didn't know the pair of you enjoy plodding through the winter night," Therese said, "I would have my carriage brought around for you. Are you sure you won't avail yourself of it?"

"Or of mine," Christian said. "It will be the work of a minute to drop the pair of you off at the vicarage."

"No, no." The reverend held up his hand. "We wouldn't hear of it—it's out of your way—but regardless, as her ladyship says, Henrietta and I do enjoy our solitary walks in the moonlight." This last was said with a fond smile at his wife, who returned the gesture.

"Oh—but wait." The reverend turned back to Christian. "I meant to ask for your help in another way. It's the carol service tomorrow, and I was hoping I could persuade you to attend. We're rather thin of male voices, you see—not much strength to anchor the sopranos and altos—and I remembered you have an excellent voice." The reverend suddenly looked uncertain. "Or at least you did."

Therese leveled her gaze on Christian; she could almost see him debating whether to seize the excuse Reverend Colebatch had left dangling. When Christian continued to hesitate, she bluntly stated, "I've heard you roar. I cannot believe your injuries have affected your vocal cords in the slightest."

Smoothly, Christian inclined his head. "What vocal abilities I was born with I still possess."

"Excellent!" Reverend Colebatch was no slouch himself. "So you will come, won't you? It's only for an hour, and it would make such a difference to the end result."

Christian knew when he was outgunned. He inclined his head again, this time to the reverend. "I'll come and do what I can to assist."

"Wonderful." Henrietta Colebatch beamed at him. "Six o'clock. We'll see you there."

Christian resigned himself to the inevitable. He could hide in the shadows—the church had plenty of those—and still contribute to the singing.

The Colebatches headed out of the front door. Lady Osbaldestone saw them off, then turned at last to him.

She eyed him with far too much understanding for his comfort. "I thought the evening went rather well."

There was a question buried in that statement. He wasn't keen on answering it, yet somewhat to his surprise, heard himself admit, "I enjoyed the evening." He paused, sensing that truth resonate within him, then bowed and quietly said, "Thank you for inviting me."

She smiled, evidently delighted. "It was a pleasure, dear boy." As he straightened, she turned to the partially open door as wheels crunched on the gravel. "And here's your carriage."

Her butler opened the door wider.

Lady Osbaldestone stood back on the other side.

As with a final nod, Christian moved past her, she murmured, "I do hope you now recognize that there's no need at all to hide away from the village—from those who've known you all your life. They don't see the scars—they just see you."

Christian halted on the porch. He sensed that she was closing the door. When he finally glanced back, it was shut.

He stared at the panel for several moments, then he turned and went down the steps to where Jiggs and his carriage were waiting.

CHAPTER 8

The next day, at close to midday, Jamie took himself off on a mission all his own.

He and George were using the bedroom above the dining room, and the fireplaces shared a flue. The previous night, once George had fallen asleep, Jamie had lain awake listening to the murmur of the conversations of those in the room below.

Gradually, his ears had grown attuned to the voices; he'd realized Lord Longfellow had to be sitting at the head of the table, nearest the fireplace, because Jamie could hear him most clearly of all.

He could also hear Miss Fitzgibbon, at least when she was speaking to his lordship and, presumably, facing the fireplace.

Jamie had felt quite chuffed at being able to listen in. He hadn't intended to pay any great attention, but then something Miss Fitzgibbon had said, and even more the way she'd said it—and his lordship's understanding responses—had struck…he supposed it was what people called a "chord." It had felt as if something rang inside him.

And he'd known what he should do.

Exactly how to approach his self-appointed task was a question he'd spent half the morning debating. When the weak sun had shone through the clouds while they'd been finishing their elevenses, he'd been struck by inspiration. He'd suggested to his grandmother that it might be useful if he and George spent an hour or so talking with the younger boys of the village, who would very likely gather on the green to make the most of the burst of finer weather.

His grandmother had studied him for an uncomfortable moment, her black gaze unnervingly sharp, but he'd met her gaze steadily, and eventually, she'd nodded. "By all means, see what you can learn. Any clue at all about the geese will be welcome."

He and George had left the manor and gone straight to the green, and as Jamie had predicted, they'd found a band of boys about their age and some a trifle older, Johnny Tooks and the two Milsom boys among them. A battered sled had sat discarded by the lane; there was insufficient snow to use it. Instead, the boys were playing marbles, and as he and George had already met some of the boys during their investigations, the group readily welcomed the pair of them into the game.

George had always had excellent aim; he quickly established himself as the one to beat.

Jamie had waited until the game had taken hold of all the boys, then had picked a moment when George was sitting out the play, leant closer, and whispered, "I'm going to walk over to Fulsom Hall. I want to see if I can have a word with Miss Fitzgibbon's brother."

George had looked puzzled. "What do you want with him?"

"You know what Lottie said—about Grandmama thinking a match between Miss Fitzgibbon and his lordship would be a good idea?"

George had nodded.

"I overheard Miss Fitzgibbon talking to his lordship last night—through the chimney. It gave me an idea."

George had frowned. "Well, don't get into trouble. You know what Mama said—we have to be good for Grandmama if we want our presents."

"I'm not going to do anything bad." Jamie had stood and brushed down his breeches. "If I'm not back by the time the church clock strikes one"—the time they were supposed to return to the manor—"go home and tell them I'll be along shortly."

"Grandmama will be cross."

Jamie had set his jaw. "I have to try this, and I have to go alone. She'll understand when I explain, but I'd rather do it first and explain later."

George had understood that reasoning; he'd screwed up his nose and waggled his head. "All right. But I'll wait here until one o'clock in case you make it back by then."

Jamie had nodded, then had turned and walked to the lane and set off for Fulsom Hall.

He heard the church clock strike twelve as he reached the Hall drive. Rather than walk along the gravel, he slipped into the trees and bushes that lined the avenue and quietly made his way toward the house. Skirting the forecourt, as he and George had done on their earlier visit, he crept into the gardens that flanked the right side of the house.

While skulking through the gardens on that earlier visit, he and George had come across a small glade, on the grass of which butts from cigarillos had been liberally scattered.

Later that day, when describing Henry and his friends to him and George, Lottie had mentioned the smell of "funny smoke" that had hung about Henry in particular. Lottie, Jamie knew, had a keen sense of smell; she could tell which of their mother's perfumes she'd used over a distance of a yard or more.

Jamie had noticed a nice big tree, perfect for climbing, to one side of the glade. Although the tree was currently leafless, a large bush thick with dark-green leaves grew near the tree's trunk and reached high enough to conceal the lowest branches. Jamie crept up to the glade, but discovered it was disappointingly empty. Undeterred, he crossed to the tree, leapt and caught the lowest branch to one side, and swung himself into the concealment of the bush.

He lay along the branch and willed Henry Fitzgibbon to show.

Unfortunately, when Henry appeared, one of his friends was with him. They were talking expectantly about lunch. Jamie prayed Henry wouldn't wait until after the meal to light up a cigarillo—and that his friend would leave him to indulge his habit alone.

Whether Cupid or some other god was watching over him, Jamie didn't know, but after a minute of chatting, the other gentleman made some excuse and took himself off, heading for the house.

Left alone in the glade, Henry drew out a silver case from his pocket and opened it.

Jamie dropped from the branch, then stepped around the bush—startling Henry. He juggled the case and only just managed to save the contents from spilling onto the grass.

Snapping the case shut, Henry frowned at Jamie. "Here—who are you? And what the devil are you doing skulking in my gardens?"

Jamie gave a slight smile—the sort of superior smile he'd seen his grandmother use. Halting before Henry, he bowed. "Permit me to introduce myself. I'm Lord James Skelton, Viscount Skelton."

Henry thought about laughing or calling what he thought was a bluff, but he saw something in Jamie's face that made him think better of it.

"I came here," Jamie smoothly continued, "because I wanted to speak with you. Privately. That was why I was hiding in the tree. I knew you smoked those things"—he tipped his head at the case Henry still held in his hands—"and that you came out here to do it, so I lay in wait."

Henry's frown had grown puzzled. "What do you want to speak with me about?"

"In a way, it's about your sister." When Henry looked taken aback, Jamie asked, "Do you know how worn out she is with managing the estate for you?"

"What?"

"I heard her talking to Lord Longfellow last night, when they were at dinner at my grandmother's house."

"Oh." Henry looked at Jamie almost with respect. "Your grandmother is Lady Osbaldestone."

Jamie nodded. "I have sisters myself, so I thought you would want me to tell you what I've heard. Not just from your sister but from others in the village, too—they all talk to my grandmother, and I've been with her for the past few days."

Henry looked uncertain. "What are people saying?"

"It's not so much gossiping as what they see and observe." Jamie leveled his most direct look at Henry. "Correct me if I'm wrong, but this estate comes to you when you attain your majority"—he knew all the right words; he'd heard them often enough, usually referring to himself—"and your sister gets none of it. When she marries—*if* she marries—she'll have a small dowry but no further call on the estate. Is that correct?"

Henry frowned. After a moment, he conceded, "That is how it goes. But what do you mean by *if*? Of course, Eugenia will marry at some point—"

"How old is she?"

Henry paused, then, in a rather more subdued tone, admitted, "Twenty-four."

"You know as well as I do that by that age, many ladies of our class are married, and if not, would already have had several offers. But your sister hasn't even had a Season in town. She's been here taking care of your inheritance."

Henry rocked back on his heels, his expression closing. "She likes taking care of the place."

"Have you asked her recently if she'd rather be doing something else?"

"Well…no."

Jamie nodded. "In her mind, she's doing her duty by you, out of loyalty to you and most likely even more for your late parents. And probably also because she feels a certain responsibility for the people—those in the household and the estate." Leading Henry that far had been simple. Now came the difficult part. "I can see it's been easy to let her carry the burden for you—she's made it that way—but what you have to grasp is that when it comes down to it, *she* is *your* responsibility. *You* have a duty toward *her*. I know all about that—I have two sisters, and I've already been told that when we're older, it might fall to me to see them properly settled. Of course, if that was the case, I would be the Earl of Winslow, but the issue is the same. Gentlemen of our class have to take responsibility for seeing that our sisters get to live the life they want and should have." He paused, then added, "Or so my father tells me, and I daresay he knows—he has three sisters himself."

Henry's expression was a study in guilt embellished by uncertainty. After several moments of staring at Jamie, Henry set his jaw pugnaciously. "You're only a boy—a child. Why should I listen to you?"

Jamie had his answer ready. "Because my grandmama is Lady Osbaldestone. And when I grow up, as an earl, I'll have far more responsibility than you ever will—and my father has already started training me in how I should behave." He held Henry's gaze steadily, then insight dawned, and he said, "But you already know where your responsibility lies. You don't need me to tell you—just, perhaps, to remind you."

After a very long moment, Henry sighed. His jaw eased; his expression softened. Several more seconds passed before he uttered the words Jamie had hoped to hear. "What do you think I should do?"

Without allowing any hint of triumph to show, Jamie told him.

Five minutes later, as Jamie made his way back to the lane, he rather thought his awe-inspiring grandmother would be proud of him. Getting people to do what one wanted them to—for their own good, of course—was a puzzle and a challenge, one with which he'd just proved he could succeed and which he had, indeed, enjoyed.

Now to see if Henry made good on his promise and started down the right track.

After conferring over a late-afternoon tea of fruitcake and scones and jam, and confirming and bemoaning that they were no closer to determining what had become of Farmer Tooks's geese, Therese and the children, along with all the manor staff, donned coats and scarves, gloves and mittens, and, with Crimmins and John Simms lighting their way with lamps hoisted on poles, set off for the church and the annual village carol service.

The event was popular, and carriages and carts from the farms and houses all around were clopping smartly up to the church. Their party had to wait for a break in the traffic to cross the lane and join the crowd streaming through the lychgate and up the short path to the base of the square tower and the church's main door, presently set welcomingly wide.

As they walked up the path, Therese looked ahead, noting the way the golden light from candles and sconces within the church spilled through the door and through the mullioned windows to pool on the cold, hard ground. The sky above was crystal clear, with a myriad of stars twinkling brightly and a close-to-full moon glowing in the ink-dark firmament.

The combined breaths of the gathering congregation hung like wispy clouds in the air, and chatter and excited comments abounded on all sides.

With Lottie's hand in hers and George and Jamie walking on her other side, Therese joined the throng with more real enthusiasm than she'd felt over the event—indeed, over Christmas—for many years. Doubtless the effect of having youngsters with whom to share the season. She glanced at them, at their fresh, innocent faces, presently turning this way and that as they took in every last detail.

"Grandmama," George said from beside her, "why is the church called St. Ignatius on the Hill when it isn't on a hill?"

"That, my dear, is a continuing mystery. There are those who maintain that when the church was built, it was on a hill of sorts, and the terrain has altered with the centuries. Others contend that it was St. Ignatius himself who was on a hill, but as to which hill that was, or what he was doing there, much less why the fact was considered of sufficient importance to commemorate, no one knows."

George uttered a sound very like a humph.

Smiling, Therese nodded to Jeremy Colebatch, fully accoutered and waiting just inside the arched doorway to welcome his parishioners as well as the many he rarely saw who nevertheless crowded into the nave for this particular event.

Therese led her small band down the central aisle. The second pew on the left had been endowed by her aunt and on occasions such as this was reserved for the manor household. Therese held the children back to allow the Crimminses, Harriet Orneby, Mrs. Haggerty, and John Simms to file into the pew, then she and the children took the places nearest the aisle.

Jamie wordlessly insisted on taking the spot closest to the aisle. George and Lottie quickly settled, with George reading his sister the order of the carols, which had been inscribed on cards scattered along the seats. Jamie, however, seemed to be waiting for something—or someone; he kept squirming and looking back up the church.

Eventually, Therese poked his shoulder. "What are you doing?"

"I'm keeping watch for Lord Longfellow. You did say he had said he would come."

"I did, and he did."

"Oh." Jamie had once again twisted to look back at the church door. "He's just come in and gone into the last pew." Frowning, Jamie glanced at the front pew on the opposite side of the aisle. He nodded toward it. "Isn't that pew where the Dutton Grange people sit?"

"Clearly, it is. No one could miss the mountainous Hendricks, and Jiggs and Mrs. Wright are there as well. So obviously that fact is well known, I expect to Christian as much as to anyone else. But of course, he's chosen to hang back in the shadows." She sighed. "It's clearly going to take more than just one dinner to make him ignore those scars."

Jamie wriggled around so he could watch the door.

Therese inwardly sighed and poked him again. When he looked up at her, his Skelton blue eyes wide, she bluntly asked, "What have you done?"

He returned her gaze, then, much to her satisfaction, replied, "I spoke with Henry Fitzgibbon. About him not…well, picking up the reins of his position. Especially not over Miss Eugenia."

"Did you now?" Therese regarded Jamie—who seemed intent on proving he was more related to her than she'd appreciated—with a degree of fascination. "And how did that go?"

Jamie lifted a shoulder. "All right, I think. But"—he looked up the nave again—"the proof will be in the pudding, I expect."

The church was filling up fast. It was almost six o'clock, and the reverend had quit his post and hurried up the nave to the vestry to join his troops—the choir, the choirmaster, and the deacon—all of whom should be congregating there. At the appointed time, the procession would form up, then circle the church to enter with all due pomp through the main tower door.

Gradually, the excited chatter faded, to be replaced by an expectant hush.

Finally, Jamie saw Henry enter the church with his sister on his arm.

Determined, Jamie stared hard at Henry, willing the young man to meet his eyes. Henry glanced down the nave and did.

Jamie signaled with his eyes—directing Henry's gaze to the last pew on Henry and Eugenia's left.

After what seemed an age but was no more than two seconds, Henry got Jamie's implied message and looked into the shadows.

Eugenia turned to Henry. She tugged at his sleeve—urging him to go down the nave to the front pew on the left, where members of their household already sat.

Mindful of Jamie's instructions, Henry shook his head and, without allowing Eugenia any chance to argue, guided her into the last pew instead.

Jamie sighed with relief. A smile curving his lips, he wriggled back around to sit facing the altar.

Therese glanced back. She couldn't see Eugenia—too many hats were in the way—but she glimpsed Henry sitting by the aisle.

Smiling, she faced forward. She caught Jamie's eye and nodded approvingly. "Good work."

At that moment, the organist pressed his fingers to the keys, and the congregation came to their feet as Reverend Colebatch, resplendent in his robes, led the small procession of deacon, choirmaster, and choristers down the aisle.

In the last pew, where he should have been safe, Christian stood beside Eugenia Fitzgibbon. What neighborly impulse had prompted Henry Fitzgibbon to eschew the Fitzgibbon pew at the front of the church in favor of the last pew where Christian had taken refuge, Christian had no clue. But when Henry had nodded politely to Christian and ushered

Eugenia into the pew, there'd been nothing Christian could do to avoid the outcome.

To avoid the nearness.

Compounding the issue, two of Henry's friends had rushed in just ahead of the procession and crammed into the pew alongside Henry. Christian had moved along as far as he'd been able, but there had already been three lads from one of the farms in the pew when he'd arrived. The resulting squeeze left him hemmed in tight beside the distracting Miss Fitzgibbon.

Along with the rest of the congregation, he bent his head for the first prayer.

It didn't help.

At Lady Osbaldestone's house, he'd managed to clamp down on his inner self's responses to what, for some reason, that younger, earlier, more hedonistic version of himself viewed as a delectably tempting morsel. He'd tried telling himself that he was far too old and far too damaged to even think of her, at least not in the way he had been thinking of her, but then he'd discovered she was actually twenty-four and apparently unperturbed by his mangled face, and that argument had crumbled to dust and blown away.

But he was adamant that, no matter the promptings of his gentler, more-carefree self, he was not going to allow that self to take control, much less dismantle the guard his older, wiser, more-hardened self had erected around his heart and his soul.

Unfortunately for his resolution, there was worse to come.

The deacon announced the first carol, and Christian, along with the others in their pew, discovered there were only three hymnals to share between them. The three farm lads took one, Henry and his two friends settled to share another, leaving Christian to share the remaining book with the female who was fast becoming his nemesis.

Not that he could accuse her of in any way pursuing him. It hadn't escaped his notice that Henry diverting into the last pew hadn't been her idea. Indeed, her murmured response to his very correct greeting had been every bit as reserved as he'd endeavored to be.

The organist completed the introduction to the carol, and the congregation filled their lungs and, led by the small choir standing in the stalls about the altar, sang.

In melody and in harmony, with full voice and full hearts, they sang of the town of Bethlehem so very far away.

And he discovered Eugenia Fitzgibbon had a very sweet soprano voice.

Discovered that she transparently enjoyed singing the old hymns, the venerated Christmas carols.

And as if a door in his mind had blown wide, he remembered how much he enjoyed that, too. He rediscovered the pleasure of lending his voice to the refrain. Remembered again the joy that welled and swelled through the interweaving of voice and organ, through the melding of notes and emotion and freely offered devotion, and its ability to lift—to buoy—his soul high.

The moment captured him again.

Yet it wasn't the past but the here and now that sank hooks into his soul.

And he couldn't draw back—couldn't find it in him to pretend, to push his other, more joyful self back into the iron cage he'd created out of pain and loss and misery. Later, he whispered to his hardened self, but even that promise was weak.

The tug of the carols was too great for him to resist, and he surrendered and sang, heart, soul, and voice.

Alongside Christian, Eugenia marveled at the quality of his voice. One part of her stopped listening to the communal song and concentrated instead on his. His effortless outpouring of note after clear note, all rendered in a baritone so true and warm she felt the sound like a tangible entity wrapping about her.

At the conclusion of the first carol, she smiled in unfeigned, unambiguous delight at him.

He smiled at her after the second carol ended—a smile more relaxed, more beguiling, than any she'd seen him give.

By the third carol, they were singing virtually as a duet, so attuned to each other's voice had they become.

She'd always enjoyed the village carol service, but this year, the experience shone like gold in her mind.

She'd been surprised when Henry had shrugged aside his friends' disparaging comments about a village carol service and had instead declared he would accompany her to the event. She'd been even more surprised when he'd kept to the time and had been waiting in the front hall when she'd come down ready to drive to the church.

Because of the press of carriages and carts trying to find a place before the church, they'd been late reaching the door, but Henry hadn't faltered in his march inside.

She'd felt more in charity with her brother than she had in a long while, but once inside the church, Henry had halted. He'd been looking intently down the aisle, then he'd looked toward the rear pew and, ignoring her wishes, had steered her that way.

She'd been annoyed with him all over again for refusing to walk all the way down the aisle to the front pew—annoyed at his ducking scrutiny by the village, which was how she'd initially interpreted his move.

Then she'd realized that Christian was in the last pew…and she'd known very well why. From that moment, she'd been wholeheartedly behind her brother's unexpected action.

She'd somewhat cynically moved up to accommodate two of Henry's friends. Roger Carnaby and George Wiley must have all but run to reach the church in time.

That, of course, had put her in very close proximity to Christian, but after having landed in his arms while decorating his house, she'd known her senses wouldn't mind.

As, indeed, they hadn't. While the service rolled on and several choristers sang piercingly sweet solos, her senses and her nerves positively basked in the warmth of Christian's presence. It was, she inwardly admitted, a rather heady feeling.

The hour-long service ended too soon, at least for her.

The reluctance with which he shut the hymnal they'd shared suggested he felt the same way.

She raised her gaze to his face and met his hazel eyes. His expression seemed less clouded, more open than before. With simple grace, he inclined his head. "Thank you for making this service especially memorable. You have a very lovely voice."

She smiled wryly back at him. "Your voice quite puts mine to shame—and you know it."

His lips twitched before he could control them, and she laughed and turned as Henry touched her arm.

She followed Henry out of the pew and into the throng of villagers queuing to exit the church.

Christian followed Eugenia out of the pew, but then retreated along the pew's back, into a spot where the shadows fell more deeply. He waited there while the rest of the congregation, smiling, laughing, and earnestly talking, filed past. While he might no longer feel it necessary to hide the destruction of his face from the elders of the village, he was still convinced the sight of his ravaged cheek was likely to give the younger children nightmares.

He hung back until everyone else had left, even the deacon, who had looked questioningly at him, but when Christian had nodded distantly, had continued on his way, transparently pleased with how the evening had gone.

Although he was the last to emerge from the church, Christian wasn't surprised to find the good reverend still at his post, farewelling his parishioners and exchanging a few words with each. However, the crowd still gathered in the church grounds took Christian aback; given the sharp chill, he'd thought that everyone would have hurried off home, but no—a very large portion of the congregation remained chatting avidly, spread along the path and over the lawns in groups of happy revelers, each group lit by the festive lanterns many men held aloft on poles.

Even as he shook Reverend Colebatch's hand, Christian was struck by the image. If he'd been at all artistic, he would have used paints to capture it—the quintessential village Christmas scene.

He'd forgotten that, too, and the memory-made-new-again stirred his latent, dormant self to life.

He was immensely thankful when immediately after their hands had parted, Colebatch was summoned to adjudicate some argument between the choirmaster and the organist. Colebatch apologized profusely, but Christian smiled and denied any need to claim more of the reverend's time.

As Colebatch turned away, Christian stepped off the church stoop, instinctively seeking the deeper shadows outside the circles of light cast by the lanterns.

Only to have Henry Fitzgibbon step into his path.

"I say, Lord Longfellow. We haven't been introduced—well, not recently. Henry Fitzgibbon, my lord." Henry held out his hand.

Perforce, Christian had to halt and grasp it. "Good evening, Fitzgibbon."

Releasing Henry's hand, Christian would have nodded and walked on, but Henry rushed to say, "I wanted to speak with you particularly—to apologize about your gate. I should have come to you immediately, but, well..."

Reluctantly, Christian waited; he had a fair idea of what would come next and, from experience dealing with subalterns, knew he had to hear Henry out.

Sure enough, Henry drew in a breath and confessed, "I regret I was foxed at the time. I didn't notice the damage to my curricle until the next afternoon, and by then…well"—Henry glanced to where Eugenia had come up to stand between them—"matters had got away from me." Henry looked again at Christian and met his eyes. "I understand you won't hear of us paying for the damages, but at least accept my very sincere apology for the damage and for any inconvenience it caused."

Christian glanced fleetingly at Eugenia. Inconvenience such as having to argue with Henry's sister? But he looked back at Henry and inclined his head. "I accept your apology, and I suggest we agree to let the matter rest."

"I say, that's dashed good of you." Henry's relief showed in an expression of unburdened happiness that forcibly reminded Christian of one of his subalterns.

He looked at Eugenia and was, once again, about to take his leave as, finally, many others were, when Reverend Colebatch came striding up, the skirts of his cassock flicking about his long legs. Lady Osbaldestone walked rather more sedately in his wake.

"Miss Fitzgibbon! Lord Longfellow! I'm glad I caught you." His face alight and rosy with the cold, Colebatch clapped Christian on the shoulder and smiled delightedly at Eugenia. "I wanted to thank the pair of you for your performance this evening. Your voices! So rich, so true—so very perfect for this night. You might not have been aware of it, standing at the rear of the congregation as you were, but your voices simply soared over the heads of us all and led us in a most magnificent celebration. I have never heard better, not even in the much larger city churches I presided over years ago."

Lady Osbaldestone had come up in time to hear the reverend's compliments; she leant on her cane and regally stated, "Your combined contribution was nothing short of a tour de force, a feat appreciated by all who were honored to hear it."

Eugenia blushed. With a sidelong glance, Christian caught her eye. Neither could demur or in any way play down their apparent accomplishment without disparaging the other—which, of course, neither would do.

Catching the satisfied gleam in Lady Osbaldestone's black eyes, Christian was perfectly certain she'd happily orchestrated their mutual trap. Yet another thing he and Eugenia had in common—their evident inability to escape her ladyship's coils.

Someone on the path leading to the carriages called for Henry. He glanced that way, then looked questioningly at his sister.

Still blushing, if anything a touch more fierily after her shared glance with Christian, Eugenia nodded and wound her arm in Henry's. "We should get on. Goodnight, everyone."

Lady Osbaldestone, the reverend, and Christian echoed the farewell, then Christian shifted, preparing to depart.

"I say, Lord Longfellow"—Colebatch turned to him as if having just remembered to ask—"do you happen to have a donkey?"

The question was so unexpected, Christian answered without thinking first. "Yes, we have one."

"Oh, thank Heaven!" The reverend's expression was all earnest supplication. "Might we borrow the beast tomorrow? Just for the middle of the day? We're in dire need of a donkey for the re-enactment of the nativity scene, you see. You must remember that tradition—it dates back to before your childhood, I'm sure."

Reluctantly, Christian nodded, although his memory of the event was sketchy.

"I wouldn't ask, what with you and your people being only recently in residence, but it transpires that with the untimely death of the Johnsons' Neddy and the Foleys at Crossley having sold their Scraggs, there's not a donkey to be had in the parish." Colebatch, his wispy gray hair standing up in tufts on either side of his head, looked almost plaintively at Christian. "Please say we may borrow your beast. Otherwise, I don't know where we might find one at such short notice, and the children will be so disappointed."

It occurred to Christian that Lady Osbaldestone, who was observing the exchange with a smile on her face, wasn't the only one in the village given to manipulation—if not outright blackmail, given the reverend's invoking of the children's happiness.

Stifling a sigh, Christian surrendered. "Yes, of course. At what time will you need the animal?"

"Thank you!" The reverend caught Christian's hand between his own and shook it heartily. "The re-enactment is scheduled for eleven-thirty tomorrow on the green. If you could bring the beast somewhat earlier?"

Christian caught the interest in Lady Osbaldestone's eyes at the reverend's assumption that he, Christian, would be delivering the animal and couldn't suppress his own small smile. "I'll make sure Hendricks gets the animal to you in good time."

The chiding look Lady Osbaldestone bent on him bounced off his emotional armor. Christian excused himself and, with a nod to the reverend and a bow to Lady Osbaldestone, stepped back, turned, and strode into the deeper shadows. The church stood not far from the border of the Dutton Grange estate. A brisk walk through the woods in the dark of the icy night would douse the lingering warmth the carol service and its aftermath had set wreathing about his beleaguered brain.

CHAPTER 9

The following morning at eleven o'clock, Christian walked toward the green along the same woodland path he'd taken the previous night to and from the church.

Behind him, at the end of a stout length of rope, trotted Duggins, the Grange donkey.

Since Christian had returned to the Grange, despite not having seen him for more than ten years, or perhaps because of that, Duggins, who had been a young jack when Christian had left for the army, clearly retained fond memories of Christian and now refused to be led anywhere at all beyond the confines of his barnyard by anyone other than the new lord of Dutton Grange.

Swearing at the beast in several languages had done not a whit of good.

That episode had brought a grin to even the stoic Hendricks's face; he and Jiggs had been the only ones within earshot who had understood the epithets Christian had heaped on the donkey's gray head.

Duggins had simply looked up at him and—if donkeys could do such a thing—smiled.

When Christian had run down, Duggins had brayed.

Jiggs had insubordinately suggested Christian take that as a sign and had handed over the rope.

And that was how Christian came to be doing the very last thing he'd intended to do—heading for the green on the other side of the vicarage, into what would surely be a crowd of the village's impressionable youngsters, all excited and impatient to get on with their re-enactment.

As he reached the edge of the woods and stepped onto the lawn surrounding the church, he glanced at Duggins. "I'll take you to the green and hand you over—it's up to whoever's in charge to make you perform as required. I won't be there—I won't be staying." How was he to get the animal back to his barn? Striding on, he pondered that, then informed Duggins, "If I know anything of you, you'll happily trot home to get warm and be fed. I'll pay a couple of the village boys—perhaps those three who were beside me in the church yesterday, if I can find them. I'll get them to bring you home." He cast a sharper glance at the donkey. "And if you make any fuss, I'll tell the boys to send for Jiggs and Johnson to come and fetch you—that will serve them right, too."

As he rounded the back of the vicarage, he looked sternly at Duggins. "Just get it through your thick skull that no matter what you do, I will not be dancing to your tune."

He was, however, talking to a donkey.

With a sigh, he faced forward and trudged on.

The village green was separated from the vicarage by a hedge and a stone retaining wall. With Duggins trotting amiably behind, Christian circled the far end of the wall and turned east toward the lane. Ahead, he saw the milling crowd gathering on the green to either participate in or bear witness to the village's traditional re-enactment of the nativity scene.

The children of Little Moseley had always been a hardy breed and not to be denied. Christian could remember similar events held in snow, in near-torrential rain, in fog so thick that Mary and Joseph had lost their way, and, memorably, once in a near-blizzard. The animals had run amok that time. Today, however, although the morning remained cool, the temperature had risen sufficiently to ward off the deeper chill of the night and melt the light frost. Although uniformly gray, the skies appeared benign, and the stiffer breeze of the early morning had fallen away.

He approached the crowd with Duggins pressing close behind him—almost as if the donkey was eager to join in the evolving melee. Christian was tall enough to see over most heads. He located Reverend Colebatch in the center of the throng, surrounded by more than twenty children.

Halting at the edge of the crowd, Christian glanced around, hunting for likely helpers, but his plan to hand Duggins over to some boys died a death as he realized that every last one of the village's children, up to and including those of fifteen or so, had claimed a role in the upcoming drama. Every lad he could see was swathed in sheets or towels or had an upturned saucepan on their head and carried a wooden sword, and most were struggling to herd sheep and goats and even a family of ducks.

A bleating, quacking, baaing chorus threaded through the cacophony of many human voices steadily rising in an effort to be heard over the barnyard din.

Then Reverend Colebatch saw Christian and, face lighting, beckoned him forward.

Jaw setting, telling himself to ignore the looks and just get on with it, he advanced through the shifting crowd with Duggins tripping eagerly at his heels.

"Excellent!" The reverend beamed. "And in perfect time, too."

Mute, half ducking his head to conceal his face, Christian handed over Duggins's rope.

Colebatch took it and waved to two of the older children. "Now, Mary —yes, I mean you, Jessie Johnson. Up with you now, and as Joseph, Ben, you get to hold the rope."

Christian glanced at Duggins, but the donkey seemed fascinated by the youngsters all around and didn't even glance Christian's way. Mentally consigning responsibility for whatever happened next onto the reverend's head, Christian backed away, leaving Colebatch, assisted by Filbert, the deacon, and Goodes, the choirmaster, working to organize the excited children into their component groups and assemble them around a ramshackle structure to which Fred Butts, the baker's husband, assisted by several of the Johnsons and Foleys from Witcherly and Crossley Farms, was still putting the finishing—stabilizing—touches.

Given the dearth of available youth, Christian glumly accepted that he would have to wait until the end of the event and retrieve Duggins himself.

Keeping his head down, angled to better hide his damaged cheek, he swiftly tacked through the distracted crowd—many now bobbing on their toes in an effort to keep their children in sight—and made for a spot at the side of the shifting mass, where it was limited by the retaining wall. The ground canted upward to the base of the wall, which at that point rose above Christian's head. He reached the wall and put his back to it. His height combined with the vantage point gave him a reasonably clear view of the proceedings.

They were just as chaotic as he remembered.

Leaning against the wall, freed of immediate duties, he took his time surveying the crowd. He started with the children and spotted Lady Osbaldestone's three scamps. Temporary interlopers they might be, but of course the village had included them. Jamie and George were garbed as shepherds, draped in striped sheets and with towels tied about their heads. Watching Jamie direct the other boys in keeping the assembled farm animals in some sort of order, Christian wryly approved Colebatch's assignment of duties; Jamie was a born…not leader so much as a director of men. The boy definitely had a way with him—very likely inherited was Christian's guess.

Lady Osbaldestone herself was standing on the other side of the sea of children. Tallish for a female, she stood upright and erect and, by her very presence, seemed to impose a degree of obedience on both children and animals alike.

Christian finally spotted Lottie with the younger Milsom boy and two others Christian decided must be the Bilson twins watching over a brood of baby chickens, ducklings, and a gosling or two.

Although the children were all there, more adults were arriving as the moment for the re-enactment to start drew near. The crowd shifted and swirled as bodies pressed in from the direction of the lane.

Then Filbert and Goodes started shooing back the adults to create a suitably large circle around the "stable" for the children and animals to move and the tableaux vivants to be seen and appreciated by the surrounding throng.

Inevitably, the crowd lapped against the wall, then pushed back, with others joining Christian hard up against the stone. There was a jostling to his left as a newcomer tried to shield a lady; Christian glanced around, away from the central spectacle—and found himself looking into Eugenia Fitzgibbon's face.

From the surprise in her eyes, she hadn't seen him until that moment.

Restricted by the wall and the press of other bodies around them, he managed a half bow. "Good morning, Miss Fitzgibbon."

Her features relaxed, and a smile, warm and encouraging, bloomed. "Good morning, Lord Longfellow." She looked out at the children, now forming up behind Mary, perched on an apparently eager-to-please Duggins. Eugenia cast Christian a sidelong glance. "Reliving youthful exploits?"

His lips twisted in a wry half smile. "It's difficult not to—the sight does bring back memories."

He leant around her to exchange nods and greetings with Henry, who had dutifully steered Eugenia around the thick of the crowd to the relative shelter of the wall.

Christian looked at Eugenia. "Were you ever Mary? I can't remember."

Eugenia nodded. "I was, but I don't think you were here that year—you'd gone to stay with school friends and didn't get home in time."

A sudden bray from Duggins as Joseph prodded him to get him moving combined with a blast from two trumpets inexpertly blown to herald the commencement of the pageant and fix everyone's attention on the spectacle, which, without further ado, got under way.

The conversations in the crowd died as everyone craned their necks to see—to watch the children they all knew perform in whatever roles they'd been assigned that year.

Eugenia laughed softly along with everyone else as, having reached the stable and halted the donkey, Joseph reached up to lift Mary down—and staggered and nearly fell, as Mary was significantly heavier than he and further impeded by the cushion tied about her middle beneath her blue robe. However, between the pair of them, they recovered, and Mary spoke her lines, then they went into the stable, and in reasonably orderly fashion, punctuated by the inevitable missteps, some of which had the audience battling to muffle their mirth, the various animals were herded in behind and to the side.

Philip Goodes, the choirmaster, who had a powerful voice, stood to one side and intoned from the script of the "play" as the children and animals went through the motions of settling down to sleep.

Christian ducked his head and murmured to Eugenia, "I wonder how long ago that script was written."

Without taking her eyes from the current tableau, she turned her head slightly and whispered back, "It's certainly older than we are." She paused, then added, "I'm fairly certain it was a part of Christmas when my father was a boy."

Christian nodded. "I believe my father took part in it, too."

Eugenia glanced at Henry, on her other side. He was grinning, his attention fixed on the children. She'd been pleased that, even though his four too-fashionable friends had declared this event beneath their notice, Henry had volunteered to accompany her and had done so with every sign of good humor.

She was even more glad that he'd seen that Christian had come. Being present at such events was an important part of building, forging, and sustaining the necessary cohesion that made a small village like Little Moseley work. Sharing the event with their neighbors, with their workers, with their neighbors' workers, and everyone else around. Seeing the children all working together and adding to the sense of collective pride as parts were successfully played, the inevitable gaffes overcome, and the whole depicted with passable grace in honor of the overarching celebration. All these were important things—especially for a man who would one day manage one of the major local estates.

The thought had her glancing at Christian Longfellow. He was standing close—inevitable in the crush—but his head was still half bowed. He hadn't straightened since speaking to her.

She realized why. She'd worn a hat—a neat cloche with an upstanding feather rising above the right side. She suspected Christian remained with his head half bowed to take advantage of the feather to screen the ravaged left side of his face.

For a moment, she studied his damaged cheek—fully revealed and quite close. And felt a tug inside—a little fillip of pleasure that he now felt sufficiently at ease with her not to worry about revealing that side to her.

She felt the sharp prick of an impulse to show him how little that disfigurement mattered.

Yes, it was quite severe—no one could deny that—but it didn't make him hideous. It wasn't simply that the perfection of the other side of his face muted or compensated but more that his personality—the man he was—overrode superficial appearance and rendered his scars of no moment.

She faced forward, but her attention was no longer on the tableau in which Mary and Joseph had awakened and discovered the swaddled babe—a doll donated by the Swindons, whose children were no longer young—in the manger set in the middle of the rickety stable.

Instead, she thought of how she felt about Christian using her as a shield, and while on her own account, she didn't mind, she had to wonder if she should allow it. But had he taken advantage of her screening feather instinctively or by conscious design? The former would be harder to address.

While she wondered how to do so, the pantomime rolled on, including several moments of hilarity sufficient to reduce both the players as well as the audience to tears. Eugenia laughed and smiled even more to hear

Christian laugh freely as well. If he could relax that far, perhaps self-acceptance wasn't that far away.

Eventually, the spectacle drew to a glorious close with the three magi —cloaked in old tapestry curtains and with gold-painted papier mâché crowns on their heads—arriving and paying tribute while the heavenly host, portrayed by the choir in their surplices, sang in the heavens.

The children held the final tableau vivant for several minutes while Mr. Goodes declaimed the last lines of the script—declaring that thus had the Messiah come to earth. Then he shut the folio containing the script's dog-eared pages, looked at the audience, and with a widening grin, uttered the words "The end."

Children whooped and cheered, and the audience clapped until their hands stung. Then the children broke from their positions, and pandemonium reigned.

Over the heads, Christian saw Duggins, made uncomfortable by the sudden jostling, tip up his head and, with lips peeled back, issue a loud, hee-hawing bray.

Startled, the sheep broke free. In a darting, baaing bunch, they rushed this way, then that, scattering children and adults in their attempts to find their way to open ground.

The older boys whooped again and chased them. That only added to the panic.

The crowd surged, backing toward the wall, jostling and unintentionally pushing.

Instinctively, Christian half turned toward Eugenia, protectively shielding her.

On her other side, Henry was pushed and gave way—shoving Eugenia into Christian and more or less off her feet.

He hesitated for only a heartbeat—shocked by the heat, the instinctive reaction that shot down every nerve—then he ruthlessly clamped down on his instincts and the impulses that roared in their wake, closed his hands firmly about her shoulders, and steadied her, shielding her from the wall and cushioning her against him, trapped between his bent arms.

He'd heard her soft gasp at the sudden and distinctly indecorous contact—they were plastered to each other from shoulders to knees—but she made no effort to pull from his hold, not even to ease away. Instead, she stood—not tense yet, he sensed, very much aware—all but pressing into him, her hands splayed on the front of his jacket as the initial wave of panic rippled through the crowd and on.

But the panic hadn't ended.

The crowd had broken up into tighter knots. The makeshift "stable" had collapsed, keeping Butts and the Johnsons and Foleys busy freeing those caught up in the crumpling structure.

Reverend Colebatch, Filbert, and Goodes, along with some of the boys—Jamie and George among them—were struggling to restrain the animals remaining within the "fold." But the sheep were still darting and dashing about, and some of the goats had decided to join them, threatening to butt anyone who attempted to corral them.

The goats were on the far side of the crowd, and of all people, Lady Osbaldestone was directing several men as to their capture. As she was wielding her cane with purpose, Christian deemed it safe enough to leave the goats to her.

He had a fleeting vision of a similar rout at the end of the re-enactment in one of the years he'd participated. In some respects, it was inevitable and not really much of a concern, but the sheep were still loose, and though in actuality unthreatening enough, certainly to those country born, a small child too young to be in the pageant had been knocked over by one of the larger ewes and was now crying inconsolably in her mother's arms…

Christian saw an older woman—very old, leaning heavily on a stick—hobbling to get out of the way of the still-darting mob.

Enough.

Over Eugenia's head, he caught Henry's eyes and, gripping Eugenia's shoulders, eased her toward her brother. "Look after your sister while I take care of this."

Not waiting to hear any response—he'd spoken in his major's voice—he pushed away from the wall and forced his way through the ranks of the crowd.

He spotted a group of older boys, sheets and towels still flapping, chasing the sheep more or less in a line following the animals. "Boys!"

At his commanding roar, the boys pulled up—shocked into instant obedience.

Christian didn't give them time to think. "You and you." He pointed to two of the boys. "Continue to chase them. Go!" The pair went. "The rest of you go that way"—he pointed diagonally across the green—"and get ahead of them. Then you and you"—he singled out the heaviest of the boys—"grab the ewes in the lead. There's two of them. Grab their heads against your bellies like this"—he demonstrated—"and hold them. They'll stop, and then the others will, too."

He waved, and the boys raced off.

He hadn't brought his cane; what with all the riding and walking he'd been doing since returning to the Grange, his left leg was growing stronger. Regardless, he still couldn't run.

It took him three minutes to catch up with the boys—and by then the ovine escapees had been recaptured. Most of the boys stood in a rough circle, corralling the submissive animals around the dominant ewes, still held close by the two boys he'd delegated to subdue them.

The boys all looked to him as he approached. One of the pair holding the ewes turned his head to ask, "Like this, my lord?"

Halting, Christian nodded. "Exactly like that. Well done!" With his gaze, he included the other boys. "You succeeded and stopped what might have become a riot."

All the boys grinned. Many exchanged proud glances.

"Now," Christian went on, "who owns the sheep?"

Informed they were from the Foleys' flock, Christian dispatched two boys to find John Foley, last seen disentangling people from the ruin of the "stable." John soon came striding up, bringing his herdsman with him. Between them, they took charge of the two ewes and, after thanking Christian and praising the boys, led the recalcitrant sheep away.

Almost smiling, Christian nodded at the boys. "Dismissed."

They grinned, and he turned away—to find Eugenia and Henry had followed him. Of course, their route home also lay in that direction, but from the manner in which Eugenia approached, her smiling gaze locking on his face, he rather thought his first instinct had been correct, and she had, indeed, come after him.

She halted before him, with Henry a few steps behind, and raised a hand to lightly touch his arm. "I wanted to thank you for saving me from tumbling."

Uncharacteristically, Christian dithered. Saying "It was entirely my pleasure," while nothing more than the truth, might be too revealing.

Then from behind him came the sound of a throat being noisily—and rather pointedly—cleared. He turned to find one of the "shepherds" he'd just instructed in how to subdue ewes standing regarding him—including taking in the disaster of his face. Prodded by instinct to act over the sheep, he'd forgotten all about his scars.

It was too late to hide the hideousness now…and the boy didn't seem overly horrified. "Yes?" His tone was a trifle sharper than he'd intended.

The boy's eyes widened, but then he firmed his jaw and raised his head a fraction.

Christian realized that all the other boys were still there, hanging back and watching a few yards behind their friend.

"If'n you don't mind, your lordship," the boy said, drawing Christian's attention back to him, presumably the group's elected spokesman, "we've been wanting to ask which battle it was that you got blown up in."

Which battle? That was one question Christian was rarely asked. "Talavera."

"Was it a big battle with lots of guns, then?"

"About six divisions involved, plus supporting cavalry and artillery." When Christian saw that didn't mean anything to the boy, he clarified, "Lots of men with guns, lots of cavalry, and lots of cannon."

He could still hear their roar when he thought of it.

The boy nodded, as if that explained things. "Thought it musta been like that. Thank you, m'lord." The boy bobbed an awkward bow, turned, and hurried back to his mates.

The group closed around him, eagerly questioning.

Christian studied them.

Beside him, Eugenia murmured, "See? They don't view your scars the way you do."

His gaze still on the boys, he frowned slightly. "I thought they would be repulsed."

"No." In a softer tone, she added, "They see the man behind the scars. The major, the man of action. That's what you are to them. When it comes to your injuries, they're just curious."

He continued to stare at the boys, some of whom had shot quick glances his way. "Just curious…huh." Then he shook aside the distraction and turned to Eugenia. "I must fetch my donkey—he's probably dug in his heels and will be refusing to move."

She grinned. "I don't think he's ever played a role in our nativity before. Next time, he'll be an old hand."

Christian arched his brows. "Heaven help us. He's such a contrary animal he's liable to consider causing a stampede an obligatory part of the show." He bowed to her. "Good day, Miss Fitzgibbon."

She dipped a slight curtsy. "And good day to you, my lord."

Henry came forward to shake Christian's hand and add his thanks to

Eugenia's, then brother and sister continued toward the lane while Christian headed for the area where the debris from the "stable" was being cleared away.

As he'd predicted, Duggins had refused to budge, and the men were having to work around him.

"Lord Longfellow!" Reverend Colebatch greeted him with relief. "Thank you for your help with the errant sheep, my lord. And for this fine fellow, as well." Beaming, Colebatch handed over Duggins's rope. "He performed as required…well, except for that last bray. But I daresay it was a protest of sorts, so we must excuse him."

Christian gave Duggins a warning look. "As you wish, Reverend. But I better get him back to his stable and allow you and your helpers to finish up here."

"Yes, indeed." Colebatch half bowed. "Thank you again, my lord. Our re-enactment wouldn't have been the same if we hadn't had the use of your beast."

And that, Christian reflected, was nothing more than the truth. He wondered how the village pundits would label this year's effort. "The year that donkey spooked the sheep" was, in his view, the most likely description.

Christian started off, and Duggins readily fell into line behind him. He'd gone no more than ten yards when he found the group of boys—most about twelve or thirteen, he judged—waiting to waylay him. He slowed.

The same boy as before—their spokesman—stepped forward to say, "We was wondering, my lord, if'n you could tell us a little of what your time in the wars was like. About being over there, away from home and fighting the Frogs."

Christian eyed their hopeful faces. The war wasn't over and wouldn't be for years, yet given their age, these boys might never be called upon to serve. That said, there were always wars somewhere, and better they heard the tales from one who knew, from someone they knew and, he hoped, would listen to.

One of the other boys shifted uncertainly. "Me dad said as how you was a major an' all, so you must know what it's like being in the thick of things."

He did know. Few better. Not many men had survived the sort of fighting he had.

Duggins nudged him in the back. Christian glanced at the donkey, then looked at the boys. "If you walk with me around the back of the vicarage and the church, I'll answer your questions."

The boys' faces lit. Eagerly, they lined up on either side of him.

Trailing his own little troop—the similarity didn't escape him—he walked on, leading Duggins, and set himself to answer the boys' questions as honestly as he could.

From the other side of the green, Therese viewed the little band departing around the far end of the vicarage's retaining wall and smiled with a great deal of satisfaction.

Lottie came gamboling up, then halted and waved goodbye to Annie Bilson, who was of similar age.

Looking around closer to hand, Therese spied Jamie and George wiping their hands on their costumes and heading her way. "Excellent work, boys. I'm sure Mr. Goodes can handle the rest. It's nearly lunchtime, and after all that excitement, you must be hungry."

Assured by all three that they were starving worse than any waifs, Therese gathered them up and herded them back to the manor.

That evening, when Therese and her three assistants gathered in her private parlor after dinner, she led them in a review of their campaigns. Ignoring the toys and games, not to mention the drawing paper, now strewn about the room, she sat back in her chair before the fire, and with Lottie curled up by her feet and leaning against her knee and Jamie and George sitting cross-legged on the hearthrug, she arched her brows at the boys. "I take it you turned up no clue this afternoon."

Both boys shook their heads. "The other boys came with us, and we searched all the buildings and barns and even Mr. Mountjoy's warehouse behind his store," Jamie reported, "but there was no sign of the geese anywhere."

"I assume you asked the owners of the properties for permission before you searched?"

George frowned. "Of course." His tone suggested he considered the question something of an affront.

"We did," Jamie confirmed. "They were all happy to let us look. Mr. Whitesheaf even allowed us to go down into his cellars, although I can't imagine how the birds could have got down there, not unless someone had left the delivery hatch open." He shrugged. "Anyway, the geese weren't there."

"Will Foley, Ben Butts, and Robert and Willie Milsom came with us," George said.

Jamie shifted. "They said they'd gone out yesterday afternoon and beaten the woods south of Crossley Farm, but didn't find even a feather."

The boys sounded rather dejected. Therese considered them, then said, "There are five more days before Christmas Day. How much do you want goose for Christmas dinner? Enough to keep searching?"

The boys exchanged a look, then glanced at Lottie, then Jamie met Therese's eyes and nodded. "Yes. If there are five more days…" He paused and frowned.

"Indeed." Therese could guess where his mind had taken him. "Although there are five more days to Christmas, Mrs. Haggerty will need time to clean and pluck the bird and properly dress it, so in fact we really have at most four days. If we don't find the flock by the twenty-third, I believe we'll need to give up."

"But not yet, Grandmama!" George and Lottie chorused.

"We should at least search until then," Jamie said. "And when you think of it, it's like long ago when everyone had to hunt for their meals. We're doing the same thing."

Somewhat relieved—for how she would occupy them if they weren't amusing themselves with the search, she had absolutely no idea—Therese regally inclined her head. "Very well. Our search goes on." She paused, envisaging the map of the area. "I suggest that tomorrow, you and however many of the other children you can collect should search the woods north of Swindon Hall. That's opposite Tooks Farm, across the road to Romsey and the Wellows. I can't remember why we didn't search there earlier, but we haven't, and we should. It's a large enough area that a flock could hide there and not be seen by anyone for some time."

Jamie and George nodded eagerly. "We can start in the morning," George said, "as long as it isn't raining."

Therese had had the thick curtains drawn tight against the icy cold of another brilliantly clear night sky. "I doubt we'll have rain, but we will have frost—possibly a hoar frost—by morning. It's been edging toward a deep freeze over the past days. I think tonight will see even the lake freeze hard. It's already frozen over, but Dick Mountjoy keeps an eye on it—he's more or less the official arbiter of when the village can skate on the lake, and he told me today that he thinks the freeze tonight will do it.

If so, he'll put up a sign in the shop window, so we'll all know the village skating party is on. The whole village gathers every year on the twentieth, as long as Dick says we can skate."

"Skating!" George cheered.

"And we packed our skates, too!" Jamie added.

"Mine are new." Lottie looked up at Therese. "I can skate all by myself, but my feet grew bigger, and I had to get new ones."

Therese smiled and passed her hand over Lottie's sleek head. "That's wonderful, my dear. I'll be able to watch you all." She looked at the boys and added, "Just as long as Dick gives us the all clear. The village rule is that there's strictly no skating unless and until Dick says it's safe."

Jamie and George returned her gaze solemnly. "Yes, Grandmama."

She eyed them for a second, then nodded. "Good. Now let's turn our mind to our other campaign."

Lottie looked up. "Is that the one where we help Lord Longfellow and Miss Fitzgibbon to see that they like each other?"

Therese looked down into her granddaughter's face and smiled. "Succinctly put, poppet—it is, indeed. And if the weather cooperates, we can hope for another event on the village calendar."

"The skating party." George rocked back and forth, a frown slowly forming on his face. "We managed at the re-enactment with Henry's help, but how are we to get them properly together on the ice?"

Slowly, Therese nodded. "A very good question. I believe that at the skating party, we'll have to rely on careful observation and our own quick wits to make the most of any opportunity that presents itself." She eyed her three helpers. "Which means we'll have to trust in Fate and be ready to seize whatever opening she gives us."

CHAPTER 10

The boys' morning search proved entirely unproductive. They returned to the manor for luncheon to learn that Dick Mountjoy had, indeed, declared the lake properly and solidly frozen over, and the village skating party was therefore convened for two o'clock that afternoon.

The news cheered them up wonderfully.

The entire household gathered in the front hall at a quarter to two. Excitement glimmered in many an eye, and anticipation abounded.

Using a large basket wrapped up in an old blanket, Mrs. Haggerty carried mince pies fresh from the oven; the aroma wafted through the air and made everyone's mouths water. Crimmins had his arms around a bundle of flagons wrapped in cloths to keep them warm—mulled wine for the adults and light cider for the children. Mrs. Crimmins and Orneby made sure all three youngsters were well wrapped up in their thick coats, hats, scarves, and gloves and were wearing their heavy outdoor shoes to which their skates could be attached.

Therese noted with approval that the three imps—although bouncing on their toes with excitement—bore with the women's fussing and checking with commendable patience.

She had to find her own portion of patience when Orneby, behaving as the first-class dresser she was, insisted on resettling Therese's warm winter bonnet more firmly over her ears and retying the fine woolen scarf draped over the bonnet to secure it.

From the corner of her eye, Therese saw her grandchildren grin at the sight of her submitting so tamely to Orneby's ministrations.

Finally, Mrs. Crimmins and Orneby picked up small piles of extra shawls and blankets, Therese nodded to Crimmins, and he opened the front door.

John Simms stood waiting on the front porch, with a stout staff in one hand and a pack on his back. The other members of the small household were also waiting—Ned Foley, the gardener, who lived with his brother and his family at Crossley Farm, Tilly Johnson, the scullery maid whose family owned Witcherly Farm, and Dulcie Wiggins, who was the orphaned niece of Martha Tooks and still lived with her aunt's family. All three had walked in as usual that morning and had redonned their heavy winter coats and boots and, in Tilly's and Dulcie's cases, were swinging the skates they'd brought in anticipation of the skating party going ahead.

"Right, then." Therese paused on the threshold, raised her cane, and pointed down the drive. "To the lake!"

The children cheered, Tilly and Dulcie giggled, everyone grinned, and they set off.

John walked ahead, using his staff to break up any small sheets of ice. The children skipped and frolicked behind him, with Tilly and Dulcie following close behind. With Orneby, the Crimminses, and Mrs. Haggerty, Therese strolled more slowly, using her cane infrequently, but grateful for the added stability nonetheless.

The sky above was ice blue with a thin veil of pearly clouds draped over the expanse by some celestial hand. The sun no doubt shone, but its light was diffused by the clouds; very little warmth penetrated the layer of chill cold that seemed to have smothered the surface of the earth.

As Therese had predicted, they'd had a hoar frost overnight, and with the temperature so low, the ice hadn't melted. It hung in icicles from the bare branches of trees, glistened on every blade of grass, and provided a constant crunch underfoot.

They reached the lane and crossed over, then walked on past the church and vicarage to turn onto the village green. Many other villagers were walking in small groups over the green, all making for the rise at the far end, beyond which lay the lake.

Therese and those of her household nodded and called greetings to the others and were greeted in return. The farther they walked, the more the company swelled. The Colebatches joined them.

"Henrietta saw you walk past," Reverend Colebatch said somewhat breathlessly. "I was working on my sermon and had quite forgotten the time."

Mrs. Colebatch smiled fondly at her spouse. "And it would never do to miss the village skating party. Everyone will be there."

Both Colebatches, Therese noticed, were carrying skates.

The rise at the far end of the village green was formed by a natural fold in the land. On the other side of the rise, the land fell gently away into a shallow valley along the bottom of which the lake spread. It was fed by several small streams running through the thick woods that bordered the lake on three sides; outliers of the New Forest, the woods were a hodgepodge of oaks, beeches, yews, and hollies, in this season forming a backdrop of stark browns and dark greens. The approach from the village green had long ago been cleared and was now a wide, grassy, gentle slope that led down to the lake's eastern shore.

The lake had been full before it had frozen, and the shimmering silver-white sheet of ice extended unbroken across the surface. The sight, lit by the soft glow of the cold afternoon sun, had everyone pausing in instinctive appreciation as they crested the rise.

Nature, her hand, seemed very close; nothing about the scene held man's touch, yet the beauty was undeniable, and they all paused to pay homage.

Then on a wave of eager excitement, the children in the various groups rushed on down the slope. The adults, smiling fondly, followed in their wake.

Being natural, the lake wasn't circular. There was a wide sweep to the left, along the southern shore, where in summer a small beach lay exposed and tempting. To the north, the lake curved east and narrowed and deepened toward the inlet from the largest stream. In Therese's mind, the lake was shaped like a pear, with the base to the south and the stalk to the north. Consequently, as along with the village's other adults, she and her household set down their burdens along the eastern shore and John Simms produced folding stools from his pack, the vista that lay directly before them was that of the widest part of the lake.

It was on that large and open expanse that the children and the others sufficiently adventurous would skate, in full view of all those settling on the shore to watch the fun.

Within ten minutes, most of the village and the families from the surrounding farms had arrived. Children quickly strapped on their skates and slid out on the ice, laughing and shouting. Tilly, Dulcie, and their friends were soon gliding on the ice, too, while many of their parents, and others like the Colebatches, rather more slowly followed.

It had been many years since Therese had skated. She'd loved the freedom, the speed and the rush of gliding so fast through the air, but the years had stiffened her joints and weakened her muscles to the point she no longer dared. But she still enjoyed watching others skate—living vicariously, she supposed.

She watched Jamie, George, and Lottie skate confidently out; even Lottie showed no hesitation, much less trepidation. They joined the others of their age on the ice—all obeying the injunctions of several mothers not to go out too far. Therese humphed to herself; she wondered how long that would last.

She glanced around and nodded to the Swindons, who came to join her.

"Always an enjoyable excursion, what?" The major set a folding stool for his wife alongside Therese. "I don't think we've missed one skating party since we've been at the Hall."

Mrs. Swindon sat and smiled up at him. "And you've never missed the chance to tie on your skates and get out on the ice, either." She waved him away. "Off you go, dear. I'll be perfectly comfortable here beside her ladyship."

"Good-oh!" The major nodded a farewell to them both and, whistling, headed for the ice.

Therese and Mrs. Swindon amused themselves by spotting the village adults who had ventured forth and passing humorous judgment on their form.

"Oh, look!" Mrs. Swindon pointed. "There's dear Eugenia and Henry."

Therese saw the pair, skating fast and confidently, streak out toward the center of the lake. She craned her neck and looked along the shore and spotted several of the staff from Fulsom Hall strapping on skates. She frowned, then looked out to where Eugenia and Henry were twirling. "I'm surprised Henry's four friends haven't put in an appearance. I would have thought having the chance to show off before a crowd would tempt them."

"Indeed." Mrs. Swindon leant forward, peering at the skaters. "Eugenia mentioned they—Henry's friends—weren't leaving until the twenty-third." She sat back. "Perhaps their ennui was too great to allow them to participate."

Therese laughed. She continued searching the crowd—both the skaters and those on the bank. After several moments, she frowned. "I can see Jiggs—Lord Longfellow's groom—on the ice, but I can't see his lordship anywhere."

"Isn't that his man—his majordomo—just arriving, along with Mrs. Wright, and their cook, and Jeffers? Jeffers was the old lord's footman."

Therese looked, saw, and imperiously waved.

Hendricks saw. He nodded to her, then spent a minute seeing his small band settled on the shore. Then Hendricks straightened and lumbered across to Therese.

Halting beside her, he bowed. "My lady."

She nodded regally back. "I noticed young Jiggs has taken to the ice. Aren't you tempted?" Hendricks hadn't brought skates.

Hendricks cast a wistful glance at the joyful, laughing crowd on the ice. "Aye—I'd like to be out there. But his lordship warned that this early in the season, although frozen over, the ice sheet's not that thick, and too much weight in any one spot might crack through it." Still staring at the lake, Hendricks concluded, "His lordship's not one you could call over-cautious, but he's always had a sixth sense about danger, so I decided to heed his advice. I wouldn't want to stand still out there and have the ice go under my feet and get dumped in the drink." Hendricks looked down and met Therese's eyes. "I'll wait until the ice builds a bit more before giving Jiggs a run for his money."

Smiling, Therese nodded approvingly, then glanced past Hendricks at the opening to the wide path through the wood from which he and the rest of the Grange household had emerged; there was no one else walking out of the trees. "And his lordship?" She raised her gaze to Hendricks's face. "Is he coming?"

Hendricks's expression set, and frustration glimmered in his eyes. "No. He told me he didn't like skating, but according to Mrs. Wright, he's a devil on the ice—or was…" Hendricks shrugged. "Perhaps now he can't, he doesn't want to watch others doing it."

But you don't believe that's the case. You think he's simply hiding. Still.

Therese looked out at the skaters on the frozen lake. "With regard to your master, it appears we have our work cut out for us. Leave it with me, Hendricks, and I'll see what I can do."

Hendricks inclined his big head. "I'll wish you good luck, my lady, but short of dragging him…"

"Here." Therese held up the box of mince pies Mrs. Haggerty had handed her. "Have a pie."

Hendricks gladly helped himself to one, then, with a polite nod to Therese and Mrs. Swindon, lumbered off.

As if somehow alerted that the mince pies had been broached, Jamie, George, and Lottie, all sporting wide grins, bright eyes, and decidedly rosy cheeks, came rushing up, followed rather more slowly by the major, equally infused with the joy of simple pleasures. All four were full of delight over the sport to be had sliding about the lake; clearly, they viewed their mince-pie break as merely an intermission.

Licking crumbs from his fingers, George looked at Therese. "Miss Eugenia is out there, but we haven't seen his lordship anywhere."

"He's not even among those by the shore," Jamie added.

With a sidelong glance confirming that Mrs. Swindon was absorbed chatting with the major, Therese told them what she'd learned from Hendricks.

Jamie frowned. "That makes it very hard for us to advance with our secondary campaign."

"Indeed." Therese fixed him with an entirely sincere, questioning look. "Do you have any suggestions?" After learning of Jamie's discussion with Henry and having witnessed the outcome, she was rather intrigued to learn what else Jamie might, if encouraged, come up with.

Still frowning, Jamie slowly said, "I think I should go and speak with him."

About what? Therese bit back the words. The look on Jamie's face reminded her so strongly of the way Gerald had looked when plotting some devious strategy…

Jamie's face cleared, and his chin set. "Leave it to me." He set his skates down beside Therese's stool. He glanced at her, then at George and Lottie. "I'll just slip up to the Grange and have a quick word—I won't be long."

Therese nodded. She pointed along the shore to where the Grange household were gathered. "Ask Hendricks to show you the path up to the Grange—there's no need to go back to the lane."

Jamie straightened his coat, nodded to his grandmother, then trotted over to where Hendricks stood.

Armed not only with the direction of the bridle path through the woods but also with the information that his lordship was holed up in his library, Jamie walked and trotted through the woods, then cut through the stable yard and the Grange gardens to fetch up on the terrace outside the library windows.

He had to tap twice before Christian appeared, stared at him through the glass, then unlocked the French doors and let him slip inside.

Relatching the doors, Christian eyed him suspiciously. "What are you doing here?"

Jamie shrugged. "The others are all at the lake, having fun skating. But I heard you were here, and I thought I would come and stay with you until it's time to go home."

Christian studied him. Jamie kept his expression open and unclouded and allowed Christian to scrutinize it.

Finally, Christian asked, "Don't you like skating?"

Jamie looked down. "Not really," he mumbled.

"Why not?"

Jamie shuffled, shifted. Eventually, he said in a rather small voice, "I fell. Hard. Last year."

Which was true. Of course, once he'd regained his wits and the use of his limbs, he'd gone straight back onto the ice, to the dismay of his mother and the approbation of his father. "It was on the lake at home at the Abbey. I knocked myself out, they said." Still not meeting Christian's eyes, he lifted one shoulder in a half shrug. "I don't like to skate anymore."

Christian remained silent for several seconds, then firmly said, "All boys like skating. You're just afraid of falling over again—of not being as confident as you used to be. But trust me, you'll be perfectly all right once you get back out there—at least after the first ten minutes." He paused, then added, "It might take a bit of courage, but hiding away from the challenge will do you no good at all."

Jamie kept his head down and fervently hoped Christian would hear his own words. In case he hadn't, Jamie glanced around—at the fire, at the big armchair beside it, at the chessboard moved to one side. "But you're here—why can't I stay with you?" Finally, he glanced up and met Christian's eyes. "I won't make any noise."

His lips set, Christian stared at him. Then he stated, "I've changed my mind. I'm going to the lake myself, and you're going to come with me. We'll stick to the south side, and you can get back on the ice there. Do you have your skates?"

Jamie ducked his head and mumbled, "I left them with Grandmama."

"Good. We'll fetch them, and you can go out where it's easiest and less crowded, then once you're comfortable, you can join the other children."

And, thought Jamie, having reached the lake, with luck you'll join the others on the shore.

Then it would be up to him, George, and Lottie to steer Miss Eugenia to wherever his lordship was.

Jamie knew well enough to pretend to be deeply reluctant, to figuratively drag his heels, but having determined on his path, Christian was ruthless in chivvying him along. After striding into the hall and returning shrugging on his greatcoat and with a thick scarf flapping about his neck, Christian tugged on his gloves, seized his cane from where it stood against the side of his chair, and bundled Jamie back out onto the terrace.

From there, they strode across the gardens, through the stable yard, and onto the bridle path leading through the woods to the lake.

As they walked, Christian continued to hear his own words ringing in his brain. *It might take a bit of courage, but hiding away from the challenge will do you no good at all.* Jamie might be hiding from skating, but he? He'd been hiding from life.

He couldn't justify doing so any longer. After the re-enactment of the nativity and his appearance among the villagers—and the response of the boys, or rather, lack of it, to his disfigured face—what was he hiding from?

Now he'd posed the question, he honestly didn't know.

"There'll be cakes and pies afterward," he said, whether to himself or to Jamie he wasn't sure.

The bridle path, along which he often rode, was reasonably well surfaced, wide, and clear of obstacles. Even with him being extra wary because of his injured leg, in less than ten minutes, they could see the lake glimmering through the trees. For the latter half of its length, the bridle path followed the rise that ran above the valley. Consequently, the end of the path lay most of the way up the slope above the lake.

As he and Jamie emerged from the woods, Christian halted to take in the sight below—the wide expanse of the lake, the ice reflecting the winter sky and so appearing a silvery gray-blue, the small figures of the village skaters sweeping, waltzing, and whirling over the surface—and the faint shushing sound made by the skates that rose in the still air in between outbursts of laughter and calls.

He was about to start walking down the slope when a flurry of movement farther up the lake caught his eye. He paused, eyes narrowing to bring the figures, even smaller due to the distance, into sharper focus…

"Good lord." He stared.

"What?" Too short to see over the trees bordering the northern section of the lake, Jamie looked up at him.

"Henry's four friends." Christian watched for several seconds more, then swore. "Damn them! The idiots have gone onto the lake at the northern end, at the outlet of the stream. The lake is deepest there, and it's protected by the trees—the ice is always thinnest in that spot, and those four are clowning about and jumping up and down." It would take only one of them to leap on one of the others in the center of that area, and they'd crack the surface.

"I don't think," Jamie said, "that anyone will care if they fall in and get soaked." Judiciously, he added, "Assuming, of course, that they can swim."

"It's not them I'm worried about." Christian scanned those on the ice—the younger half of the village spread out across the middle of the lake where it was widest and, in general, safest—and felt a chill touch his soul. "If they crack the ice at the northern end this early in the season, the cracks can spread… I've seen it happen before."

Long, long ago, yet the memory was too vivid to ignore.

Jaw setting, he started down. "Come on—first things first. I'll have a word with those idiots before we see about getting you on your skates again."

Jamie gamely kept pace as Christian strode determinedly down the slope, more or less forgetting to use his cane. He was halfway down and almost jogging when an incredibly loud, ear-splitting *crack!* splintered the moment.

Activity on the ice slowed. People looked around, confused as to where the sound had come from. Christian was already too far down the slope to see into the northern arm of the lake, but he knew where the danger lay, knew where next to look.

Thin jagged lines started appearing on the surface of the ice sheet, crack by small crack extending south from the lake's northern end, second by second insidiously creeping toward where half the village now stood unsuspecting on the ice.

Christian doubled his pace. Running, he waved his arms and roared, "Everyone off the ice! It's cracking! Get everyone to shore—*now!*"

His voice carried clearly in the sudden hush. His tone left no one in any doubt of the threat. For a split second, those on the ice remained frozen…then they leapt to obey.

Christian slowed as he saw the adults on the ice gathering the children and directing the older ones to pick up the youngest and skate quickly for the shore. He could still see the cracks advancing, but it seemed everyone would be off in time.

His gaze scanning the line of skaters reaching the shore, without conscious thought, he searched for one particular head…then he saw Eugenia Fitzgibbon skating slowly in, scanning the retreating backs as she came toward shore.

Ensuring the safe retreat, making sure everyone was there.

Then one little boy—was he Daniel Bilson's Billy?—called out something and pointed—past Eugenia.

She came to an abrupt, ice-scraping stop and swung around.

Christian had reached the shore by then; he had to stand on his toes to see what she was looking at…

Then he heard her call—and she pushed off and skated out again.

As she leant forward, skating fast, he saw what she was so frantically skating for—a little girl crouched on the ice, right out in the middle of the lake, farther than most of the skaters had gone. The child was hunched, head down, apparently scratching patterns in the surface with a twig.

Why hadn't the child reacted? Regardless, she hadn't, and she didn't seem to hear any of the frantic cries from shore.

Christian looked at the encroaching cracks. Then he looked at the child and Eugenia.

Danny Bilson, a man of about thirty and as heavy as his father, the butcher, grabbed someone's skates and struggled to put them on; from the murmurs, Christian gathered the girl was his daughter, Annie.

"Don't!" Christian's sharp order had Danny looking up; Christian caught his eyes. "You can't go out there. None of us can." He looked out at Eugenia Fitzgibbon as she neared the child and slowed. "Any extra weight will only make it more certain the ice will crack through, and they won't get back."

Danny Bilson stared at him, then the big man's shoulders slumped. Together with everyone else, he looked helplessly out at the lake.

Eugenia had halted a foot from the girl. From the direction of Eugenia's gaze, she'd seen the approaching cracks and recognized the danger. Wisely, she didn't pick up the little girl, nor did she panic her. But she had to crouch down to get the little girl's attention. Once she did, she spoke to the girl's face, then took the girl's hand.

When Eugenia straightened, the little girl stood with her. She wobbled on her tiny skates, but then steadied. She was small and young—barely five, Christian thought. The second of twins; it was her brother who had raised the alarm.

Slowly, talking to the girl as she drew her along, Eugenia started back to the shore.

A deeper, menacing *crack* from the lake's northern arm, followed by a faint slapping sound, told those who knew that the ice sheet was broken through, at least in that spot.

The villagers collectively held their breaths.

The cracks continued to inch across the lake, spreading like a spiderweb.

Christian studied them, then he turned his head. Hendricks and Jiggs were at his back. "Rope," he said, his voice low, his tone urgent. "As much of it as you can find—as fast as you can, bring it here."

Reverend Colebatch appeared beside Jiggs. The minister's face was pale, but composed. He'd held the living there for nearly all of Christian's life; he knew the danger two of his flock were in. "The vicarage is nearest. The shed at the end of the garden. There's two long ropes coiled just inside on the left."

Christian looked at Jiggs. "Fetch them."

Jiggs was off on the instant. He grabbed Rory Whitesheaf, groom at the Arms, as he went past; Jiggs gabbled his mission, then Rory raced with him up the slope.

Christian returned to watching Eugenia and the child's slow progress.

He'd been in too many battles to have much faith left, yet along with everyone else there, he prayed.

There was barely a murmur as, stride by slow stride, Eugenia led the little girl closer.

Logic and reason told him the pair wouldn't make it to shore, that the ice would crack beneath them when they were still over deep water, but along with everyone else, he still hoped…

It happened in a blink. The ice shattered all around the pair, and they fell into the inky blackness of the freezing lake.

A collective agonized gasp rose from those watching.

Then Eugenia's head bobbed up; she wrestled and struggled, and then she was grimly holding Annie's head above the freezing water.

"No! Stop!" Christian shouted at Henry and Danny, both of whom had instinctively started forward onto the ice. "You'll only make it worse."

Eugenia and the child had only minutes left before they froze too badly to help any rescuer, and lifting a dead weight out of a hole like that would be well-nigh impossible. Not before they were too far gone to be revived.

A pounding rush and a flurry behind him told Christian that Jiggs and Ray had brought the ropes.

Christian turned. He grabbed the end of one rope and tied it about his waist. As he did, he said to the men who were gathering around, "I'm the slightest—the tallest and leanest—of the lot of you. Barring only Jiggs, and I'm stronger than Jiggs. So it's me who has to go out." He handed the other end of his rope to Hendricks. "Wait for my signal, then pull me back."

He seized the end of the second rope and held it out to Henry and Danny Bilson. "Here—I'll tie the other end about them, and then you can pull them in."

All protests died. At the very last instant, Christian's gaze fell on his cane, lying at his feet where he'd dropped it. An image flashed into his mind. He bent and swiped up the cane in one gloved hand.

He didn't even risk stepping onto the ice—he crawled onto it. On hands and knees, concentrating on what he could feel of the movement of the ice beneath him, as fast as he could, he headed for the hole where Eugenia still doggedly clung to the side and, with her other hand, kept the child's face, already blue, above the water.

Ten yards from the hole, Christian felt the easing of the ice beneath him, heard the quiet little pops, and went flat on his stomach. As rapidly as possible, he pulled himself along.

When he was a yard from the edge of the hole, Eugenia's lips set, and with an almighty effort, she hauled the little girl up and free of the water and half flung, half pushed her at Christian.

He caught the girl's sodden skirts and pulled her to him. He set aside his cane and rapidly tied the second rope securely about the girl's limp form, then he swiveled and looked back, signaled, and Danny Bilson, aided by Henry and others, rapidly pulled the unconscious child to shore.

Turning back to the hole, Christian grasped his cane and edged forward. Of course, now they had only one rope, but they would manage. He just had to get Eugenia clear of the hole.

He felt the ice crack, and the section beneath his shoulders and chest dipped. For a second, he held his breath, held still. He could feel the edge of the section that had broken free poking upward under his rib cage. When nothing more dramatic happened, he raised his gaze and locked his eyes on Eugenia's.

Her teeth were chattering uncontrollably, but she clung to his gaze with…hope.

She believed in him. In that moment, he believed in himself.

Moving slowly, he extended the cane. With his arm stretched to its full length, the head of the cane hovered a foot before Eugenia's face.

"I can't come closer. The ice will crack if I do. You need to grab the cane and hold on—"

She dragged her arm up. In her current condition, the sodden weight of her sleeve made even that a massive effort. But she was still wearing her fine kid gloves. The leather allowed her to grip the cane tightly.

Christian recaptured her gaze. "Good. Now the other hand."

She needed to trust him and release her grip on the side of the hole—the only thing keeping her head above water.

"As soon as you get both hands on the cane, I'm going to pull you toward me. I think the ice in front of me will dip, and you'll be able to slide on your front onto it. Then we can both get pulled back—"

She'd dropped her gaze from his face to the head of the cane, to her left hand wrapped about the silver head. Her breaths were coming short and fast. Whether she'd heard his words, or whether she'd understood without them, she suddenly let go of the ice and locked both hands about the cane.

She went under the surface again.

His own breath stuck in his chest, Christian hauled on the cane. Hand over hand, as quickly as he could while keeping the pull even, he drew her toward him.

Her weight on the other end of the cane didn't ease; she hung on—desperately clung to life.

And as he'd hoped—as he'd prayed—her head rose above the black water again, closer now, on his side of the hole, and then the ice at the edge of the hole dipped, the edge beneath his ribs rising even as he started to squirm backward as fast as he could.

She slumped onto the ice, her head, her shoulders, almost to her waist. Her eyes were closed, her features tinged blue. Her lips were parted. But still she clung to the cane.

He paused to take rapid stock, then he pulled her closer still until he could lock his hands about hers where they gripped the head of the cane.

"I can't risk pulling you nearer." She might not be conscious, yet if she was, she would hear. "Our combined weights might be too much." He lifted one hand and, without turning to look back, signaled to those on shore. "Just hold on." He'd started to shiver, too. He clamped his hand about both of hers again and gripped hard as the rope attached to his waist went taut.

He heard shouting; he thought it was Hendricks, the ex-sergeant booming orders, then the rope started to drag him slowly toward the shore. Her legs and feet came out of the hole without catching, then he and she were sliding freely and smoothly over the ice, back to safety.

How many hands were on the rope he couldn't see, but once free of the hole, they were whisked across the ice as fast as if they'd been skating.

Then his boots hit the bank, and willing hands reached to help them up.

To lift them up and gather them in. Hendricks and Jiggs supported him between them while the major untied the rope. Henry and the footman from the Hall—James—had hold of Eugenia, but she slumped limp and apparently unconscious in their arms.

It was an effort and a wrench to peel his hands from over hers, but once he had, hers slid bonelessly from the cane.

The cane fell to the grass. Instinctively, he bent to pick it up. As he straightened, his legs almost went from under him. The cold struck him then; he felt chilled to the marrow and strangely lightheaded.

Jiggs took the cane; someone—he thought it was Hendricks—shoved Christian down to sit on a stool.

Someone wrapped a blanket around his back and shoulders. Someone else thrust a flask of brandy into his hand.

He took a long swig. The brandy burned, but it did the trick. His lightheadedness receded. His faculties returned. After a fashion.

Rory Whitesheaf had rushed back to the Arms, hitched the carthorses to his father's dray, and in contravention of village regulations but with the wholehearted approval of everyone there, he'd driven the dray over the green, up the rise, and down to the lake.

Henry looked stricken and helpless, then Mrs. Fitts, the Hall's housekeeper, pushed her way through the crowd. She took one look at Eugenia lying unconscious in Henry's arms and barked, "You and you!" She pointed at James and Billings, Henry's groom. "You help Mr. Henry get Miss Eugenia into the back of the dray."

Mrs. Fitts turned her gaze on Christian, then looked to where his own housekeeper, Mrs. Wright, was bustling up.

"Come on with you now, my lord." Mrs. Wright tugged at his shoulder. "Best you get in the dray and go to the Hall, too. M'sister will see you warm and dry, and when you come home, I'll have your dinner ready. Nothing more for you to do other than get warm and dry and that as fast as possible, so off with you now."

Christian recalled that Mrs. Wright was Mrs. Fitts's sister.

Apparently now taking their orders from Mrs. Wright, Hendricks and Jiggs got their hands under his arms and hoisted him to his feet. Not that he had any intention of resisting Mrs. Wright's directive. He wanted to—needed to—see Eugenia to safety. All the way safe—until she was dry and warm and no longer lying like one dead, silent and so pale.

Henry climbed into the dray, and the others lifted Eugenia, now swathed in countless blankets, to him. He settled her on his lap. Christian slowly clambered up and, with Hendricks's help, slumped down with his back against the dray's low side.

More blankets were piled atop him; he thought that between them, he and Eugenia now wore every last blanket not on a bed in the village.

Instead of giving in to the urge to giggle inanely, he took another swig from the flask, which he was rather surprised to find he still held. He recorked it, then held it up to study it.

"Mr. Colebatch, my lord." Hendricks and Jiggs both climbed up and sat on the end of the dray's bed.

"Really?" After a moment, Christian said, "I didn't know clergymen carried such things."

"Neither did we," Jiggs quipped. "Just glad he did."

The dray lurched, and the horses started the slow climb up the rise. But once they reached the top, it was an easy roll down and across the green, then into the lane. It wasn't that far to Fulsom Hall.

CHAPTER 11

They were rocking along the Hall's drive when Henry, who had spent the short journey until then with his gaze locked on his sister's pale face, raised his head and looked at Christian. "Will she live, do you think?"

Christian found it curious that he hadn't thought to ask the same question himself. He considered why, then said, "She held to consciousness until she was free of the hole. If she hadn't…I might not have been able to get her out. She's a fighter—she won't give up." And at some unfathomable level, he felt sure she wouldn't leave. "Once she's warm and dry, she'll wake up."

He sensed that in his soul. Fear…seemed to have lost its hold on him. At least in the here and now.

As the hall came into sight, he wondered if he should tell Henry that it was his friends' thoughtless actions that had caused the ice to break, then the dray slowed, and he decided that piece of news could wait until later. It seemed much less important than seeing Eugenia open her eyes again.

The instant the dray drew up before the front steps, the door flew open, and Mrs. Woolsey, trailing draperies, fluttered out at the head of a small army of Hall staff; the household must have been alerted by someone sent running from the lake.

Hendricks and Jiggs hopped down from the dray and helped Christian alight. As he straightened and the Hall staff, paying no attention whatever to Mrs. Woolsey's disjointed and often contradictory instructions, pushed past to lift their mistress and carry her inside, the staccato clop of horses' hooves had him turning to look down the drive.

Three carriages came bowling up. The first, the vicarage gig driven by Reverend Colebatch, carried Lady Osbaldestone and her very correct maid, both looking exceedingly determined. The second gig was driven by Major Swindon. While Colebatch halted his horse and Jiggs, summoned by an imperious wave, went to help Lady Osbaldestone down, Swindon drew up across the front of the dray. The major leant over and called, "I say, shall I go and fetch Dr. Berry?"

Dr. Berry was the current medical man for the area and lived in East Wellow, several miles away.

Henry, to whom the major had addressed the question, still looked blank—too shocked to respond.

Seeing that, Mrs. Woolsey attempted an answer. "Possibly. That is—well, it might be just a swoon, do you think? It seems wrong to get the doctor until we know…"

"Yes." Across the dray, Christian caught the major's eyes. "If you would, Major. There's no sense risking an inflammation of the lungs."

"Just so." With a nod and a salute, Major Swindon backed his horse, then turned and drove quickly away.

The third carriage had been the cart the Hall staff who had gone to the skating party had used to drive as far as the green; it had bypassed the forecourt and driven on toward the rear of the house and the stable.

Mrs. Woolsey was still flittering about Henry as he slowly and somewhat stiffly descended from the dray; the front of his clothing was sodden from cradling Eugenia.

The Hall staff had already whisked Eugenia inside, and Lady Osbaldestone was disappearing in her wake.

With a nod to Rory Whitesheaf, Christian left Henry to deal with Mrs. Woolsey—she'd finally got to asking what had happened—and, flanked by Hendricks and Jiggs, made his way carefully into the house.

He hadn't been inside Fulsom Hall for a very long time, but little had changed.

He halted in the front hall; he could hear Lady Osbaldestone giving orders upstairs and Mrs. Fitts agreeing and embellishing further. A patter of footsteps drew his attention to a line of maids and footmen carrying pails of hot water along the upstairs corridor.

Then Lady Osbaldestone appeared at the gallery railing. Looking down into the front hall, she spotted him. "There you are, my lord. Please come upstairs. We have a bath awaiting you. While you're bathing, the staff will dry your clothes. Come along now."

He went. Not only did he suspect resistance would be futile, but also he was so cold, he wasn't sure he was thinking clearly.

Hendricks and Jiggs flanked him up the stairs, no doubt in case he stumbled and fell. He appreciated the thought; his legs still felt weak.

The room a footman led him to had been Henry's father's. With heavy, dark furniture, it was large and accommodating. A huge tin bath had been set before a roaring fire and filled with steaming water.

With Hendricks's help, Christian stripped, stepped into the tub, and lowered himself into the water with a heartfelt sigh. Warmth permeated his skin and sank into his frigid muscles, and finally, the frozen tension that had gripped him started to ease.

An hour later, warmed all the way through, his hair mostly dry, and dressed in clothes that had been dried and ironed, together with Hendricks, he descended the main stairs to find Jiggs waiting in the front hall.

Jiggs straightened from his slouch and handed Christian his cane. "The doctor's with Miss Eugenia. He hasn't said anything yet, but apparently she woke when she got warmed up and said she's well enough, just tired."

Christian felt a weight he hadn't known was there lift from about his heart. He nodded. "Thank you. That's good to know." He paused, then asked, "And the little girl? Has anyone heard?"

"Danny Bilson sent a message. Seems she's taken a bad fright, as anyone would have, but she's otherwise right as rain. They got her out of her wet clothes right quick and rubbed her dry, and seems she's taken no lasting harm." Jiggs nodded down the hall to a closed door. "Mr. Henry asked if you'd stop by the library when you came down." Jiggs glanced questioningly at Christian. "I'm thinking I should go and fetch the carriage before it gets darker. You won't want to be walking home in the pitch dark."

Christian glanced at the windows on either side of the front door and realized the short winter twilight had fallen. He nodded. "Yes, go—and Hendricks." Christian turned to meet his majordomo's eyes. "Thank you for your help." He glanced at Jiggs. "Both of you. But I'm capable enough of sitting in Henry's library without aid, so both of you can return to the Grange. Jiggs can drive back and fetch me."

Hendricks studied his face, then nodded. "Aye, then we'll both go."

Jiggs tipped his head toward the library. "Quite a crowd in there, waiting on the doctor's verdict."

Thus warned, after watching his men depart, then allowing the footman to show him to the library, Christian wasn't surprised to find Major and Mrs. Swindon, along with the Colebatches, sitting with Henry. He was, however, somewhat taken aback to find Jamie, George, and Lottie beside Mrs. Colebatch on the chaise, and quite half the village, and even some from the nearby farms, dotted about the room, propping up bookshelves or leaning against the desks or the backs of chairs.

Henry waved vaguely. "Everyone wanted to know how you and Eugenia are." He smiled faintly. "I told them they could stay and find out."

Christian felt his lips twitch. He glanced around at the eyes trained on him. "As you can see, I wasn't hurt—just made a trifle damp, a minor inconvenience from which I am now fully recovered."

That raised a few strained smiles.

It was Jamie who informed him, "The doctor is with Miss Eugenia right now."

Christian smiled and crossed to the armchair beside the sofa. It had been left empty, he assumed for him. "So I heard." He sat and leant his cane against the side of the chair. He hadn't been using it all that much; it was fast becoming a mere fashion accessory.

Bilson, the butcher, the grandfather of the little girl, pushed away from the bookshelves, lumbered to Christian's side, and with his old cap in his hands, bowed. "We—my family—want to thank you, my lord. My son and his missus would have been gutted to lose their girl, and if it hadn't been for Miss Eugenia and you, they'd be attending a corpse at this very moment."

Christian met Bilson's eyes. "I was there and knew what had to be done. I'm glad to have been able to help." He directed an easy look around the room. "And we wouldn't want one of our most cherished village Christmas traditions to be touched by tragedy."

"No, indeed" and "Right enough" came from all around the room.

Bilson bobbed again and retreated.

The door opened, and Lady Osbaldestone walked in. She glanced around, nodded regally in a general fashion, then went to sit in the corner of the chaise beside Lottie.

Henry sat up, his gaze on her ladyship's face, and asked the question on all their minds, "Any news of Eugenia?"

Having settled herself, Lady Osbaldestone regarded him calmly. "Dr. Berry's still with her, but I believe we're all satisfied that she has taken no harm but is merely—and it's hardly to be wondered at—drained to the point of exhaustion." She glanced at Christian. "She was in the icy water for as long as she could bear. It was providential that she was rescued in time."

Christian inclined his head fractionally in response.

Deciding that he would most likely not welcome further expostulations of gratitude, and it wasn't really her place to offer such anyway, Therese glanced around at the assembled company. "What I would like to know is why little Annie Bilson didn't hear all of us calling her."

She brought her gaze to rest on old Donald Bilson, the only member of his family present.

Bilson shuffled, then offered, "I don't rightly know the way of it, but they—the twins, her and her brother—got mumps early in the year. Billy threw the illness off and was right as rain in days, but little Annie got a fever and all, but eventually she came good again. But ever after, we've been wondering if she can hear as good as she ought. Apparently, that can happen with mumps—that it dulls the hearing."

Therese nodded. "That's true."

"Annie can't hear if she's not looking." It was Lottie who made the pronouncement. Everyone stared at her, but she looked solemnly up at Therese and said, "I noticed when we played. If she looks at me and I talk, she knows exactly what I say, but if I speak from behind her or when she's not looking at me, it's as if she can't hear me at all."

Therese took that in, then glanced at Donald Bilson. "Annie's deaf, but she can understand well enough. That's something the whole village needs to know—so we can make sure to speak to her face."

"And so we can keep an eye out for her if she has her back to some danger." Christian glanced at Bilson. "I know men who lost their hearing through the war. There's no reason they—or in this case, Annie—can't live a full life if those around them know."

Slowly, Bilson nodded. "I'll tell Daniel and his missus. And the boy."

Henry glanced around the room. "And I'm sure all those here will spread the word around the village."

Nods and murmurs of agreement came from all around the room.

A heavy footstep in the corridor drew all eyes to the door. A second later, it opened, and Dr. Berry, a large-framed, bluff, no-nonsense practitioner, walked in. He halted and blinked at the crowd.

Henry rose and waved at the company. "Everyone wants to know how Eugenia is, sir. Will she recover?"

Berry humphed. "As to that…" He broke off to acknowledge Christian, Lady Osbaldestone, the Colebatches, and the Swindons with bows and nods, then resumed, "I would say she's more or less recovered already, thanks to the prompt actions of all those involved. That said, strenuous physical exertion while immersed in ice water is a massive drain on anyone's reserves—she needs to regroup. To that end, I've given her a sleeping draft—she'll sleep until morning, which is the best thing for her. After that, I envisage no further complications, but I'll return tomorrow to check, just to make sure."

Henry went forward to shake Berry's hand. The doctor confirmed he had nothing to worry about regarding Eugenia, then turned his professional eye on Christian, who rose and exchanged greetings.

"I heard you were involved in the rescue, my lord." Berry gripped Christian's hand. "Miss Fitzgibbon inquired how you were. Lady Osbaldestone said you'd merely got a trifle wet and were in no danger of succumbing to anything at all. Is that correct?"

"Entirely correct," Christian assured him. "After the rigors of campaigning, a little water, iced or not, isn't liable to have much effect on me."

Berry studied his face, then nodded. "Your color's good, your eyes are clear, and your grip's firm." He smiled and released Christian's hand. "You'll do."

With that, Berry took his leave. Henry saw him to the door and into the care of the footman who was waiting in the corridor.

As Henry turned back to the room, Gordon Whitesheaf, the proprietor of the Cockspur Arms, said, "What I want to know is why the ice cracked. Thanks to his lordship, we had warning enough to get all the nippers off 'cept for little Annie, but it coulda been much worse. If his lordship hadn't been coming down to the party late and hadn't looked and seen what was happening, half the danged village would have gone in, and that lake's plenty deep. A grand tragedy it woulda been and no mistake."

There were murmurs all around.

Dick Mountjoy, his usually rosy cheeks pale, stepped forward from his position at one side of the hearth. He held his cap in his hands and started turning it around and around. "I checked as I always do—like me granddad taught me, and his father afore that. The ice was sound. It shouldn't've cracked. I'd take me oath on it."

For a minute, silence reigned, then Reverend Colebatch cleared his throat. "Perhaps we need to…er, revise how we test the lake?"

"We need to be sure," Major Swindon put in, "that it truly is going to be safe to skate. Virtually the whole village gets on the ice at some point. Can't risk this happening again."

"No blame to you, Dick." Peggy Butts, her heavily muscled baker's arms crossed beneath her impressive bosom, eyed him sympathetically. "But there's too many kiddies sneak away to skate at any old time, and we need to be sure they're safe."

Christian let the discussion run, listening to both the words and their tone. Concern over the safety of skating on the lake continued to escalate, although only a few asked the critical question of why the ice had cracked *today*.

He'd reached the point of speaking up and giving them the answer to that question—he couldn't allow Dick Mountjoy to shoulder so much guilt even though no one was blaming him, nor allow the rising tide of anxiety to spur the adults into trying to keep the village brats from skating—when across the library, he met Jamie's eyes. The boy's gaze held his steadily, then Christian nodded fractionally. He opened his mouth—and was forestalled by a tap on the door.

Before any response could be uttered, the door opened, and Henry's four friends filed in.

Christian scanned the young gentlemen's faces, then shut his lips and waited.

All four looked even more upset than the villagers. Led by Viscount Dagenham, they lined up across the end of the room, facing the assembled villagers and Henry and Christian.

Dagenham inclined his head with a wary courtesy far removed from his usual arrogance. "Our apologies for interrupting, but…" Dagenham glanced at Kilburn, Carnaby, and Wiley, all of whom looked back at him, then Dagenham squared his shoulders, looked up the room at Henry, and said, "We've come to apologize. It was us who broke the ice. We didn't mean to—we had no idea the stuff wasn't thick enough to hold our combined weights."

Christian glanced at Henry. His already pale face had set at his friend's words. He stared at the four men. "You? It was *you* who were responsible for my sister falling into the lake and nearly freezing to death?"

He might as well have struck them—all four flinched.

Seeing from the darkening faces all around that the exchange might get out of hand, Christian spoke up. "How, exactly, did you break the ice? I saw you leaping about at the northern end of the lake."

Kilburn nodded and, as if glad to have been asked—glad to be able to say something—rushed to explain, "We were horsing around, then I piled onto Dags"—he glanced at Dagenham and amended—"Dagenham, and then Roger and George piled on top of me. And then the ice cracked."

"Right beneath our feet," George Wiley said. "Well, under Dagenham to be precise. We'd had no idea it might."

"We'd heard it was safe," Roger Carnaby added. "Then when it happened"—he gestured weakly—"we panicked."

"We didn't know what to do." Thomas Kilburn looked embarrassed and ashamed, as did the other three. "We…er, scrambled off the ice."

When Kilburn fell silent and didn't go on, Dagenham drew in a tight breath and said, "The cracks were spreading by then, but we had no idea—didn't dream—they'd continue to spread across the lake." His face was grim but resolute as he admitted, "We'd got wet, so we came back to the Hall to change."

"If we'd known the danger," Kilburn added in a quieter voice, "we would have raised the alarm. But we didn't, so we just came away." He glanced around the faces. "You have to believe us. We wouldn't have knowingly left people to drown."

Christian, for one, believed them; he appreciated what it said of them that having eventually learned what had happened, they'd come to face the music of their own accord.

The four weren't bad, they were simply immature. Or they had been.

Christian glanced at Henry's face. He had aged years in the past hours.

Once again, Dagenham raised his head and spoke for all four. "We are truly sorry and offer you"—he nodded to Henry—"and the village"—with his gaze, he swept the room—"our unqualified apologies."

Murmurs of various sorts greeted those words, but Christian was ready to accept them at face value. He steepled his fingers before his face, studied the four—all pale and somewhat trepidatious; he noted Lady Osbaldestone was studying them through narrowed eyes, much as he was, yet hers would be a distinctly more uncomfortable scrutiny, he felt sure. Finally, over the rumblings and grumblings, he raised his voice and said, "You are here as Henry's guests, yet in this instance, he couldn't be with you but instead was doing his duty by the village and his sister, as he should have been."

The room had fallen silent, everyone listening to see where he intended steering the exchange. Evenly, he continued, "You are all strangers to the locality and couldn't have known that the northern end of the lake is the deepest spot, and because the stream feeds in at that point, the ice is always weakest there, so it could well crack, especially if the weight of the four of you was applied at one point. It's clear today's near-tragedy was an accident, albeit one initiated by you. However, regardless of how belatedly, you have by your admissions and apologies demonstrated an understanding of the responsibilities that accrue to the position in society you hold."

He paused. All four young gentlemen had listened closely; if the faint color rising in their cheeks was any guide, all four had understood his oblique reference to growing up and acting as adults and as befitted their stations in life. He met their eyes, one after another, then nodded. "I believe I can speak for the village in saying we accept your apology. I will add that I hope you will learn from the incident the lessons inherent within it."

Christian glanced around at all the others. "Has anyone anything to add?"

Most of the villagers shook their heads. The major had listened with approval and indicated he had nothing to say. The reverend shook his head. Lady Osbaldestone had raised her brows and—to the four young men's intense discomfort—had deployed her quizzing glass, but she said nothing to Christian's prompt.

Finally, Christian turned to their host. "Henry?"

Henry had been staring at his friends. Slowly, he shook his head. "No. I have nothing to add."

For a second, an awkward silence held sway, then Dagenham came to everyone's rescue. He bowed, and the other three followed suit. "Thank you. We'll take ourselves off." Dagenham looked up the room. "Henry—we'll speak with you later."

After a second's hesitation, Henry somewhat stiffly nodded.

The four left the room.

On a soft tide of murmurs and comments, the villagers came to bid

Henry, and then Christian, farewell, and, with nods and bows to the other landowners, to take their leave.

Henry, to Christian's eyes, seemed to have shed a skin and become his father's son. He spoke to each villager, acknowledging their help at the lake and thanking them for coming and showing their support.

Christian had merely to add his tuppence-worth at the end.

Finally, Henry went to see the villagers out.

The Swindons and Colebatches trailed behind, hanging back no doubt to make their farewells and assure Henry of any support he or Eugenia might need. Christian waited while Lady Osbaldestone gathered her three grandchildren, then fell in beside her as they quit the library and followed the others into the front hall.

They halted by the foot of the stairs. Lady Osbaldestone glanced up the long flight, then looked at Christian. "I've a mind to check on Eugenia." She studied him for a moment, then turned to her grandchildren. "Orneby said she would walk home and send John with the carriage—no doubt it will be waiting in the forecourt. Jamie and George, please go with Lottie, get in, and wait for me—tell John I won't be long."

"Yes, Grandmama," the three chorused. The boys took Lottie's hands, and the three turned and headed for the door.

Christian hid a smile. "Are they always so obedient?"

"I'm sure I can't say, but I suspect they generally are even when they're plotting insurrection."

He laughed, then sobered as he met her ladyship's black eyes. "I'm coming, too. To check on Eugenia."

Lady Osbaldestone's finely penciled eyebrows rose. "Are you now? Well, I suppose I can't stop you. This isn't my house, after all."

Christian grunted in disbelief. If she'd wanted to deny him… But of course, she wouldn't. He wasn't sure he could level an accusation of matchmaking against her, yet when it came to him and Eugenia, the sense of some éminence grise having pushed a little here, then there, lingered.

He followed her ladyship up the stairs. In the gallery, he glanced over the balustrade. Henry was still at the front door, seeing the last of the villagers out, and the Swindons and Colebatches were waiting in line.

Christian followed Lady Osbaldestone down the corridor. He reviewed the recent events and murmured, "If I hadn't intended to stay away—and Jamie hadn't come to winkle me out of the Grange—I wouldn't have been on that path above the lake at that precise moment in time. I wouldn't have seen the cracking start and wouldn't have known to alert everyone to the danger."

"Hmm." After a moment, Lady Osbaldestone said, "I have often observed that Fate moves in mysterious ways."

"One question." It had been nagging at him. "Jamie loves to skate, doesn't he?"

"Yes." Lady Osbaldestone glanced back at him. "Why? Did he tell you he didn't?"

"He told me he'd grown frightened of skating after a serious fall."

"Well, if he had, he's outgrown it." Her ladyship's black eyes passed over his face.

Christian was grateful when she said nothing of what she presumably could read there. He'd been frightened, too, but he'd outgrown the emotion. In truth, since Jamie had arrived at the Grange, he hadn't thought of his damaged face at all. It wasn't important, not anymore, not within the village, and that was all he cared about.

Lady Osbaldestone paused outside a door. She lowered her voice. "I left Mrs. Woolsey lying down on her bed in her own room. She was quite overcome by the excitement and stress. Incoherent, although I'm not convinced that isn't her customary state."

"Let us hope she's still resting," Christian murmured back.

"Indeed." Lady Osbaldestone opened the door and quietly walked into the room.

Christian followed and silently shut the door behind him.

The curtains had been closed. A small lamp with its wick turned low had been left on a table near the window; it shed a soft glow across the room, enough for him to see Eugenia lying fast asleep in the pretty tester bed.

The honey-gold mass of her hair was spread across the white pillow. Her complexion was pale, but not unnaturally so, with the promise of roses blooming in her cheeks. Her features were relaxed, serene in sleep, her brown lashes, tipped with gold, forming gilded crescents above her cheekbones, and her lips, plump and rosy, gently curved and tempting.

Christian realized he'd drawn closer to the bed. He halted, straightened, but couldn't drag his gaze from salvation's face.

He'd found her, and he wasn't going to let her go.

He'd recognized that he was finished with fear, that he'd overcome the fears that had dogged him. Yet here was one fear with which he would have to live if he wanted what he desperately desired—a family, a hearth and home, a wife.

This fear, the one that lay before him, was different from the rest. It was a fear one had to embrace—knowingly, willingly—if one wanted the greatest of joys life had to offer.

In that moment, as he looked down at Eugenia's delicate face, he felt as if he finally understood—fear, and himself, and everything he needed to know about the future.

It was there, lying in front of him, both physically and metaphorically.

Silent and still, Therese watched the thoughts wash over Christian Longfellow's face. She gave him as long as she dared, then she reached across and tweaked his sleeve. When he looked at her—and pulling away from his absorption took a moment—she tipped her head toward the door.

His lips firmed, and reluctantly, he nodded.

He followed her from the room.

They made their way downstairs, where they found the Colebatches just departing. They joined Henry in waving the couple off, then made their farewells. Therese left Henry with the information that Eugenia was sleeping peacefully and a reminder that she shouldn't be disturbed until morning.

Christian walked with Therese to her carriage and opened the door. The running lamps had been lit, and inside, the children were lined up like robins perching on the seat, waiting as instructed, with John on the box, holding the reins.

Therese smiled at her three helpers. She glanced to where Jiggs waited with the Grange carriage, then turned to Christian. "That was well done today—and I especially liked your lecture to those four young men." She trapped Christian's hazel eyes. "I do hope you'll take your own words to heart. Little Moseley needs you not just in emergencies, although you are well qualified to take charge of such events, as you proved today. And we don't need you only to provide a sound baritone in the church choir, to lead a recalcitrant donkey, or even to pull a young lady from a frozen lake—although we're all very glad you did those things." Relentlessly, she held his gaze. "The village needs you as a fully functioning part of our community. Without you, we would be less. You have contributions to make—that you should make and need to make—to life in Little Moseley."

In the flickering light cast by the carriage lamps, he studied her face, then he humphed. "You do realize you said 'we.'"

She blinked, replayed her words, then slowly nodded. "I did, didn't I?"

"Several times." He gave her his hand and, when she grasped it, helped her into the carriage.

The children made space for her between them, and she sat and released Christian's hand.

He stepped back, closed the door, and saluted her.

John shook the reins, and Therese settled back as the horses plodded across the forecourt and on down the drive.

As the shadows of the avenue closed around them and the children snuggled against her sides, she smiled to herself.

Christian Longfellow hadn't argued. Her work was—almost—done.

CHAPTER 12

"Excuse me, Miss Eugenia."

Eugenia looked up from the embroidery hoop that lay neglected in her lap; she'd been sitting staring at it for the past half hour. After saying she would sit quietly and embroider, she'd taken refuge in the morning room to escape the smothering attentions of Henry, his suddenly exceedingly polite and attentive friends, and every member of the household who could find a reason to be in her vicinity.

She was no wilting flower; a night of untrammeled sleep had restored her to her customary rude health. Clearly, her being carried inside unconscious the previous afternoon had shaken everyone, but their continued solicitousness was getting on her nerves.

And now here was Mountjoy, standing at the door and looking at her questioningly.

She inwardly sighed. "Yes, Mountjoy?"

"Lord Longfellow has called, miss. He asked how you were and inquired if you were well enough to speak with him."

Would he fuss over her, too?

On the other hand, he was the one person whose concern over her well-being was warranted. Justified, even. He'd rescued her from certain death—that gave him a freedom she would extend to no other.

And the notion of him being worried enough to come and inquire didn't irritate her at all.

"Thank you, Mountjoy." She set aside the embroidery hoop, stood, and shook out her new teal kerseymere gown. "Did you put him in the drawing room?"

"Yes, miss." Mountjoy hesitated. As she walked toward him and the door, he cleared his throat and asked, "Would you like me to summon Mrs. Woolsey, miss?"

Eugenia met Mountjoy's eyes. "No, thank you." Cousin Ermintrude had remained abed, insisting her nerves were too overset to permit her to venture downstairs. "I'm sure I'll do better dealing with his lordship without unnecessary distraction."

Mountjoy's lips twitched, but he stilled them. "As you say, miss."

He bowed her out of the room, then led her to the drawing room and opened the door.

She walked in to see Christian Longfellow dressed more formally than she'd previously seen him in a coat of Bath superfine that fitted his broad shoulders to perfection, worn over buff breeches and highly polished Hessians.

He was standing at the wide bay window, looking out at the side garden. He heard the click of the latch as Mountjoy shut the door, glanced over his shoulder, then turned to face her.

His cravat was elegant, in keeping with the rest of his attire. His gaze remained steady on her face as she slowly crossed the room to him. With a little skip of her heart, she noticed he no longer ducked his head to the side to hide his scars.

Halting before him, she smiled warmly, dipped a curtsy, and held out her hand. "Good morning, Lord Longfellow."

He took her fingers in his and bowed. "Miss Fitzgibbon." With a hint of reluctance, he released her hand.

Still smiling, she captured his gaze. "Put simply, my lord, I cannot thank you enough for your rescue yesterday. Quite literally, you saved my life." She spread her hands to either side. "I am forever in your debt."

He studied her, her eyes, her face, for several seconds, then quietly said, "I would take it very kindly if you would call me Christian…and if you would promise me that you will set aside all notions of gratitude, of being in my debt or repaying me in any way whatever, for the duration of this visit."

She frowned. "Why? You were the epitome of heroic—"

"Yes, well…" He paused, then with his eyes still on hers, he drew in a breath and declared, "I don't want what happened yesterday to influence you."

"Influence me in what?"

"In how you respond to what I wish to say to you." Frustration sharpened his tone. His chin set, his lips fleetingly compressed to a thin line, then they eased. "Please—can you just listen to what I have to say and forget all the rest?"

She searched his eyes. A frisson of hope, of anticipation and expectation fizzed along her veins, but did he truly mean to ask…

With effort, she reined in her galloping imagination, refocused on his face, and considered his request—and his tone. He was used to commanding; every now and then, that shone through. Yet…he had said please. She nodded. "All right." She folded her hands before her and looked at him steadily. "What do you wish to say to me?"

Christian had rehearsed all he wanted to say, but as for how to lead into that… He held her gaze, let himself sink into the summer blue, and allowed the words to flow. "I know some would say that this is too soon —that especially given the events of yesterday, I should hold back in case you feel obliged to agree—but I'm relying on your good sense to know I would never want you to feel compelled over anything and especially not over this." He paused for breath, then doggedly went on, "I acknowledge that although we've been aware of each other's existence for most of our lives, we haven't really known each other in the true sense—as people, as individuals—for very long at all. Yet if my years in the Peninsula taught me anything, it's that life is fragile, and it can be fleeting, and that we should seize whatever chance of happiness comes our way and not hang back thinking our eagerness not quite nice."

She tipped her head, her eyes steady on his. "So far, I agree with everything you've said. Especially about seizing happiness when it offers. When I sank beneath the waters of the lake…that made a lot of things much clearer. What was important, truly important, and what was merely superficial and not really worthy of my time."

He nodded. "Yes. Exactly. That moment when I saw you sink under the water the first time was bad enough. The second time…" He stared at her, then looked to the side. Then his chest swelled as he drew in a deep breath, and he brought his eyes back to hers and simply said, "I'm a soldier. I've been largely absent from society for the past decade. I don't know if my proposal is socially acceptable or not—if this is the right time or the right way. If this is what you want or would like."

To his surprise, she stepped forward, into him, grasped his lapels and tried—unsuccessfully—to shake him. "Just tell me."

His eyes locked with hers, he licked his lips. "I should go to one knee at least, but my injured leg makes that awkward…" He read her surging impatience in her glare and evenly, quietly, said, "I wanted to ask you if you would do me the inestimable honor of agreeing to be my wife."

Eugenia stared into his hazel eyes, read the depth of his sincerity, saw the straightforward, honest, *good* man he truly was. And that good man wanted her as his partner in life. His helpmate. His wife.

Her gaze grew misty. Regardless, her voice low but clear, she replied, "I don't care what anyone says now or later—that this is too quick, that I must have felt beholden—I don't, and what do I care what people say or think? I *know*. I know to the bottom of my heart and my soul that you are the husband I never knew I wanted—never had time to think of or dream of. But you're here now, and all I want to do is say *yes*. Yes, please—"

She didn't manage to say anything more because Christian had swept her into his arms and slanted his lips over hers.

He kissed her as if she were precious, a gift from the gods. She wound her arms around his neck and returned the kiss with fervor, as if he was and always had been the man of her dreams.

When he finally raised his head and looked down at her, a smile the like of which she hadn't seen for more than a decade wreathed his face. Lighthearted, joyous, it was the smile of the devil-may-care, devilishly handsome young gentleman he had once been. Yet he was no longer that young man; the rough and pocked skin of his left cheek resting beneath her palm testified to that.

She saw in his eyes, now shining with simple happiness, the man he now was. A man who had walked through cannon fire and survived, who had, at last, found his way home.

As if to prove that, he reached into his pocket and pulled out a bedraggled sprig…

She stared, then laughed. "Mistletoe?"

"It is the season." He held it up, over their heads. "It's even got berries, so I can claim a kiss." As he bent his head, he whispered, "We shouldn't let our matchmaking crew's efforts go entirely to waste."

She was still laughing when his lips claimed hers.

She tightened her arms, sank against him, and let her heart and soul flow into the kiss—one of dreams undreamt, of passion yet to be spent, and an unwritten, unscripted promise for a shared future of laughter and tears, of children and home and family. Of a shared life they would both take delight in living.

Of a love still burgeoning, still growing and evolving—a reality they needed no more words to claim.

After the adventures of the previous afternoon, that morning, Therese found herself at something of a loss. Jamie and George had asked permission to go to the green and play with the other boys; she'd granted it, more than anything else to get them out from under her feet while keeping them appropriately occupied. With Lottie drawing by the fire, Therese tried to settle at her escritoire, but found the ink drying on her nib while her thoughts wandered.

She had, she suspected, done all she possibly could regarding Christian and Eugenia. Really, no one seeing the pair together—how each looked at the other—could fail to comprehend that they should carve out a life together, but how long it would take for one or the other to broach the subject was anyone's guess.

With no further action pending on that front, there remained the vexing mystery of the missing geese. Earlier, Mrs. Haggerty had delivered the news that although Bilson had hoped to get in sufficient extra cuts of beef to tide the village over, he was no longer so sure he would be able to satisfy the unexpected demand.

Mrs. Haggerty was now conning her cookbooks, trying to find recipes that might serve to dress up the capon she had hanging in her larder. To Therese's mind, and she felt sure everyone else's, capon was a poor substitute for goose.

She frowned at the letter she'd started. She'd barely got past the salutation.

The clocks throughout the house chimed the hour—eleven o'clock.

As the peals and chimes faded, she realized another peal was ringing in the servants' quarters, then she heard Crimmins's measured tread cross the hall to the front door.

The clatter of footsteps and a medley of piping voices reached her. Lottie stopped her drawing and looked up, then she picked up her paper and crayon and came to Therese's side.

The door opened, and Crimmins looked in. "Lord James, Mr. George, and some of their young friends, my lady."

Therese raised her brows, then Jamie and George were leading a small band of village boys into Therese's sanctum. She made a mental note to explain to Jamie and George what the word "sanctum" meant.

Then she took in her grandsons' faces and instantly came alert. Both Jamie and George looked…transformed. Eager and urgent and not at all like the halfway-bored boys who had trooped out to play. "What is it?" she asked.

Jamie and George came to stand beside her. Jamie made the introductions. "This is Johnny Tooks." He gestured to each boy in turn. "And Roger and Willie Milsom, and Ben Butts, and Will Foley."

As Jamie said his name, each boy performed what was doubtless his best bow.

Therese nodded at them all. "Good morning."

"Good morning, my lady," they chorused, and all of them bowed again.

Therese glanced at Jamie. "And…?"

Jamie all but puffed out his chest. "And Johnny has something to say."

"Oh?" She focused on Johnny and did her best not to look intimidating but merely interested.

She must have succeeded, because Johnny solemnly nodded and said, "The day the geese went missing, Dad went off to market like he always does—real early, he goes, long before the sun is up. And I'm supposed to feed the geese morning and evening while he's away—we've been fattening them up for the past month, you see—but…" Johnny stopped and looked at Jamie.

From the corner of her eye, Therese saw Jamie level a determined look at Johnny, who was several years the elder.

Johnny looked pained, yet he shifted his gaze back to Therese's face and went on, "But that day, soon as Dad was off, I left to go fishing with some lads from Romsey."

Therese waited. When nothing more was forthcoming, she prompted, "Yes?"

Johnny blinked and looked at Jamie.

Who quietly sighed and explained, "He didn't feed the geese. He left them hungry, and because they'd been feeding on extra for the past weeks, they would have quickly got very, very hungry."

"At least that's what we think," George put in.

"And then," Roger revealed, "Johnny didn't get home until late. Until dark."

Again, Therese looked to her grandsons for clarification.

Jamie obliged. "It was after six when Johnny got home and went to feed the flock—that was when he found they were missing. But he should have fed them earlier, before it got dark and they roosted for the night."

"Ah." Therese looked at Johnny. "So the geese had, in effect, missed two feedings?"

Johnny hung his head and nodded. "Me dad's gonna skin me."

"That," Therese briskly informed him, "is an excellent reason to do all you can to help us locate the geese." When Johnny glanced up warily—hopefully—and met her eyes, she said, "I gather this means the geese would have been exceedingly hungry." When all the boys nodded, she asked, "Would they have—could they have—gone looking for food?"

"That's what we think must have happened, my lady," Will Foley said.

"Terrible hungry, they musta been," Johnny added.

Therese sat back and ran her eye over her now-expanded band of searchers. "Very well. It appears we have to think like hungry geese. Let's assume they were hungry enough that they wandered off looking for food. Where would they have gone?"

"They might hunt for grain," Johnny said, "but more likely scraps. They love those."

"But," George pointed out, "we know they're not in any of the barns or stables or anywhere else around the village."

Therese considered, then said, "There has to be somewhere we haven't thought to search—somewhere with food that would satisfy geese."

"But where?" Jamie demanded.

She was saved from having to shrug by the doorbell pealing. They all waited as Crimmins went to the front door, then he tapped on the parlor door, opened it, and looked in. "Mr. Fitzgibbon and friends, my lady." He lowered his voice. "They appear quite excited and say they have something to show you."

Therese blinked. This seemed a morning for the unlikely. "Very well, Crimmins. Show them in." She waved the younger boys deeper into the room. "Stand over there, if you please."

The five village boys cautiously shuffled toward the fireplace, leaving just enough space for Henry and his four friends to get through the door and line up facing Therese.

Five more enthused and excited faces looked at her.

"Lady Osbaldestone." They all bowed.

She waited until they'd straightened to ask, "Yes, gentlemen?"

Henry's guests looked to him. But before Henry could even open his mouth, the doorbell pealed again.

This time, when the parlor door opened, Crimmins announced, "Miss Eugenia Fitzgibbon and Lord Longfellow, my lady."

"Good heavens!" Therese muttered. She waved and more loudly said, "Further in, boys." She flicked her fingers at Henry's friends. "You, as well, if you would. We appear to be getting a trifle crowded."

All her guests complied, allowing Eugenia and Christian to come in and Crimmins to pull the door closed behind them.

Therese looked at her latest guests, read their news in their faces, and beamed.

Christian saw her understanding and smiled. "As you've guessed, we've come to share our news." He glanced at Eugenia. She looked up and met his eyes, and her face positively radiated happiness. Christian glanced at Therese. "Miss Fitzgibbon has done me the honor of agreeing to marry me."

"Excellent!" Therese's smile couldn't grow any wider.

Congratulations erupted from Henry, from his friends, and even from the village boys.

Jamie, George, and Lottie sang their felicitations, then, beaming, turned to share a thoroughly triumphant look with Therese.

Still smiling—indeed, beaming, too, which she rarely did—she looked up as Christian said to Henry, "We looked for you at the Hall, but you'd already left. I take it you have no objections?"

"Of course not! None at all." Henry beamed, too. "I literally couldn't be happier." Henry looked at Eugenia and caught her eye. "I'm very happy for you both." He kissed his sister's cheek, and she patted his.

Therese let the excitement run for a moment more, then lightly rapped her cane on the floor. When the occupants of her parlor fell silent and looked her way, she fixed her gaze on Henry and his friends. "You gentlemen were about to share some news, I believe."

"Yes, indeed." With a nod, Henry invited Dagenham to speak.

Transformed by his enthusiasm and for once looking younger than his years, the viscount suddenly appeared shy, but then he drew breath, inclined his head to Therese, and said, "We"—he indicated the other three —"felt…well, guilty over cracking the ice and spoiling the village's day of fun, and we'd heard about the missing flock of geese, so we thought to make what amends we could by scouting around and making absolutely certain that the geese weren't anywhere on the Hall estate at least. Only the boundaries aren't marked, and it seems we ended in the woods at the back of the estate, but the long and the short of it is that we found these"—like a conjurer, Dagenham held up four largish, mostly white feathers—"on a narrow path through the woods to the west and a bit south of the Hall."

Everyone stared at the feathers.

Then Jamie, his eyes shining, stepped forward, plucked one feather from Dagenham's hand, and showed it to Johnny. Johnny touched it, then nodded eagerly.

Jamie held the feather aloft and announced, "At last! A clue!"

CHAPTER 13

By the time Therese and company—Jamie, George, Lottie, the village boys, Eugenia, Christian, and Henry and his friends—reached the stretch of path along which the feathers had been found, quite half the men of the village and several of the women had joined them.

Farmer Tooks, summoned by Johnny, came plodding along the footpath from the direction of his farm. "I knew this path existed—it skirts around the back of the Hall and the back of my fields and goes north all the way to the West Wellow lane—but even if they was driven mad with hunger, I can't see why the birds would have come this way."

"Regardless," Therese said, "we now have a direction." With her cane, she pointed southward along the path. "I suggest we follow and see where your vagrant birds have taken themselves off to."

There was a rumble of assent from all those there.

"We should spread out as best we can," Christian said, "and keep our eyes peeled for further signs. Just in case the flock veered off the path at some point."

Those in boots duly spread out to either side of the path beneath the trees. With Therese, Eugenia, and Mrs. Colebatch keeping to the path, the company set off.

They advanced purposefully in a southwesterly direction, with the path paralleling the banks of the stream that fed the lake. Although the skies were gray and the temperature hovered only a little above freezing, under the trees, they were protected from the chilly breeze. Everyone was bundled up appropriately, and although the footpath was clearly not well frequented, the going was easy enough.

When the woods to her left thinned, Therese glanced in that direction and saw they'd drawn level with the meadows behind the Mountjoys' property.

A little way ahead, the path swerved west and, via an old single-person bridge, crossed the stream, which was swollen and sullen and running only sluggishly, half choked with ice. From a liberal scattering of droppings and several more feathers, it was obvious the flock had congregated on the bank there. Tooks studied the area, then pointed to a patch where the winter grass had been flattened. "Looks like they spent that first night there."

The rickety bridge spanning the stream was constructed from the sawn bole of one large tree trunk fitted with a timber handrail on one side. Henry's friends had already crossed. Heads bent, they'd been studying the ground on the other bank.

"Yes!" Raising his head, Thomas Kilburn looked across the stream at the bulk of the company and pointed to the ground near his feet. "There are webbed prints in the softer ground here."

"And bits of down!" George Carnaby triumphantly held up a few whitish-gray wisps he'd picked from some bushes along the next section of the path.

That was good enough for the rest of the group. The younger boys and Lottie scampered fearlessly across the ramshackle bridge, their steps light and sure. The others crossed more carefully, with Christian instructing that no more than two adults should be on the somewhat ancient structure at any one time. Reverend Colebatch assisted his wife across, Christian followed, leading Eugenia, and Rory Whitesheaf grinned, bowed, and offered Therese his hand, which she accepted with gracious thanks.

They crossed the stream without mishap and continued on. The path twisted and turned. Roughly one hundred yards farther on, they came out on the shore of the lake. They all halted and looked around, getting their bearings.

"This is the western side of the northern arm." Christian looked right, then left. "I'd completely forgotten this path was here." He glanced at Dagenham. "I take it you four didn't come via this path yesterday?"

Dagenham flushed slightly, but shook his head. "We used the path on the eastern side of the woods, running along the edge of those meadows we passed."

"I'd showed them that path," Henry said. "It's the one the Hall household always uses to get to the lake." He glanced back along the path they'd followed. "I never knew this path was here."

Tooks grunted. "Skirts your boundary, it does, so it's not on Hall land, and the path's not so easy to see unless you're on it."

Christian turned to look on along the path. "My memory of this path isn't perfect, but as I do remember being on it as a child, then I suspect—I think—it must go on and at least come close to the Grange holdings."

"More down!" Roger Milsom waved from farther along the path where it curved around, following the lake shore.

Therese gestured with her cane. "As it seems our feathered friends went that way, I suggest we continue on."

They tramped steadily on, with the younger members of the company forging ahead to search for feathers, down, and droppings. And by all such signs, Farmer Tooks's flock had, indeed, doggedly plodded on.

"Where the devil are these wretched birds going?" Tooks grumbled. "They must have been ready to eat twigs by the morning of the day after they left."

Therese considered, then said, "Presumably they found sufficient fodder to sustain them along the way, but I take your point in that it seems they must have had some place—some destination—in mind. Which seems odd."

"Devilish odd," Tooks agreed. "Contrary, they are, geese. I can't see them going off somewhere for any other reason than food, but how would they know?"

"And what was it they knew," Christian said, "given that none of us can guess?"

They might, finally, be on the trail of the geese, might at last be able to postulate that the flock had gone in search of food, yet the birds' intended destination remained a confounding mystery.

They walked around the western shore of the lake all the way to the southwestern corner, and still the path led on, a narrow path barely one person wide plunging deeper into the woods. Encouraged by continuing discoveries of signs the flock had passed that way, they trudged on in a generally southerly direction, but gradually, the path swung to their left, toward the southeast, and climbed the low ridge that was the extension of the rise that separated the lake from the village green.

Of necessity, the company slowed as they toiled upward; Therese was glad to avail herself of Rory Whitesheaf's assistance again. But once they reached the top of the ridge, the path continued along it, more or less flat, and the children raced ahead until Christian called to them to remain within sight.

Not long after, he said, "We're nearing the rear boundary of the Grange estate."

Tooks grunted. "If memory serves, the path passes by your rear boundary, just as it does with the Hall and my farm. Then it heads on past the back of Milsom Farm, and a while after, it splits—one arm runs down the east face of the ridge to our lane, and the other goes west and all the way down to the Salisbury road."

His gaze distant, Christian continued walking. After a moment, he said. "Yes, I believe you're right." He refocused and glanced at the other village men. "I haven't yet caught up with George Milsom. Are all his fields currently under the plow?"

"Aye," Ned Foley replied. His brother John ran Crossley Farm, another of the outlying farms of the village. "George has two tenant farmers as work the fields closer to the ridge, if that's what you're thinking. Not much by way of anything to attract geese there, I'd've thought."

"Exactly," Christian said. "Which makes me wonder if this wayward flock was making for Allard's End."

"Old Allard's farm at the back of the Grange?" Rory asked.

"Yes." Seeing Therese's mystification, Christian explained, "Allard was an old tenant farmer in my father's day. He worked a small acreage tucked away against the woods at the rear of the Grange estate. Allard died…it must have been a few years before I joined the army. More than a decade ago. When I returned and took charge of the estate, I found that my father hadn't got around to re-tenanting the land. I believe he intended to incorporate it into the Home Farm—it's a small acreage by today's standards—but he never actually started working the fields again."

"As I recall," Ned Foley said, "old Allard's farmhouse was a wreck even while he was still living there."

Christian nodded. "He was a crusty old beggar and used to chase us off whenever Cedric and I ventured that way. He had an old orchard with wonderful damson plums and the sweetest apples, which was what attracted us, of course."

Tooks came to an abrupt halt, forcing those behind him to halt, too.

They grumbled, but, oblivious, Tooks stared at Christian's back. "Orchard? I didn't know Allard had an orchard."

Puzzled by his tone, Christian stopped and turned to look at Tooks. "I have to admit I have no idea if the orchard still exists, but…do geese eat fruit? Deadfall?"

"These geese would," Tooks averred. "They love scraps—anything vegetable and soft, and the sweeter the better. It's what we fatten them with—the vegetable scraps from all over the village. I'd say they'd gobble up old fruit fast as you could feed it them."

"Well." Christian turned and led the company on. "It sounds as if we might have identified one possible place the flock might have gone. Assuming the plum trees and apple trees are still there and still bearing."

Not fifty yards on, they found further evidence that the flock was making for Allard's End.

Jamie and the younger boys were scouting ahead, and as the path there was completely overhung by the woodland canopy, the surface was soft enough to carry occasional imprints of the webbed feet of their quarry, so the boys had no difficulty confirming the trail.

They noticed within yards that the geese had turned aside and left the footpath they'd been following to that point.

Everyone helped search through the surrounding bushes, then Henry called a halloo. "It's this way." He popped his head around a large tree and grinned. "Just come around this tree, and there's another little path." He glanced at Christian. "It leads toward the Grange, doesn't it?"

Everyone followed Henry around the tree and onto a very narrow, poorly surfaced track that angled eastward out of the woods, with open fields glimmering ahead.

"Yes," Christian said. "Our boundary's the ridge line, so we're now on the Grange estate. And it certainly seems the birds are heading for Allard's End."

It wasn't far at all to the ruins of the farmhouse.

Therese halted with the others in front of the remains of an ancient farm cottage that must have been barely held together before the last occupant had died. A decade and more of weather had pummeled the structure until sections of three of the walls had collapsed and the roof had caved in. Weeds and field grasses had blown in and taken hold. From the brown stalks all around and the winter-bare tendrils crisscrossing the still-standing walls, in summer, the place would all but disappear beneath the engulfing greenery.

"Well," Christian said, "clearly no person has been living here." He started for the right end of the building. "If it still exists, the orchard's at the back."

Eagerly, the boys hurried to keep up with Christian's long strides. Everyone else followed.

They tramped over the encroaching weeds and stepped over fallen branches, eventually rounding the rear corner of the tumbledown cottage to line up along the remains of a low stone wall and stare at the sight beyond.

Allard's orchard was definitely still there, and if the thick carpet of leaves was any indication, then despite the broken and dead branches scattered here and there, the trees were still thriving. They stood well spaced, two by two stretching away from the cottage—a total of eight trees, all ancient, with gnarled trunks and twisted branches, many of which had dipped to the ground.

In this season, barely a leaf, even withered and brown, remained clinging to the twigs. It was therefore easy to spot the white-and-gray birds dotted throughout the orchard. Some were settled amid the leaves, contentedly snoozing. Others ambled, with their beaks tossing aside dead leaves, then greedily pouncing on the fallen fruit beneath.

As the company massed along the low wall, the geese came alert. Some issued the faint hissing sound that was the birds' equivalent of a warning growl, but when all the members of the company halted at the wall and no one ventured into what the geese plainly considered their territory, feathers settled, and the flock returned to the twin occupations of contented contemplation and foraging.

Therese looked at Tooks. His fingers were flicking; he was plainly counting.

Then Tooks heaved a massive sigh. "Blow me down, but they're all here. Every last one."

Many of the company shook their head in wonder.

The younger boys were grinning and whispering about how, now, they would all have goose for their Christmas dinner.

Ned Foley voiced the question circling Therese's brain. "How did they know? They're birds. Hardly any of us in the village—only really his lordship here—knew about this place. Yet these blinking birds knew—they must have, to come here so…well, determinedly."

Everyone looked at Tooks, who appeared as puzzled as they.

The boys had wandered off to explore the crumbling cottage.

Noticing, Christian called them back with a warning the place was dangerous and could collapse further—on their heads—at any time.

The boys returned, and Jamie announced, "The geese have been nesting in there."

"There's a spot where two walls are still standing, with a bit of roof angled over," Johnny Tooks reported. He looked at his father. "The flock has been roosting in there."

Tooks nodded absentmindedly, then his expression cleared. "That's it! Gladys and Edna knew."

Everyone looked at Tooks in bemusement.

All but laughing, he explained, "I haven't always kept the village geese—I only took them over after old Johnson died. Before that, he kept the flock at the Grange. When he died, our Johnson, his son, had too much to do with learning all the ropes and keeping the Grange gardens and grounds right for his late lordship, so I took over the flock. That was…" Tooks screwed up his face, then pronounced, "Eleven years ago, it would be." He smiled at his audience. "I knew—well, all the village knew—that old Johnson had some special way to fatten up the geese for Christmas. They always tasted special, but he never would say what he fed them. He promised to tell Johnson before he passed the flock on to him, but old Johnson died suddenly, so our Johnson never learned the secret."

Tooks turned to the orchard and waved at the geese, fat and plump and looking almost drunk with their bellies full to bursting. "What odds old Johnson brought them up here? Allard occasionally brought fruit down for the Mountjoys to sell, but in his later years, he grew to be a cantankerous old beggar and often didn't bother. Old Johnson would have known. Bet he offered Allard a few pennies to let him fatten the flock on the deadfall."

"That sounds very likely," Christian said. "But who are Gladys and Edna?"

"Ah, well," Tooks said, a grin splitting his face. "That's how those of us who keep geese run a flock. Naturally, we don't kill all of the birds. We keep those who'll be our breeders for the next season, and we also keep two or three of the older ladies, see. They help—well, I suppose you could say they anchor the flock. Keep it more settled, make the rules and run the roost, teach the young ones how things are done—that sort of thing."

"What you mean, I think," Therese said, "is that the older birds keep the collective memory and the accumulated wisdom of the flock." She glanced at the birds settled in the orchard. "I take it Gladys and Edna are your old ladies." With her cane, she pointed to two older-looking birds nestled together in the leaves in the middle of the orchard. "Those two, are they?"

"Aye, your ladyship." Still grinning, Tooks nodded. "That's them—at the center of everything, keeping their beady eyes on all the younger ones. And when the flock got over-hungry the other day, well, Gladys and Edna, they hail from the days old Johnson had the flock. Live to a ripe old age, geese do—well over twenty years."

"So they remembered and came here!" Jamie looked out at the two old geese, then looked up at Therese and grinned.

Yes, indeed, she thought. She felt entirely at one with Gladys and Edna. Old ladies were excellent at keeping collective memory and accumulated wisdom and anchoring their flock. That, after all, was the role she'd claimed.

Christian looked at Tooks. "What do you want to do with them now? If it's easier, you're welcome to leave them here for as long as you want. And indeed, by all means use the orchard in the years to come."

"Thank ye." Tooks bowed his shaggy head. "I can see they're happy here, and we've no foxes about this area at present, so it'd be best if I could leave them undisturbed until...well, it's the day after tomorrow I'll need to start preparing the ones for the village's ovens." He glanced at Johnny. "We can come up with the cart and the cages then and round them all up."

"Do you need help?" Jamie promptly asked—backed by the keen and eager faces of the rest of the younger boys.

Tooks smiled. "Aye—that'd make it all go faster, but you'll need to bring thick gloves. Those birds do peck, but I can teach you how to handle them."

"So now we'll all have goose for Christmas dinner!" The chorus welled from all the children's throats.

Led by Gladys and Edna, the geese squawked loudly, more in censure than alarm.

The children snickered and quieted.

Christian glanced at Henry's four friends and smiled. "You gentlemen have certainly redeemed yourselves in the eyes of Little Moseley. If you hadn't thought to go hunting through the woods in that direction, we would likely not have found the flock, certainly not in time and possibly not at all."

The four looked both relieved and pleased.

Henry did, too. Indeed, everyone was smiling.

Leaving the geese once more settled and content, the company re-formed and headed down the cart track that would take them to the stable of Dutton Grange and the village beyond.

Smiling at her three grandchildren boisterously skipping with the rest of the village youngsters, laughing and calling, all thoroughly thrilled over the successful conclusion of their quest to find the geese, Therese walked with the adults at a more sedate pace down from the ridge and on between the fallow fields. Along the way, she invited Henry, Eugenia, and Christian to join her, her grandchildren, and the couples she'd already asked to celebrate Christmas—the Swindons and the Colebatches. "And by all means, bring Mrs. Woolsey as well."

"Thank you." Eugenia smiled at Christian, then turned her smile on Henry. "We'll be delighted. All of us."

Therese smiled serenely. "Excellent. That's settled, then."

To her mind, everything had fallen into place, all was as it should be, and like Gladys and Edna, she was thoroughly content.

The seating about Therese's Christmas table was almost the same as the dinner she'd hosted a week earlier, with the addition of Henry and of Jamie, George, and Lottie, who had been granted special dispensation to join the adults in celebrating the day and in toasting the village's success in hunting down the geese appearing in pride of place on every table in the village.

As under her direction the company settled in their designated chairs, with Christian once more at the head of the table and Therese presiding from the foot, and the company oohed and aahed over the plethora of dishes Mrs. Haggerty had slaved for the past two days to prepare, with an inner serenity, Therese smiled upon them all.

She'd returned to the village ostensibly to stay, to make Hartington Manor her permanent home. That had always been her intention, yet in her heart she hadn't been sure whether the village and the small pleasures of village life would prove absorbing enough, engaging enough, to satisfy her.

She was delighted to have had that niggling inner question decided in the affirmative. Those in the village and the farms around about might not be haut ton, might not belong to the sort of families and society she was accustomed to reigning over, however, they were still people—fine, upstanding, and interesting people—many of whom, like the gentleman at the head of the table, had difficulties to overcome.

Hurdles to clear, obstacles to surmount, fears to conquer.

And that, Therese knew, had always and forever been her calling. To understand and steer and guide those who needed her help in turning their lives around and making those lives the best they could be.

Crimmins, aided in this instance by Mrs. Crimmins, efficiently served the soup—a clear broth prepared from wild morels. They proceeded smoothly to the next course of roast spatchcocks and partridges in aspic.

As with much exclaiming and compliments being dispatched to Mrs. Haggerty, the company ate, Therese looked at her grandchildren, took in their bright faces, their eager chatter as without the slightest shyness they interacted with the adults around them, and approved; village life had proved to be an arena in which the three could expand their horizons, stretch their wings, and develop the experience they would need when they graduated to their destined places in society—and just look at the strides Jamie had made during his short stay in Little Moseley.

When the trio had arrived sixteen days ago, she had had no real inkling of their abilities. What she'd seen over the past days had left her impressed. All three had the strength to forge their own places in society, their own lives; all they would need was encouragement and perhaps a helpful hand here and there.

She glanced around again and felt her heart swell—with happiness, with joy, and something more…anchoring.

Smiling to herself, she inwardly acknowledged that she was as deeply content as Gladys and Edna.

"So exciting"—Mrs. Swindon leant forward, her face alight with that emotion—"that you've decided to marry tomorrow!"

Eugenia, seated at Christian's right, smiled brilliantly, then shared a more personal look with her fiancé.

"So useful," Henrietta Colebatch said, "that dear Christian is distantly related to the Bishop of Salisbury."

After Christian and Eugenia had decided that now they had made up their minds they saw no reason to waste further time, Christian had ridden to Salisbury Cathedral and returned with a special license in his pocket.

"The whole village is cock-a-hoop!" Reverend Colebatch smiled beatifically. "Mr. Filbert has had the bell-ringers practicing a special peal, and Mr. Goodes and the choir are delighted to be able to present those hymns they so rarely get to sing."

"And"—Major Swindon fixed Jamie, Lottie, and George, seated on the opposite side of the table, with an interested eye—"I hear that you three young people have been recruited into the wedding party."

Jamie nodded solemnly. "I'm to carry the ring into the church. On a small velvet pillow." He glanced at Eugenia and wrinkled his nose. "I hope the ring doesn't roll off."

Everyone knew he was teasing; even Mrs. Woolsey saw it and laughingly assured him that the ring would behave and all would go smoothly.

"I'm to be flower girl." Lottie beamed.

Looking at her granddaughter's face, Therese felt she owed Eugenia and Christian a special favor. True, she had been instrumental in bringing the pair together, but it was the goodness of their hearts that had seen them both go out of their way to make one little girl's Christmas so very extra special.

"And I," George proudly said, glancing at Therese, "will escort Grandmama to the front pew."

Christian looked down the table, met Therese's gaze, and smiled, his eyes twinkling. He had insisted she sit in place of his departed parents. She suspected he, for one, had been awake to her machinations all along.

Not that she had forced anything on him—quite the opposite. As she took in the softening of Christian's gaze as he looked at Eugenia, Therese was more than delighted with the results of her most-recent manipulations.

Since the aborted skating party, Christian appeared to have lost all consciousness of his injuries. He rarely used a cane anymore, and Therese was certain he wouldn't when he walked down the aisle, but most importantly, he no longer ducked his head and had, it seemed, accepted that all those in the village knew him so well they literally saw past his scars.

That, more than anything else, was, she felt, her principal triumph of this festive season.

Then the double doors behind her were flung wide, and she turned and, with everyone else, saw Crimmins, with Mrs. Crimmins and Mrs. Haggerty assisting, bearing in a large platter on which reposed their Christmas goose.

With all due ceremony, his face wreathed in a beaming smile, Crimmins carried the platter down the table and placed it triumphantly before Christian. Mrs. Haggerty set down the boat of her special apple-and-brandy sauce, and Mrs. Crimmins handed Christian the carving set.

Christian took the implements. He glanced down the table, and, at Therese's encouraging nod, rose to his feet the better to attack the bird.

Therese reached for her wine glass; the others saw and did the same.

As Christian made the first cut and the scent of roast goose set their mouths watering, Therese raised her glass and declared, "To our Christmas goose and the friendships and understandings our quest to reclaim it has brought us."

There were cheers all around the table.

Christian picked up his glass and joined with the others in echoing loudly, "To our Christmas goose!"

Then Christian carved, and the Crimminses and Mrs. Haggerty proudly passed the plates and platters, then Reverend Colebatch said grace.

After uttering "Amen," the company looked around the table, meeting each other's gazes, all thoroughly pleased with their present and looking forward to their future.

Then cutlery rattled as they all claimed their knives and forks and settled to the serious business of doing justice to this year's Christmas goose.

THE END

Dear Reader,

I know many of you have long wondered about the redoubtable Lady Osbaldestone's earlier life. I haven't yet traipsed back in time to her own romance, but when I thought of doing a series of Christmas tales, she was the principal character that leapt to mind, and she brought her grandchildren along with her! I hope you've enjoyed this small insight into Lady O's own family, of whom you will see more in subsequent volumes in this series, and have also enjoyed a lighthearted Christmas-of-long-ago tale.

Next year, 2018, will see the release of The Legend of Nimway Hall books, commencing with the first installment from me, to be released March 15, 2018 – this is a series of historical romance novels from five of your favorite historical romance authors that documents the romances of successive generations of the ladies who are born to become the guardians of Nimway Hall. The first five stories will be released a week apart, commencing on March 15. The five of us are having great fun getting together to write this series and we all hope you'll enjoy the result!

In addition, the first of the romances of the Cavanaugh siblings – Ryder Cavanaugh's half brothers and sister, who you met in *The Taming of Ryder Cavanaugh* – will be released on May 29, 2018. In that book, Lord Randolph Cavanaugh meets his match, quite literally over the workings of a steam engine.

Then to keep you amused, we'll be releasing two more Casebook of Barnaby Adair novels in July and August.

And to round out the year, we'll have the second volume of Lady Osbaldestone's Christmas Chronicles to delight you in the lead-up to Christmas. So lots more fun and games ahead – stay tuned!

And from me and mine to you and yours: we wish you a happy and safe festive season and a productive and prosperous New Year.

Stephanie.

For alerts as new books are released, plus information on upcoming books, exclusive sweepstakes and sneak peeks into upcoming novels, sign up for Stephanie's Private Email Newsletter
http://www.stephanielaurens.com/newsletter-signup/

The ultimate source for detailed information on all Stephanie's published books, including covers, descriptions, and excerpts, is Stephanie's Website www.stephanielaurens.com

You can also follow Stephanie via her Amazon Author Page at
http://tinyurl.com/zc3e9mp

Goodreads members can follow Stephanie via her author page

https://www.goodreads.com/author/show/9241.Stephanie_Laurens

You can email Stephanie at stephanie@stephanielaurens.com

Or find her on Facebook
https://www.facebook.com/AuthorStephanieLaurens/

COMING NEXT

The first volume in
THE LEGEND OF NIMWAY HALL
1750: JACQUELINE
To be released on March 15, 2018

The opening tale in a series of romances through the ages from five bestselling historical romance authors.

RECENTLY RELEASED

The first volume of the Devil's Brood Trilogy
THE LADY BY HIS SIDE

A marquess in need of the right bride. An earl's daughter in search of a purpose. A betrayal that ends in murder and balloons into a threat to the realm.

Sebastian Cynster knows time is running out. If he doesn't choose a wife soon, his female relatives will line up to assist him. Yet the current debutantes do not appeal. Where is he to find the right lady to be his marchioness? Then Drake Varisey, eldest son of the Duke of Wolverstone, asks for Sebastian's aid.

Having assumed his father's mantle in protecting queen and country, Drake must go to Ireland in pursuit of a dangerous plot. But he's received an urgent missive from Lord Ennis, an Irish peer—Ennis has heard something Drake needs to know. Ennis insists Drake attends an upcoming house party at Ennis's Kent estate so Ennis can reveal his information face-to-face.

Sebastian has assisted Drake before and, long ago, had a liaison with Lady Ennis. Drake insists Sebastian is just the man to be Drake's surrogate at the house party—the guests will imagine all manner of possibilities and be blind to Sebastian's true purpose.

Unsurprisingly, Sebastian is reluctant, but Drake's need is real. With only more debutantes on his horizon, Sebastian allows himself to be persuaded.

His first task is to inveigle Antonia Rawlings, a lady he has known all her life, to include him as her escort to the house party. Although he's seen little of Antonia in recent years, Sebastian is confident of gaining her support.

Eldest daughter of the Earl of Chillingworth, Antonia has abandoned the search for a husband and plans to use the week of the house party to decide what to do with her life. There has to be some purpose, some role, she can claim for her own.

Consequently, on hearing Sebastian's request and an explanation of what lies behind it, she seizes on the call to action. Suppressing her senses' idiotic reaction to Sebastian's nearness, she agrees to be his partner-in-intrigue.

But while joining the house party proves easy, the gathering is thrown into chaos when Lord Ennis is murdered—just before he was to speak with Sebastian. Worse, Ennis's last words, gasped to Sebastian, are: *Gunpowder. Here.*

Gunpowder? And here, where?

With a killer continuing to stalk the halls, side by side, Sebastian and Antonia search for answers and, all the while, the childhood connection that had always existed between them strengthens and blooms...into something so much more.

The first volume in the trilogy. A historical romance with gothic overtones layered over a continuing intrigue. A full length novel of 99,000 words.

The second volume of the Devil's Brood Trilogy
AN IRRESISTIBLE ALLIANCE

A duke's second son with no responsibilities and a lady starved of the excitement her soul craves join forces to unravel a deadly, potentially catastrophic threat to the realm - that only continues to grow.

With his older brother's betrothal announced, Lord Michael Cynster is freed from the pressure of familial expectations. However, the allure of his previous hedonistic pursuits has paled. Then he learns of the mission his brother, Sebastian, and Lady Antonia Rawlings have been assisting with and volunteers to assist by hunting down the hoard of gunpowder now secreted somewhere in London.

Michael sets out to trace the carters who transported the gunpowder from Kent to London. His quest leads him to the Hendon Shipping Company, where he discovers his sole source of information is the only daughter of Jack and Kit Hendon, Miss Cleome Hendon, who although a fetchingly attractive lady, firmly holds the reins of the office in her small hands.

Cleo has fought to achieve her position in the company. Initially, managing the office was a challenge, but she now conquers all in just a few hours a week. With her three brothers all adventuring in America, she's been driven to the realization that she craves adventure, too.

When Michael Cynster walks in and asks about carters, Cleo's instincts leap. She wrings from him the full tale of his mission—and offers him a bargain. She will lead him to the carters he seeks if he agrees to include her as an equal partner in the mission.

Horrified, Michael attempts to resist, but ultimately finds himself agreeing—a sequence of events he quickly learns is common around Cleo. Then she delivers on her part of the bargain, and he finds there are benefits to allowing her to continue to investigate beside him—not least being that if she's there, then he knows she's safe.

But the further they go in tracing the gunpowder, the more deaths they uncover. And when they finally locate the barrels, they find themselves tangled in a fight to the death—one that forces them to face what has grown between them, to seize and defend what they both see as their path to the greatest adventure of all. A shared life. A shared future. A shared love.

Second volume in a trilogy. A historical romance with gothic overtones layered over a continuing intrigue. A full length novel of 101,000 words.

The thrilling third and final volume in the Devil's Brood Trilogy
THE GREATEST CHALLENGE OF THEM ALL

A nobleman devoted to defending queen and country and a noblewoman wild enough to match his every step race to disrupt the plans of a malignant intelligence intent on shaking England to its very foundations.

Lord Drake Varisey, Marquess of Winchelsea, eldest son and heir of the Duke of Wolverstone, must foil a plot that threatens to shake the foundations of the realm, but the very last lady—nay, noblewoman—he needs assisting him is Lady Louisa Cynster, known throughout the ton as Lady Wild.

For the past nine years, Louisa has suspected that Drake might well be the ideal husband for her, even though he's assiduous in avoiding her. But she's now twenty-seven and enough is enough. She believes propinquity will elucidate exactly what it is that lies between them, and what better opportunity to work closely with Drake than his latest mission, with which he patently needs her help?

Unable to deny Louisa's abilities or the value of her assistance and powerless to curb her willfulness, Drake is forced to grit his teeth and acquiesce to her sticking by his side, if only to ensure her safety. But all too soon, his true feelings for her show enough for her, perspicacious as she is, to see through his denials, which she then interprets as a challenge.

Even while they gather information, tease out clues, increasingly desperately search for the missing gunpowder, and doggedly pursue the killer responsible for an ever-escalating tally of dead men, thrown together through the hours, he and she learn to trust and appreciate each other. And fed by constant exposure—and blatantly encouraged by her—their desires and hungers swell and grow…

As the barriers between them crumble, the attraction he has for so long restrained burgeons and balloons, until goaded by her near-death, it erupts, and he seizes her—only to be seized in return.

Linked irrevocably and with their wills melded and merged by passion's fire, with time running out and the evil mastermind's deadline looming, together, they focus their considerable talents and make one last push to learn the critical truths—to find the gunpowder and unmask the villain behind this far-reaching plot.

Only to discover that they have significantly less time than they'd thought, that the villain's target is even more crucially fundamental to the realm than they'd imagined, and it's going to take all that Drake is—as well as all that Louisa as Lady Wild can bring to bear—to defuse the threat, capture the villain, and make all safe and right again.

As they race to the ultimate confrontation, the future of all England rests on their shoulders.

Third volume in the trilogy. A historical romance with gothic overtones layered over an intrigue. A full length novel of 129,000 words.

If you haven't yet caught up with the first books in the Cynster Next Generation Novels, then BY WINTER'S LIGHT is a Christmas story that highlights the Cynster children as they stand poised on the cusp of adulthood – essentially an introductory novel to the upcoming generation. That novel is followed by the first pair of Cynster Next Generation romances, those of Lucilla and Marcus Cynster, twins and the eldest children of Lord Richard aka Scandal Cynster and Catriona, Lady of the Vale. Both the twins' stories are set in Scotland. See below for further details.

BY WINTER'S LIGHT
A Cynster Special Novel

#1 New York Times bestselling author Stephanie Laurens returns to romantic Scotland to usher in a new generation of Cynsters in an enchanting tale of mistletoe, magic, and love.

It's December 1837 and the young adults of the Cynster clan have succeeded in having the family Christmas celebration held at snow-bound Casphairn Manor, Richard and Catriona Cynster's home. Led by Sebastian, Marquess of Earith, and by Lucilla, future Lady of the Vale, and her twin brother, Marcus, the upcoming generation has their own plans for the holiday season.

Yet where Cynsters gather, love is never far behind—the festive occasion brings together Daniel Crosbie, tutor to Lucifer Cynster's sons, and Claire Meadows, widow and governess to Gabriel Cynster's daughter. Daniel and Claire have met before and the embers of an unexpected passion smolder between them, but once bitten, twice shy, Claire believes a second marriage is not in her stars. Daniel, however, is determined to press his suit. He's seen the love the Cynsters share, and Claire is the lady with whom he dreams of sharing *his* life. Assisted by a bevy of Cynsters —innate matchmakers every one—Daniel strives to persuade Claire that trusting him with her hand and her heart is her right path to happiness.

Meanwhile, out riding on Christmas Eve, the young adults of the Cynster clan respond to a plea for help. Summoned to a humble dwelling in ruggedly forested mountains, Lucilla is called on to help with the difficult birth of a child, while the others rise to the challenge of helping her. With a violent storm closing in and severely limited options, the next generation of Cynsters face their first collective test—can they save this mother and child? And themselves, too?

Back at the manor, Claire is increasingly drawn to Daniel and despite her misgivings, against the backdrop of the ongoing festivities their relationship deepens. Yet she remains torn—until catastrophe strikes, and by winter's light, she learns that love—true love—is worth any risk, any price.

A tale brimming with all the magical delights of a Scottish festive season.

A Cynster novel – a classic historical romance of 71,000 words.

THE TEMPTING OF THOMAS CARRICK
A Cynster Next Generation Novel

Do you believe in fate? Do you believe in passion? What happens when fate and passion collide?

Do you believe in love? What happens when fate, passion, and love combine?

This. This…

#1 New York Times *bestselling author Stephanie Laurens returns to Scotland with a tale of two lovers irrevocably linked by destiny and passion.*

Thomas Carrick is a gentleman driven to control all aspects of his life. As the wealthy owner of Carrick Enterprises, located in bustling Glasgow, he is one of that city's most eligible bachelors and fully intends to select an appropriate wife from the many young ladies paraded before him. He wants to take that necessary next step along his self-determined path, yet no young lady captures his eye, much less his attention...not in the way Lucilla Cynster had, and still did, even though she lives miles away.

For over two years, Thomas has avoided his clan's estate because it borders Lucilla's home, but disturbing reports from his clansmen force him to return to the countryside—only to discover that his uncle, the laird, is ailing, a clan family is desperately ill, and the clan-healer is unconscious and dying. Duty to the clan leaves Thomas no choice but to seek help from the last woman he wants to face.

Strong-willed and passionate, Lucilla has been waiting—increasingly impatiently—for Thomas to return and claim his rightful place by her side. She knows he is hers—her fated lover, husband, protector, and mate. He is the only man for her, just as she is his one true love. And, at last, he's back. Even though his returning wasn't on her account, Lucilla is willing to seize whatever chance Fate hands her.

Thomas can never forget Lucilla, much less the connection that seethes between them, but to marry her would mean embracing a life he's adamant he does not want.

Lucilla sees that Thomas has yet to accept the inevitability of their union and, despite all, he can refuse her and walk away. But how *can* he ignore a bond such as theirs—one so much stronger than reason? Despite several unnerving attacks mounted against them, despite the uncertainty racking his clan, Lucilla remains as determined as only a Cynster can be to fight for the future she knows can be theirs—and while she cannot command him, she has powerful enticements she's willing to wield in the cause of tempting Thomas Carrick.

A neo-Gothic tale of passionate romance laced with mystery, set in the uplands of southwestern Scotland.

A Cynster Second Generation Novel – a classic historical romance of 122,000 words.

A MATCH FOR MARCUS CYNSTER
A Cynster Next Generation Novel

Duty compels her to turn her back on marriage. Fate drives him to protect her come what may. Then love takes a hand in this battle of yearning hearts, stubborn wills, and a match too powerful to deny.

#1 New York Times bestselling author Stephanie Laurens returns to rugged Scotland with a dramatic tale of passionate desire and unwavering devotion.

Restless and impatient, Marcus Cynster waits for Fate to come calling. He knows his destiny lies in the lands surrounding his family home, but what will his future be? Equally importantly, with whom will he share it?

Of one fact he feels certain: his fated bride will not be Niniver Carrick. His elusive neighbor attracts him mightily, yet he feels compelled to protect her—even from himself. Fickle Fate, he's sure, would never be so kind as to decree that Niniver should be his. The best he can do for them both is to avoid her.

Niniver has vowed to return her clan to prosperity. The epitome of fragile femininity, her delicate and ethereal exterior cloaks a stubborn will and an unflinching devotion to the people in her care. She accepts that in order to achieve her goal, she cannot risk marrying and losing her grip on the clan's reins to an inevitably controlling husband. Unfortunately, many local men see her as their opportunity.

Soon, she's forced to seek help to get rid of her unwelcome suitors. Powerful and dangerous, Marcus Cynster is perfect for the task. Suppressing her wariness over tangling with a gentleman who so excites her passions, she appeals to him for assistance with her peculiar problem.

Although at first he resists, Marcus discovers that, contrary to his expectations, his fated role *is* to stand by Niniver's side and, ultimately, to claim her hand. Yet in order to convince her to be his bride, they must plunge headlong into a journey full of challenges, unforeseen dangers, passion, and yearning, until Niniver grasps the essential truth—that she is indeed a match for Marcus Cynster.

A neo-Gothic tale of passionate romance set in the uplands of south-western Scotland A Cynster Second Generation Novel – a classic historical romance of 114,000 words.

And if you want to catch up with where it all began,
return to the iconic
DEVIL's BRIDE

The book that introduced millions of historical romance readers around the globe to the powerful men of the unforgettable Cynster family – aristocrats to the bone, conquerors at heart – and the willful feisty women strong enough to be their brides.

ABOUT THE AUTHOR

#1 *New York Times* bestselling author Stephanie Laurens began writing romances as an escape from the dry world of professional science. Her hobby quickly became a career when her first novel was accepted for publication, and with entirely becoming alacrity, she gave up writing about facts in favor of writing fiction.

All Laurens's works to date are historical romances ranging from medieval times to the mid-1800s, and her settings range from Scotland to India. The majority of her works are set in the period of the British Regency. Laurens has published more than 60 works of historical romance, including 38 *New York Times* bestsellers and has sold more than 20 million print, audio, and e-books globally. All her works are continuously available in print and e-book formats in English worldwide, and have been translated into many other languages. An international bestseller, among other accolades, Laurens has received the Romance Writers of America® prestigious RITA® Award for Best Romance Novella 2008 for *The Fall of Rogue Gerrard*.

Laurens's continuing novels featuring the Cynster family are widely regarded as classics of the historical romance genre. Other series include the *Bastion Club Novels*, the *Black Cobra Quartet*, and the *Casebook of Barnaby Adair Novels*.

For information on all published novels and on upcoming releases and updates on novels yet to come, visit Stephanie's website: www.stephanielaurens.com

To sign up for Stephanie's Email Newsletter (a private list) for heads-up alerts as new books are released, exclusive sneak peeks into upcoming books, and exclusive sweepstakes contests, follow the prompts at Stephanie's Email Newsletter Sign-up Page.

Stephanie lives with her husband and two cats in the hills outside

Melbourne, Australia. When she isn't writing, she's reading, and if she isn't reading, she'll be tending her garden.

Made in the USA
Middletown, DE
16 October 2017